Praise for

THE BOOK OF IVY

"*Thought-provoking, poignant, and sexy! Readers will burn the midnight oil to finish* The Book of Ivy *and fall asleep with the name Bishop Lattimer on their lips.*"

—Regina at Mel, Erin, and Regina Read-A-Lot

"The Book of Ivy *has every ingredient you look for in an epic novel: from the spine-tingling plot and exhilarating characters, to every entrancing word penned by Amy Engel.*"

—Kris at Insightful Minds Reviews

"*I enjoyed this novel so much that I polished it off in two sittings. There is no insta-love! There is no love triangle! Best of all, the protagonist actually has common sense, and she uses it! The slow-to-develop relationship is believable, and both Ivy and Bishop are easy to relate to. Waiting anxiously for Book 2!*"

—Julie at Magna Maniac Café

"*With her debut, Amy Engel has pulled off one of the best dystopian romances that I have ever read. It was impossible to put down.*"

—Kayla at Bibliophilia, Please

THE
BOOK
OF

THE
BOOK
OF

AMY ENGEL

Entangled Publishing, LLC
2614 South Timberline Road
Suite 109
Fort Collins, CO 80525

Visit our website at www.entangledpublishing.com

Edited by Alycia Tornetta and Stacy Abrams
Cover design by Alexandra Shostak
Interior design by Jeremy Howland

Paperback ISBN 978-1-62266-465-8
Ebook ISBN 978-1-62266-466-5

Manufactured in the United States of America

First Edition November 2014

10 9 8 7 6 5 4 3 2 1

For my father, who always believed

No one wears white wedding dresses anymore. White cloth is too hard to come by, and the expense and trouble of securing enough to make several dozen dresses, or more, is too high. Not even on a day like today, when it is our leader's son who will be one of the bridegrooms. Not even he is special enough to be allowed to marry a girl dressed in white.

"Stand still," my sister says from behind me. Her knuckles are icy cold against my spine as she tries to force up the zipper on the back of the pale blue dress. It was made for the wedding day she never had and it doesn't fit quite right on my taller frame. "There." She gives the zipper one last yank. "Turn around."

I turn slowly, smoothing my hands down the soft material. I'm not used to dresses. I don't like how naked

I feel underneath, already longing for pants and a breath not hemmed in by a too-tight bodice. As if reading my thoughts, Callie's eyes roam downward. "You're bigger in the bust than I am," she says with a smirk. "But I doubt he'll complain."

"Shut up," I say, but there's no force behind my words. I didn't think I would be this nervous. It's not as if this day is a surprise. I've known my whole life that it was coming, spent every minute of the last two years preparing. But now that it's here, I can't stop the tremor in my fingers or the sick fall of my stomach. I don't know if I can do this, but I also know I have no choice.

Callie reaches up and tucks a stray strand of hair behind my ear. "You'll be fine," she says, her voice firm and even. "Right? You know what to do."

"Yes," I say, pulling my head back. Her words make me feel stronger; I don't need to be babied.

She looks at me for a long moment, her mouth a tight line. Is she angry that I'm taking the spot that should have rightfully been hers, or is she glad to give it up, to be rid of the burden of being the daughter who holds so much hope on her shoulders?

"Girls." My father's voice floats up the stairs. "It's time."

"You go," I tell Callie. "I'll be right down." I need one last minute of quiet, one last chance to look around this room that will never be mine again. Callie leaves the door ajar when she goes, and I can hear my father's impatient voice from downstairs, Callie murmuring something reassuring to him.

On my bed is a well-worn suitcase, the wheels broken off long ago, forcing me to carry it. I heave it off the mattress, turn in a slow circle, knowing I will never sleep in this narrow bed again, never brush my hair in front of the mirror above my dresser, never listen to the sound of rain tapping against my windowpane as I drift to sleep. I close my eyes against a sudden press of tears and take a deep breath. When I open my eyes, they are dry. I walk out of my room and I don't look back.

The weddings are performed on the second Saturday in May. Some years there is rain and with it the faint, acrid scent of burning, even after so many years. But today dawned clear, the sky a bright, hectic blue, wispy clouds floating on a mild breeze. It is a beautiful day to become a bride, but all I can concentrate on is the heavy thump of my heart and the line of sweat forming between my shoulder blades as we walk toward City Hall.

My father and Callie flank me, almost as if they are penning me in to keep me from bolting. I don't bother telling them I'm not going anywhere. My father's swinging hand brushes mine, and he clasps my fingers in his own. He hasn't held my hand since I was a little girl, and the gesture shocks me so much that I stumble over my own feet, the pressure of his hand balancing me at the last moment. I'm grateful for his touch, even though touching is not something he does often or easily. He is not an offerer of comfort. When your fate is predetermined, there's not much benefit in coddling. His job was to make me strong, and I like to think he did it well. But maybe that is just wishful thinking.

"We're proud of you," he says. He squeezes my hand once, hard, almost to the point of pain, and lets go. "You can do this."

"I know," I tell him, my eyes straight ahead. The limestone facade of City Hall is less than a block away now. There are several other girls climbing the steps with their parents. They must be nervous, anxious to find out if they will end today as someone's wife or if they will go home and slide between their own sheets again. My anxiety is different. I know where I will be sleeping tonight, and it won't be in my own bed.

As we reach the sidewalk in front of City Hall, people begin to turn, grinning at my father, reaching out to shake his hand, clap him on the back. A few women give me reassuring smiles as they tell me how pretty I look.

"Smile," Callie whispers near my ear. "Stop scowling at everyone."

"If it's so easy, why don't *you* try it?" I hiss back, but I do as she says and plaster a smile onto my face.

"I would have, remember?" she says. "But I didn't get the chance. Now you need to do it for me."

So she is jealous after all, angry at having her birthright stolen. I expect her eyes to be cold, but when I turn my head, she is looking at me with a softness I have rarely seen.

She is the female version of our father, with his chocolate eyes and dark chestnut hair. I always longed to look like the two of them, instead of being the odd one out with my not-quite-blond, not-quite-brown hair and gray eyes, both gifts from my long-dead mother. But as little as we resemble each other, looking at Callie has always been like staring at a fiercer, more disciplined version of myself. Looking at her reminds me of who I am expected to become.

We follow the long line of brides into City Hall. All around me are girls in pale dresses, some with hands clutching small bouquets, others, like mine, empty. We are ushered into the main rotunda where a stage has been set up at one end. There is a dark curtain across the back, and I know that, even now, the boys are gathering behind it, lining up before they are revealed to find out who they are destined to marry.

The potential brides sit in the first few rows of chairs, the families of both brides and grooms seated behind them. President Lattimer and his wife, however, are seated on the stage, as they are every year. Even with a son behind the curtain, their status does not change. My father gives my hand a final squeeze before moving away. Callie brushes a quick, dry kiss against my cheek. "Good luck," she says. If my mother were still alive, maybe she would hug me, give me final words of advice that I could actually use instead of a worn-out platitude.

I slide into an empty seat in the front row, avoiding eye contact with President Lattimer and the girls on either side of me. I keep my gaze straight ahead, focusing on a slight tear in the stage's dark curtain until the girl next to me presses something into my hand. "Here," she says. "Take one and pass it on."

I do as she says, sliding the stack of programs to the girl on my left. It is the same program they give out every year. Only the color of the paper and the names inside change. It hardly seems worth the effort; I'm sure we all have it memorized by now. This year the program is a washed out pink, the words WEDDING CEREMONY across the front in curly, slightly smudged script. The first two pages are a history of our "nation." Personally, I think it's ridiculous to refer to a town of fewer than ten thousand people as a nation, but no one's ever asked for my opinion.

The history includes talk of the war that ended the world, the floods and droughts that followed, the diseases that almost finished us off. But we, of course, rose from the ashes, ragged, war-weary survivors who managed to find one another across a vast, barren landscape and carved out a spot to begin anew. Blah, blah, blah. Our rebirth, though, was not without conflict and more deaths as two sides fought to determine how our tiny nation would go forward. The winning side, the side led by President Lattimer's father, prevailed. But the loser, my grandfather Samuel Westfall, and his followers were welcomed into the fold, promised forgiveness, and granted absolution for their sins.

I have to resist the urge to make gagging noises as I read.

And that is why we have the wedding day. Those who came from the losing side offer up their sixteen-year-old daughters to the sons of the winners. There is a second wedding day in November, when the sons of the losing side marry the daughters of the winning side. But that wedding day is more somber, the nation's most prized daughters forced to marry subpar boys under a bleak winter sky.

The theory behind the practice of the arranged marriages is twofold. There is a practical purpose: people don't live as long as they used to, before the war. And having healthy offspring is a much dicier proposition than in the past. It's important that we procreate, the earlier the better. The second is even more pragmatic. President Lattimer's father was smart enough to know that peace only lasts when the unhappy side still has something left to lose. By marrying our daughters to his side, he ensured we would think twice about rising up. It's one thing to slay your enemy; it's another thing entirely when that enemy wears your daughter's face, when the man you cut down is your own grandson. The strategy has worked thus far; we have remained at peace for two generations.

It is hot in the rotunda, even with the doors open and the cool limestone walls. A small bead of sweat slides down the back of my neck and I wipe it away, pushing my hair up again as I do. Callie did her best to twist it into submission, but my hair is thick and unruly and I don't think it cooperated as she would have liked. The girl to my right gives me a smile. "It looks good," she says. "Pretty."

"Thank you," I say. She has a crown of sad yellow roses in her red hair, the petals already withering in the heat.

"It's my second year," the girl whispers. "My last

chance."

If you aren't matched with anyone your sixteenth year, you are put back into the pool for the next year. This also happens on years when there aren't enough girls to match with all the available boys, or visa versa, to give everyone the best chance of finding a match. If after two tries you aren't matched, then you are free to marry someone of your own choice who has similarly never been chosen. Or, if you're a woman, you can apply for a job as a nurse or teacher. Men, married and unmarried alike, work. Once women are married, they are expected to stay home and have babies, so traditional "female" jobs are filled with the ranks of the unmatched.

"Good luck," I tell the girl, although personally I don't think not finding a match would be such a terrible fate. But I know it will not be mine. My name has been in an envelope ever since Callie's was removed. There is no suspense for me. The other girls here today have the benefit of personality tests and endless interviews so that there is at least the *possibility* of compatibility with their new husbands. With me, all that matters is my last name.

"Thanks," the girl says. "I know who you are. My dad's pointed your dad out to me before."

I don't respond. I turn my eyes back to the stage, where the curtain is beginning to rustle. I take a deep breath in through my nose, let it out slowly through my mouth.

A man approaches the podium at the side of the stage. He looks nervous, glancing from the audience to President Lattimer and back again. "Ladies and gentlemen," he calls. His voice breaks on the last syllable and there is a smattering of laughter from the room. He clears his throat and tries again. "Ladies and gentlemen, we are here today to celebrate the marriages of the eligible young men from Eastglen and the lovely ladies from Westside. Their unions represent the best our small nation has to offer and symbolize the peace we have fought for and achieved together." It's not always this same man, but it's always this same speech, so sad and ridiculous I am torn between laughter and tears.

The redheaded girl next to me clasps her hands together so tightly her knuckles turn white, her toe tapping a nervous rhythm against the floor. The man at the podium gestures to someone offstage who I cannot see, and slowly the curtain begins to move to one side. It screeches on the metal pole, a long, high shriek that sets my teeth on edge. The first boys to be revealed fidget nervously, taking their hands in and out of their pockets, rocking on their heels. A small, dark-haired boy who looks more twelve than sixteen is suffering from a fit of giggles, tucking his chin into his chest while his shoulders heave. I am glad, at least, that he won't be mine.

They've put the one who will be mine right in the middle, so much taller than the other boys that they seem to flow out from him like water from a rock. He doesn't even look like a boy compared to them, which makes sense given his age. At eighteen, he's two years older than everyone else, but it's more than just his years. I'm not convinced he's ever been boyish. There is a gravity about him that none of the others possess. He does not fidget. I cannot imagine him giggling. His gaze is fixed—cool, impassive, and faintly amused—on some spot in the distance. He does not so much as glance at me.

He should have stood here two years ago. He was meant for Callie all along. But the day before the ceremony, we were notified that he was not attending, would not marry until he turned eighteen, and that it would be *me* standing next to him on that day, not my sister. Such whims are indulged, I suppose, when you're the president's son. As a consolation prize, Callie was given the option of having her name removed as a potential bride in the marriage ceremony. An option she took and one I wish were mine.

"Oh my God," the redhead breathes, glancing at me. "You are so lucky!"

I know she means well and I try to smile at her, but my lips don't want to cooperate. The man at the podium turns things over to the president's wife, Mrs. Erin Lattimer. She is auburn-haired and full-figured in the way that makes men's eyes follow her wherever she goes. But her voice is tart, cold even. It reminds me of the first bite of a sour green apple.

"As you all know," she says, "I will read the name of a boy, who will step forward. I will then open the envelope and read the name of the girl who will be his wife." She looks down at us. "Please come onto the stage when your name is called. If, at the end, your name is not called, it simply means the committee determined you weren't a good match for any of the boys this year." She gives us a brisk smile. "There's no shame in that," she says, "of course." But it is shameful not to be chosen; everyone knows that. No one ever says it out loud, but it's always the girl's fault if she's not matched to anyone. Always something in her that was found lacking, never the other way around.

The first name called is Luke Allen. He's blond, with a spray of freckles across his nose like brown sugar. His eyes widen briefly as Mrs. Lattimer tears open the envelope with his name written across the front and pulls out the creamy card stock. "Emily Thorne," she calls. There is rustling behind me, excited murmurings, and I turn my head. A petite, toffee-haired girl slides past the knees of the girls seated in her row. She stumbles a bit on her way up the stairs to the stage, and Luke hurries forward to take her hand. Some of the girls behind me sigh as if this is the grandest romantic gesture they've ever seen, and I will my eyes to stay still in their sockets. Luke and Emily stand awkwardly, giving each other sidelong glances, until they are shooed to the edge of the stage so the next couple can be announced.

It takes what feels like hours to get through the thick stack of envelopes. And even then there are plenty of girls left sitting, including the one next to me. Tears slide down her cheeks as Mrs. Lattimer holds up the final envelope. I want to tell her to be glad, to be happy that she can go back home tonight and figure out what she wants to do with her life beyond being a bride. But I know my words will be cold comfort. Because all anyone will ever remember about this girl is that she came home unmarried, that at the end of the day she was unchosen.

Mrs. Lattimer looks over her shoulder at her husband, and the president stands and approaches the podium. He is a tall man; it's easy to see where his son gets his height. His dark hair is sprinkled with premature gray at the temples, his cleft chin strong. His pale blue eyes scan the crowd, lingering on me. A shudder works its way up my spine, but I hold his gaze.

"Today is a special day," he says. "Even more special than usual. Years ago, after the war, there was disagreement about how we should rebuild. Eventually, the two sides managed to come to an accord."

I find it interesting that he turns a battle into a disagreement, a forced hand into an accord. He has always been masterful at twisting words to fit the stories he tells us.

"As you all know, it was my father, Alexander Lattimer, who led the group that ultimately took control. And it was Samuel Westfall who opposed him but who, with time, came to agree with my father's vision for the future."

That is a lie. My grandfather never agreed with the Lattimers' vision for Westfall. He wanted a democracy, for people to have a vote and a say in their own lives. He spent years keeping an ever-growing band of survivors alive and moving until they found this place to settle. Then he had it all ripped away from him by Alexander Lattimer, who wanted a dynasty for himself and his descendants.

I don't dare turn my head to find my father or Callie in the crowd. They are skilled, after all these years, at hiding their emotions, but I will be able to read the rage in their eyes, and I cannot let it show in mine.

"And today, for the first time, we have a marriage between a Lattimer and a Westfall," President Lattimer says with a smile. It looks genuine to me, and maybe it is. But I also know what this marriage means to him. It's another way to cement his power, which is what he is really happy about. After my father, there will be no more Westfalls. It's not enough for President Lattimer that the Westfall line has run out—he has to turn my children into Lattimers, too.

"Up until now, neither one of our families has been very good at producing girls," President Lattimer continues. There is a rumble of laughter from the crowd, but I can't bring myself to join in, even though I know I should. When the chuckles die down, President Lattimer holds up the envelope for everyone to see. "The president's son and the founder's daughter," he calls.

My father was not the founder, of course. It was his father who founded this town and was then usurped by Alexander Lattimer and his followers. But it was established early on that the original founder's descendant would take on the title of founder, the same way Alexander Lattimer's descendant is called president. It's a meaningless title. The founder has no say in how the nation is run. He's only a ceremonial figurehead, trotted out to prove how peaceful we are. How well our system of government works. The title of founder is like giving a beautifully wrapped present with nothing inside. They hope we'll be so distracted by the shiny outside, we won't notice the box is empty.

"Bishop Lattimer," the president calls out in a clear, ringing voice. The sound of the envelope, the paper tearing, seems as loud as a scream to my ears. I can feel hundreds of eyes on me and I hold my head high. President Lattimer draws the paper out with a flourish and smiles in my direction. He mouths my name, *Ivy Westfall,* but I can't hear him over the ringing in my ears and the pounding of my heart.

I take a final deep breath, trying to draw courage into my lungs like air. Trying to stomp down the anger that buzzes through my veins like poison. I stand, my legs steadier than I thought they would be. My heels click on the tile floor as I make my way to the stairs. Behind me, the crowd claps and shouts, a few irreverent whistles punctuating the chaos. As I start up the stairs, President Lattimer reaches down and takes my elbow.

"Ivy," he says. "We're glad you're joining our family." His eyes are warm. I feel betrayed by them. They should be icy and indifferent, to match the rest of him.

"Thank you," I say, with a steady voice that doesn't sound like my own. "I'm glad, too."

Once I'm onstage, the other couples move even closer to the edge so that I can make my way to the center, where Bishop Lattimer waits for me. I hold his unwavering gaze. He is even taller than I thought, but I am tall, too, and for once my height is a blessing. I would not want this boy to dwarf me. I feel powerless enough already.

He has dark hair, like his father. Although up close, I can see lighter streaks in among the coffee brown strands, as if he's spent a lot of time outdoors, under the sun. That makes sense given the rumors I've heard about him over the years: that he prefers to be outdoors rather than in, that his father has to force him to attend council meetings, and that he's more often found rafting on the river than inside City Hall.

His eyes are a cool, clear green, and they study me with an intensity that makes my stomach cramp. His gaze is neither hostile nor welcoming but appraising, like I am a problem he is figuring out how to solve. He doesn't come toward me, but when I get close enough to hold out a hand, as I've been coached to do, he takes it in his. His fingers are warm and strong when they close over mine. He squeezes my hand briefly, which startles the breath in my throat. Was he trying to be kind? Reassure me? I don't know, because when I glance at him, his eyes are on the minister waiting in the wings.

"Let's begin," President Lattimer says. Everyone on the stage shifts into position, standing across from their intended spouse, Bishop and me in the center where everyone in the audience can watch. Bishop takes my other hand in his, our hands joined across the small space between us.

I want to shout out that this is wrong. That I don't know this boy across from me. Have never had a single conversation with him in my entire life. He doesn't know that my favorite color is purple or that I still miss the mother I don't remember or that I am terrified. I shoot a panicked glance out to the audience but see only smiling faces reflected back at me. Somehow, that makes it even worse, the way everyone goes along with this charade. How no one ever cries out or tries to stop their child from marrying a stranger.

Our compliance is the strongest weapon President Lattimer has in his arsenal.

And, in the end, I'm just as bad as the rest of them. I open my mouth when everyone else does, repeat the words I can't even hear over dozens of louder voices around me. I tell myself that none of it matters. I have to get through this part, and so I do. I slide the plain gold band that was my father's onto Bishop's finger and he does the same with mine. The ring feels foreign against my skin, tight and confining even though the sizing is correct.

When the minister pronounces us man and wife, Bishop doesn't try to kiss me, not even on the cheek, and I am thankful. I don't think I could have stood it if he had. It would be like someone on the street grabbing me and planting his mouth on mine. An assault, not affection. But all around us, couples hug and cheer and most of them have no trouble kissing as if they've known each other for much longer than an hour. Will these girls be so happy in a few months when their bellies are heavy with babies and they realize they are stuck forever sleeping next to a boy they barely know?

For them this ceremony is about keeping the peace, about honoring a tradition that has worked to stabilize a society for more than two generations. But unlike them, I know how fragile that peace is, how it hangs by only a few slender threads that are even now being snipped. I am different from all these other girls surrounding me because marrying Bishop Lattimer has not fulfilled my destiny. My mission is not to make him happy and bear his children and be his wife.

My mission is to kill him.

After the ceremony, everyone files down to the basement of City Hall, where long tables are set up against the walls, cups of bright pink punch lined next to a single large wedding cake. There will only be enough for the brides and grooms to have a bite or two, but just the thought of the sweet icing clinging to my teeth makes me feel nauseous.

Bishop's parents greet us almost as soon as we enter. His father pulls me into a hug and kisses me on the cheek. I try not to flinch, but my smile is tight across my face. His mother is not as demonstrative. She lays her hand briefly on my upper arm and then snatches it away, more the idea of a touch than a touch itself. "Be good to him," she tells me, and I don't have to strain to hear the warning in her voice.

"Mom," Bishop says. He gives her a sharp look that I pretend not to see. Bishop puts his hand on the small of my back, guiding me away from his parents.

"Where's your family?" he asks, tilting his head down so I can hear him over the din of happy congratulations all around us. They are the first words he's spoken to me other than our vows, which don't really count, even though in a different world they would matter most.

I point to the far corner of the room where my father stands stiffly, Callie leaning against the wall next to him.

"Let's go say hello," Bishop says, and I glance up at him, surprised. Our families pretend to get along, we fake smiles and clasp hands and all the while we seethe under our skin. But his voice sounds easy, his eyes sincere. He is a good actor. I will have to be careful around him, even more than I anticipated.

Callie pushes herself away from the wall as we approach, taking a spot next to my father, a bright smile on her face. My father smiles as well, but his is more reserved and doesn't come close to touching the dark depths of his eyes.

"Dad," I say, "you know each other, I think." I cannot bring myself to introduce Bishop formally, to call him my husband. "This is my father, Justin Westfall."

They shake hands. "Nice to see you again, sir," Bishop says. "It's been a while." His eyes hold my father's. He doesn't blink. My father does not intimidate Bishop the way he does most people.

"You, too, Bishop," my dad says, clapping him on the shoulder with his free hand. "And this is my older daughter, Callie."

"I'm sure he knows who I am, Dad," Callie says with a

laugh. She looks up at Bishop from under her dark eyelashes. "I'm the one you almost married two years ago."

I'm not sure what she's doing, whether she's flirting with him or simply trying to remind him of the fact that his original obligation was to her. All I know for sure is that she wanted to be the one to take his life and now she's been robbed of the chance. One more thing she will never forgive him for. I glance down at the floor, hoping he can't feel the turmoil swirling around us, so strong I can practically taste it on my tongue.

But all he says is, "I remember." His smile reveals even white teeth. A future president's smile. "But it is nice to officially meet."

We make the rounds of the room, accepting congratulations from friends and strangers alike. I watch the other brides, most of them with shining eyes and wide smiles. They never stray far from their new husbands, proud to show off and be shown off in return. Do they worry about what comes later? Tonight and all the nights to follow, the endless hours they must fill with these boys they don't know? The children of my grandfather's original group go to schools on the opposite side of the city, in Westside. Mingling is not forbidden, but it is not encouraged. Adults constantly chaperone those under sixteen, just to ensure they don't develop crushes or begin romances that will only make the arranged marriages more difficult. I have no doubt the majority of these girls have never set eyes on their husbands before today. How can they smile so broadly? How can they be so convinced of their own happiness?

"Are you ready to go?" Bishop asks me. "I don't think I

can stand one more handshake."

I'm as ready as I'll ever be. Part of me wishes I could just kill him right here and now. Grab the knife off the cake table and bypass all the steps in between, jump straight to the final result. "Yes," I say. "I need to say good-bye to my family."

Bishop nods and I breathe a sigh of relief when he doesn't follow me. I want to say my farewells in private.

"Well," I say, once I'm next to my father and Callie again. "This is it."

"You can do this," Callie says. Her hand grabs mine and squeezes until my bones grind together. "He's good looking. He seems nice enough." Her sneering voice belies her words. "Just get through it. Get through tonight and tomorrow will be easier. I promise."

But how can she promise me that? She is not the one who has to go home to a strange house with a strange boy and let him…

My father catches my gaze. "Remember the plan," he says, voice barely a whisper. "And remember I love you."

I can count on one hand the number of times he's said that to me. I don't doubt his love, but a bitter, angry part of me I try hard to silence questions what that love is tied to—my obedience, my allegiance, my success? Will he still love me if I fail?

I nod, lips pressed together, because I'm not sure what will come out if I open my mouth.

Bishop and I are among the first couples to leave, and several older boys in the crowd catcall as we climb the stairs from the basement.

"Leaving so early?"

"Can't wait, huh, Bishop?"

"Somebody's in a hurry to see what's under that dress."

My cheeks burn at their words. I would like to march back down the steps and slap them all. Slap Bishop, too, while I'm at it, just for being a part of this. I stumble on a step, and Bishop reaches out and steadies me with a hand on my upper arm. "Ignore them," he says, voice tight. "They're idiots."

They may be idiots, but I can't imagine they're wrong, either. He's an eighteen-year-old boy and this is his wedding night. I don't think he's taking me home to play checkers. My heart leaps hard in my chest, like it's going to tunnel out, right through my ribs. I wish, for the millionth time, that it was Callie standing here instead of me.

After I point it out, Bishop grabs my suitcase from the row lined up outside the doors to City Hall. "Is this it?" he asks. "Only one?"

"Yes," I say. "We don't have as much on my side of town," I can't resist adding, even though Callie told me countless times not to antagonize him. I have to fight my natural inclination to provoke.

But he doesn't seem angry or even surprised at my words, he just follows me down the steps, suitcase clutched in his hand as though it weighs nothing. "You know it was your grandfather who wanted to keep the two sides separated, right?" he asks, voice mild.

Callie told me there was no point in pretending our families love each other, that he'd see right through that. But I have to hide the true depth of our hatred. It's like walking a tightrope with no net, every step a huge risk. "At first, yes," I say finally. "But that was only a temporary plan, a way to calm things down between the two sides. He never wanted it to continue for this long."

Every year my father approaches President Lattimer and suggests it's time to end the arranged marriages and co-mingle the two sides of town. He keeps his ideas reasonable, doesn't ask for a democratic government, which will never be granted. And every year President Lattimer smiles and nods and does exactly nothing.

"What's the difference?" Bishop asks. "It's all one town, it's not like you were living in a prison."

Easy for him to say, this boy who's grown up knowing the best of everything, who from birth has been the cho-sen one. Even this marriage is something he orchestrated, swapping my sister for me as easily as he changes clothes.

"It doesn't always feel like one town," I tell him, because that seems like the only safe thing I can say. He's right in that there is nothing glaringly different between his side of town and the side I grew up in. The physical differences are subtle—a little more shade, the houses slightly bigger and set back a little farther from the sidewalks, the streets a few feet wider. They are the kind of differences that aren't obvious enough to breed outright resentment, but the mere fact of their existence is a way to remind us of our rightful place.

Once on the sidewalk, we turn right, venturing farther into his side of town, illustrating my point, even if Bishop doesn't get it. I've been past City Hall before, the informal line that separates Westside from Eastglen, but not often. And I've never been inside Bishop's parents' large home, but I know my father has.

Before the war, Westfall had another life as a small town in southern Missouri, the Ozarks, as this part of the state was called back then. This town was the county seat, and the town square still remains, anchored at the south end by City Hall and the courthouse to the north. That's part of the reason my grandfather picked this place to settle. He lived in Chicago when the war started, survived the first wave of nuclear and EMP bombing, and headed inland. Along the way, he met fellow survivors, and three years after the war, in 2025, he founded Westfall with an initial population only slightly less than what it is now, around eight thousand people. This part of the country was hit hard by disease and famine, but only a few bombs fell here, leaving enough remaining infrastructure that they weren't forced to start over from scratch.

The sun casts dappled shadows on our faces as we walk, sidestepping cracks in the sidewalk where the roots of giant oaks poke through the pavement. It would be nice to have some kind of transportation, especially today in high heels, but there are no cars anymore. The EMPs rendered them all useless, and we have no access to gasoline, anyway.

And now, fifty years on, the streets are too cracked, weeds pushing their way through the uneven asphalt, for cars to be of any use to us regardless. Now, everyone walks or rides bikes or sometimes horses, although there aren't enough of them to make it a practical mode of transportation.

The strap of my high heel is rubbing against my foot and I wince as I walk, trying to shift my weight off the sore spot. Bishop looks at me, switching the suitcase from his left hand to his right. "Why don't you take those off?" he asks. "They look painful."

"They are." I take his advice and slip off my shoes, hanging them over my index finger. The sidewalk is rough and warm under my bare feet. I breathe out a tiny sigh of pleasure before I can stop myself.

"Better?" he asks, the edge of his mouth lifting.

"Much," I say.

When we reach the corner of Main and Elm, I turn left. The president's house looms in the distance, its brick facade partially obscured behind a black wrought-iron fence.

"Where are you going?" Bishop asks from behind me. I glance over my shoulder. He is halfway up the path to a tiny bungalow.

I stop, confused. "Your parents' house."

He shakes his head. "We aren't living with them." He hooks his thumb toward the bungalow. "This is ours."

"But I thought—" I cut myself off. Callie and my father told me we would be living in a wing of the president's house. They never even considered another option. Last week a contact of Callie's on this side of town told her they were moving in new furniture, changing curtains, and painting walls.

Panic floods through me, thick and vicious. If my father was wrong about this part of the plan, what else doesn't he know? Where else will he lead me astray? I have the urge to flee, back to City Hall, back home, anywhere but here. I can only do this if I am not required to improvise. I am not Bishop. I am not Callie. I am not that skilled an actor.

Bishop's eyebrows pull together as he stares at me where I am rooted in place. "Are you coming?"

I nod. "Yes," I say, my voice too quiet. "Yes," I repeat, louder this time.

He holds the front door open and follows me inside. The door closing is very loud in the empty silence of the house. He is standing right behind me, and I move forward so he can pass. The entryway opens up directly into a small living room, and he sets my suitcase down next to a beige sofa. Straight back is the kitchen, complete with a round table under a row of windows. To the right of the living room is another doorway, leading to the bedrooms, I assume. I cut my eyes away quickly.

I have no idea what to do with myself. In giving me guidance, Callie concentrated mainly on the big moments, not the day-to-day interactions I will be forced to have with this boy. I drop my high heels to the floor, where they land with a clatter. "So," I say, crossing my arms. "What now?" My voice comes out louder than I intended, and I can picture Callie wincing at my words.

Bishop raises his eyebrows at me. "Are you hungry?"

he asks. "You didn't eat any cake." He unbuttons the cuff of his shirt and rolls the sleeve up, exposing a tan forearm. He has the kind of muscles you only get by using them, lean and strong. He goes to work on his other sleeve, waiting for me to answer.

I can't imagine eating. Chewing and swallowing are beyond me. But fixing something to eat means a reprieve, at least, a few minutes where I don't have to worry about what's coming next.

"Maybe," I say finally. "What is there?"

Bishop shrugs. "I have no idea. But I'm sure my mother had them stock the icebox." I trail behind him into the kitchen. It's warmer and brighter in here, and he crosses to the windows, pushing one up so that a breeze ruffles the lace curtains. The icebox is fancier than the basic wooden box we had at home. This one looks like a piece of furniture, scrollwork carved into the wood. Refrigerators are just one more thing that didn't survive the war. Even if we had enough electricity to power them continually, we ran out of Freon long ago. So we use handmade wooden iceboxes and ice blocks are delivered every few days, harvested in winter and kept in an ice house year round.

I pull open the icebox, just to have something to do with my hands. There is a block of cheese, meat of some kind wrapped in paper, a glass jug of milk and one of water on the top shelf. Below that are a dozen eggs, lettuce, and carrots in a bin at the bottom. A bowl of fresh berries. We never went hungry in my house, but there was never this much food, either. Always just enough and no more.

"There's more fruit here," Bishop says from the counter. "And bread." He flips the dial on the stovetop. "Electricity is out, so nothing we have to cook." Electricity was one of the first things my grandfather and the other survivors worked to restore. But it still runs intermittently and we are prone to outages, sometimes short, sometimes lasting for days. Only government buildings, City Hall, the courthouse, are always guaranteed power. We are all encouraged to use our electric appliances sparingly—no lights unless it's necessary, fans running only when it's so hot we don't have any choice.

"Sandwiches?" I suggest.

"Sure."

I pull out the meat—turkey, it turns out—and cheese and set them on the counter next to Bishop. He hands me a knife and I slice the bread while he does the same with a tomato. His fingers are long and he wields the knife easily, his movements deft.

We work in silence, assembling two sandwiches, one of which I know will go uneaten. "Do you like to cook?" Bishop asks. He pulls two yellow glass plates down from the cabinet. "There's not a right answer," he says when I don't respond. He sounds amused. "It isn't a test."

But he's wrong. This is all a test. Every second, every interaction, has the potential to blow up in my face. I remember what my father told me: to be myself as much as I can. The truth, where it can be told, is always more effective than a lie.

"I don't mind it," I say. He's probably picturing me in an

apron, making him food all day long. "Why?"

Bishop looks at me, his eyes doing that appraising thing again. "I was just making conversation, Ivy. Trying to get to know you."

It's the first time he's said my name. To be honest, I wasn't entirely sure he even knew what it was.

We eat without speaking. Well, he eats. I pick at the edges of my bread, rolling little balls of dough between my fingers. I keep my gaze mostly on my plate, but every time I look up, his eyes are on me, making the pit in my stomach expand. I wait for him to speak, demand something of me, but he seems content with the silence.

I don't know how long we sit there, but shadows are starting to slide down the walls when he finally gets up and puts our plates in the sink. Through the open window, I hear someone calling a child in for the night, the slam of a trash can lid, the faint strains of music from a guitar. The normality of it only reminds me how alone I am.

"Do you want to unpack?" Bishop asks.

"Okay," I say, smoothing my dress down as I stand, wishing I could glue it to my body. My legs feel cold and exposed, even in the mild evening air. I hear Callie's voice in my head: *Just get through it.*

He carries my suitcase down the short hallway to the bedroom. I follow a few paces behind, my fingers trailing against the wall, like maybe I can find something to cling onto that will save me. There is a bathroom to the left and a single bedroom to the right. The fading daylight reveals a large bed with two matching nightstands and a dresser on the opposite wall.

"There are hangers in the closet," he tells me. "And half the dresser is empty."

I nod, hovering in the doorway, fists clenched. He stands at the foot of the bed, his hands shoved in his pockets, watching me with careful eyes. I know what Callie would do. She would flirt and laugh. She would make the first move. She would seize the reins of a situation that is completely beyond her control and bend it to her will, happy to sacrifice herself for the good of the cause. But I am not like that. Despite what I've been taught, I know that if he tries to touch me, tries to take off my dress, I will fight him. Even though it won't do any good, I will fight. I don't know if that makes me weak or strong.

But he doesn't touch me, doesn't come any nearer. He opens a dresser drawer and pulls out a pair of shorts and a T-shirt, bunching them in his fist. "I'll sleep on the couch," he says.

I have been so tense, so prepared for a battle, that at first his words don't register. "Wait… What… You don't…" I'm not even sure what I'm asking.

He gives me a wry smile, his eyebrows raised. "You do?"

"No," I say, and instantly regret how quickly I answered. I should be more worried about insulting him, but right now sheer relief overshadows my training.

He nods. "That's what I thought."

We stare at each other. I've never heard of the groom sleeping on the couch on his wedding night. Maybe it happens all the time and I don't know it. But I doubt it, remembering the other couples with their greedy lips and flushed cheeks at the reception today. If he is disappointed, though, or angry, he doesn't show it.

I move out of the doorway so he can slide past me. He pauses briefly and tips his head down to me. "Good night, Ivy," he says.

"Good night."

He closes the door behind him as he leaves. I walk to the bed and sit on the edge, press my fingers between my knees to stop their trembling. If there was a chair I could wedge under the doorknob to make sure he can't come back, I would feel better. But deep down, I don't believe he'll come in. I don't think he will hurt me and I don't know what to make of that. It might be easier if he had.

3

have never lingered in sleep. When I wake, it is with a bang, one second eyes closed and asleep, the next eyes open and mind aware. It is no different here, in this strange bedroom in this new and too-big bed. I blink up at the white ceiling and hold my body still, listening for any sign of him. I think I hear the rattle of a dish from the kitchen, but I can't be sure.

It is hard to believe that only yesterday morning I was waking up in my own bed in the house I've lived in my entire life and now I have a new house, a new bed. A new husband. He is not what I expected. I knew what he looked like, at least from a distance, so that was no real surprise. But after all the angry words I've heard about his father and his family's barely concealed disdain for mine and everything we stand for, I thought Bishop would be crueler behind closed doors. His restraint surprised me. I did not think he would be patient. Perhaps I'm not what he expected, either.

I will have to find a way to let Callie know we are not living at the president's house. Although, knowing Callie, she already has the information and is formulating a new plan. I will need to get to the market soon, to check if there is a message for me. I could always go and visit her, of course, but it was decided that the less contact between my family and me, the better.

"Ivy?" Bishop's voice calls me from the other side of the door, a quiet knock against the wood to go with it.

"Yes?" I scramble up to a sitting position.

He opens the door slowly, only his head and upper body appearing in the crack. "I'm leaving. I wanted to let you know." His eyes skate over my hair, which is loose now, tumbling halfway down my back, before settling on my face.

"Okay," I say. I am trying hard to sound normal, to think about how a wife would talk to her husband, but my voice sounds too high, strained, like I'm playing a part. Which I guess I am. In more ways than one.

After he's gone, I think I probably should have asked where he was going, shown more of an interest in his day. But right now, I am too exhausted to care. This was all so much easier when it was only an idea in my head.

I lay in bed and watch the sun sneak through the edges of the curtain, spread its warm fingers across the floor. When my legs start to sweat under the blanket, I make myself get up, stretching my arms above my head, trying to work the tension out of my neck and shoulders where it's settled like a leaden scarf.

The bathroom is small, like the rest of the house, and spotlessly clean. I take a shower as fast as I can, for once not a consequence of the lack of hot water. I don't want to be naked for any longer than I have to; I have no idea when Bishop might return.

After I'm dressed in a T-shirt and shorts, my hair dripping down my back, I go ahead and finish unpacking. It's strange to see my small collection of clothes hanging next to Bishop's in the closet; the sight makes our marriage seem more real than anything else that's happened so far.

I wander through the house, opening drawers, letting my hands touch and my eyes roam. I need to get more comfortable here, somehow. He's never going to talk to me, trust me, if I keep acting like I can't wait to get away. There's a lot of room between willingly giving myself over to him and closing myself off completely. I just have to find a way to live in that space.

On the living room wall is a large version of the hand-drawn map of our town that hangs in City Hall. I kneel on the sofa to get a closer look at the bird's-eye view. The map shows all our major landmarks, both manmade and natural: City Hall, the courthouse, the river, the greenhouses where we grow most of our food, the solar panels that help provide our electricity, the water treatment plant, the fields of cotton we use to make clothing. The fence.

According to my father, the fence was originally constructed to keep predators out, both human and animal. It was never meant to keep us inside. And, even now, we are always free to leave. But hardly anyone ever does. Because no one knows what lies beyond the stretch of land we can see. What horrors might lurk over the horizon. Most people are content here, where at least there is food on the table and four walls to sleep behind. The memory of the war and the stories our grandparents told of starvation, radiation poisoning, and neighbors slaughtering neighbors in blind panic has made people reluctant to explore.

The only people who go beyond the fence are those who are forced to, put out as punishment for crimes, both real and perceived. Occasionally, someone manages to get back in, by tunneling under the fence or ripping a hole in the metal. But there are no second chances. If you return once you're put out, the punishment is death, no exceptions. My father said in the early days bandits breached the fence a few times looking for food or weapons, but we were always able to overpower them and drive them out again. Nothing like that has happened in my lifetime, though.

I know I can't sit in this house all day, staring at the walls, or I'll go crazy. I might as well try the market even if it's too soon for Callie to reach out to me. If nothing else, I can get some fresh air and stop chasing the thoughts inside my own head.

I've never been to the market on this side of town, but I know where it is. I go the long way, so I can walk past the president's house. It's another warm, sunny day, and although the sidewalks aren't crowded, there are other people out walking and riding bikes. Some of them give me furtive second glances that unnerve me until I remember who I am now. I duck my head and walk faster, letting my hair fall around my face like a curtain.

The president's house is dark and still, no movement behind the sheer curtains. A lone man works on the lawn, pushing a wheelbarrow of mulch. I stop and let my hands curl around the iron bars keeping me outside the grounds. Is Bishop inside the house right now, learning from his father the way I learned from mine? When the gardener catches my eye, I release my hold on the fence and move away.

I smell the market before I see it. The scent of apples, overripe vegetables, fresh earth float on the breeze, making my throat clench with longing for the market near my family's house. Even more than my own home, I always felt comfortable there, where everyone knew me by name. My father, although a leader in our section of the city, was always insular, keeping Callie and me contained in our little unit of three as much as he could. He believed in home-schooling, never encouraged friendships beyond each other. But in the market I felt a part of something bigger, a community that cared about me.

But this market is foreign to me, even though to an outsider it probably wouldn't look much different than the one I used to frequent. The stalls are bigger and the awnings brighter, and there isn't a single face I recognize. No one is rude to me, but I'm aware I don't belong with every step I take. I stand on the outside edges of the crowds around the stalls, observing but not participating. A woman in a printed dress hands me a pastry as I pass by her table.

"Oh, no," I say, shaking my head. "I'm not buying any-thing."

She smiles. "No charge. Enjoy it." She keeps her hand extended, and it would be rude to keep walking. I take the pastry from her.

"Thank you," I say, smiling back.

"You're welcome, Mrs. Lattimer," she says, and the smile slides off my face. Are they going to try and give me gifts now? Is that what it means to be Bishop Lattimer's wife, everyone wanting to give me things I don't deserve because of my name? Is this what Bishop's life is like? And how long does it take before you start thinking you *do* deserve it, that it should all belong to you?

I hand the pastry to the next child I pass, a little girl who looks up at me with delighted eyes. Weaving through the crowd, I find the small stall at the end where an older man sells jars of jelly and mustard. Even those are fancier here, scalloped edges on the labels and colored twine tied around the lids.

"Hello," I say. I pretend to study the jar of mustard in my hand.

"Hello," he says in return, his eyes taking in the crowd behind me. "Anything I can help you with?" One of his arms curls uselessly against his chest, the hand withered and hooked like a claw. Such birth defects are common in Westfall, an ongoing casualty of nuclear war.

"No." I set down the mustard. "Just looking." As I scoot over to make room for the family on my right, the man gives me a quick shake of his head. No message from Callie. I didn't think there would be, but disappointment still courses through my blood, leaving me tired and defeated.

But I cannot afford to be discouraged. She will contact me when the time is right. Until then, I have to figure out how to play Bishop's wife in a way he will believe.

He is still not home by six o'clock. I made scrambled eggs a half hour ago and now they are congealing on the stove. It is ridiculous to be annoyed with him, since I was the one who didn't ask any questions when he left this morning, simply glad for him to be gone and not staring at me with those eyes that seem to be constantly sizing me up with every glance.

I go ahead and set the table, concentrating on lining up the forks and napkins so I don't have to think about anything else. When the front door opens, I move to the stove and flip the burner back on.

"Hi," I call out, "I'm in here," wincing at the stupid sing-song note of my voice.

He doesn't answer, but I hear his footsteps crossing the living room. "Hello," he says from the doorway. I didn't notice it yesterday, when I was strung tight with nerves, but his voice is deep and slightly sleepy, like the words he speaks come from some cavern inside him and are in no particular rush to leave his mouth.

"I made dinner," I say, glancing at him. He's leaning in the doorway, arms crossed. He's wearing a dark gray T-shirt and worn jeans and he looks more at ease in casual clothes, the same way I suspect I do. His thick dark hair is slightly messy, like he's been running his fingers through it or been out in the wind. I return my attention to the eggs I'm trying to unglue from the bottom of the pan.

"I hope you're hungry," I say. "Because I am. Starving. I barely ate anything today." I'm rambling, trying too hard, and snap my mouth closed.

He doesn't respond. I risk another look at him and he's giving me a small half smile, his gaze curious. "What are you doing?" he asks finally.

"Cooking," I say, the beginnings of exasperation licking around the edges of my patience. I'm trying, at least. Why can't he just go along with it? So far he hasn't lived up to any of my imaginings. Replacing commands with silence, violence with patience, superiority with what feels like empathy. I am hit with a sudden wave of anger at my sister. I need her here to tell me what to do in the face of a boy who is not acting in any of the ways she prepared me to expect.

"Hmmm…" is all he says. The quiet grows around us until I can't take it anymore. I have to fill it up with something, even if it's misplaced anger. I slam the spatula down on the counter with a little too much force and small bits of egg fly off, spattering my arm. It is this, of all things—hot egg smearing across my skin—that brings tears to my eyes. I turn away, fumbling for the rag at the end of the counter.

Behind me, I hear the burner click off, the frying pan sliding to the back of the stove. He puts a hand on my shoulder and I try very hard not to flinch, but he must sense it anyway because his hand drops away.

"Come on," he says. "Let's go sit down."

I turn around but keep my face averted, concentrating on cleaning my arm. "What about dinner?"

"I think it can wait."

I follow him into the living room and wait for him to sit in one of the armchairs before I take a seat on the couch across from him. I fold my legs up under me and pick at a loose thread on the cushion. It is still light out, but the sun has begun its slow descent. Because this room faces east, the shadows are beginning to creep in, masking both of us in twilight. He doesn't turn on the lamp and I'm glad. Maybe it will be easier this way, with something to hide behind.

"I know this is difficult," he says. He leans forward and puts his elbows on his knees, stares at his laced hands. "It's hard for me, too."

I don't know what to say, so I say nothing.

He lets out a frustrated sigh. "You don't…you don't have to be any certain way with me, Ivy. I don't expect anything. I want you to be yourself." He leans back and scrubs at his face with one hand. He sounds tired. "I just want to know who you are."

"Okay," I say, while my brain searches for all the hidden meanings behind his words, trying to figure out what it is he really wants. Because it seems impossible that he is coming into this relationship without an agenda of his own. "What do you want to know?"

Bishop leans forward again and stares at me. "Everything," he says quietly, and my stomach clenches. "Anything."

I know I have to tell him something, but I need to be careful. And even beyond the worries about all the secrets I hold, there is the nagging feeling that I'm not even sure who I am, apart from my family. For most of my life, I was the spare daughter, the one who would stay by my father's side and work behind the scenes while Callie took center stage. And then, unexpectedly, two years ago, I became the focus. I've spent my whole life becoming the girl they need me to be, and I've shoved any parts that don't fit so far down inside myself I don't think I can find them anymore. It is one more violation to have to reach down and offer myself up to this stranger.

I force my fingers to stop worrying the cushion thread. "Umm...I don't know." I take a deep breath. "I like strawberries. I wish I were a few inches shorter. I'm scared of snakes. I like to read. My mother died when I was a baby." I say the words fast, as if the sheer speed at which I spit them out will render them less personal, although they are hardly deep, dark secrets. I wonder if he knows what his father did to my family? How he took away my mother—had her killed—to remind us who has the power. Just thinking about it makes heat rush into my cheeks, my heart thundering against my ribs. I should stop, but instead, I look up at him, hold his eyes. "I don't like the things your father does." Callie may be the fiercer one, but there is a recklessness in me that cannot be contained. "Is that what you wanted to know?"

The expression on Bishop's face doesn't change, his eyes still and calm. "It's a start," he says eventually.

I know he is waiting for me to ask him questions in return, to express curiosity about him and his life. But I don't care. I already know everything about him that's worth knowing. I know who his father is and what his family stands for. Anything beyond that doesn't matter to me. But I can hear my father's voice in my head: *Step one is establishing trust. Talk to him, get him to open up to you.*

"What about you?" I ask, trying hard to sound interested. "It's your turn now."

"Okay," he says. "I like pecans. I wish I had my father's cleft chin." His eyes gleam and I know he's teasing me. I'm not sure whether to be annoyed or relieved. "I'm scared of confined spaces," he continues. "I like being outdoors. My mother drives me crazy." He pauses, looks right at me. "I like the way your eyes flash when you're angry. Is that what you wanted to know?"

Something flutters in my chest. "It's a start," I say.

4

wake the next morning to an empty house. Bishop is already gone, a note left on the kitchen table telling me he'll be back by five. I'm hit with a small flare of disappointment as I read it. Not that I'll miss him or wanted him to stay, but I don't know what to do with myself for another day. I've never been good at sitting still unless there's a book in my hand. Too long without activity and my mind races, something Callie says can only lead to trouble. She always said it with a smile, but I never once thought she was joking.

Alone in the house, with a long day stretching in front of me, I realize how truly isolated I am. Other than my sister, I don't really have a single friend in the world. My father home-schooled us, not trusting President Lattimer's influence over the curriculum. He also worried that we might slip up and tell someone our intentions if we became too close to other children. Although there were people on our side of town who grumbled about President Lattimer and his policies, my father thought it safer to keep our plans private, an army of three. He never spoke outright of revolution and warned us not to, either.

For the last two years, he's kept me particularly segregated, while he and Callie have worked hard to build up relationships on our side of town, shoring up alliances by helping people when they ran short of food or speaking with President Lattimer on behalf of those with small grievances. They've also done some good deeds for those on this side of town, like the man in the market whose daughter they were able to help when she fell sick last winter and who now happily acts as a messenger. My father always says that once he takes over, people will remember those good deeds and we'll have plenty of support behind us. But until then, true friends outside the family are discouraged, too many ways those relationships can come back to haunt us. But today I would do almost anything to have someone to talk to, a friend who could occupy my spinning mind for even a few minutes.

After a breakfast of oatmeal and raspberries and a quick shower, I wander out onto the screened porch off the kitchen. It's a large room with a floor covered in once white-washed planks, now faded to a tired gray. Two wicker sofas topped with yellow cushions face each other across a low wrought-iron table. My namesake grows up the sides of the screens, giving the porch a cozy, cocoon-like feeling. I can see out, but the ivy gives the illusion that no one else can see in.

The back door of the neighboring house opens and a girl emerges, carrying a basket over one arm, gardening gloves clasped in her fist. Her hair is long and stick straight, a shiny, pale blond. The kind of hair I've always secretly wanted instead of my tumbled and tangled mass of waves, my own color more plain honey than spun gold. I recognize her from my side of town, although I'm sure I've never officially met her. It's possible she was at the marriage ceremony, but I was too preoccupied to pay close attention. She is halfway down her back steps when the screen door opens again and a boy leans out, grabbing her forearm.

"What about my breakfast?" he asks her.

"I left cereal out," she says. Her voice is high and child-like. "And I made fruit salad."

From where I stand, concealed by the greenery, I see his hand tighten on her arm. She winces and tries to pull away, but he jerks her back toward him. "That's not breakfast," he says. His voice is reasonable, not raised, which makes it more frightening. "I want eggs. Or pancakes. Something hot."

"All right," the girls says. "Just let me—"

"Now," he says.

I push open the screen door to the porch and bound down the steps toward them.

"Hi," I call out. Both their heads whip in my direction.

The boy's eyes narrow briefly, then clear. He drops the girl's arm and comes down the steps toward the low fence separating our yards. "Hi there," he says with a smile.

I smile back at him, although it costs me something

to do it, and find the girl's eyes over his shoulder. "I'm Ivy…Lattimer," I say. The name still sounds foreign on my tongue, like I'm introducing a girl I've never met, "We just moved in."

"Sure," the boy says, "I know who you are. I went to school with Bishop, although he was a few years ahead of me." He holds out his hand. "I'm Dylan Cox." He hooks a thumb back over his shoulder. "And this is my wife, Meredith. We're new to the neighborhood, too."

"Hi," Meredith says. Her eyes ping-pong between her husband and me.

"It's nice to meet you," I say. "Well, I just wanted to introduce myself."

Dylan smiles at me again. It's an infectious smile, one that's difficult to resist. Looking at it makes me think maybe I'm wrong about what I saw, wrong about what kind of boy I think he is.

"Don't be a stranger," he tells me. I stand at the fence and watch until he and Meredith go back inside, the dark doorway swallowing them whole.

By afternoon, I have to get out of the house, even if I have no particular destination in mind. I'm bored and restless and I can't stop replaying the scene with Dylan and Meredith in my head. *That* is exactly the type of relationship my father always talked about when he railed against the arranged marriages. He said that forcing young girls to marry boys they'd never met and who were considered a better class, even if no one said it out loud, set up an unbalanced power structure that often resulted in abuse and violence. And now I've seen evidence of it first hand. I want to help Meredith, but I'm not sure how. Once my father's plan is fully in place, it might be too late for her.

Without any conscious thought, I find myself wandering to the green space that separates the populated sections of town from the uninhabited woods. It's more than twenty acres of grass and rolling hills, dotted with trees and a large pond. There is a path for bicycles, and a wider one for walking, but today, a Monday afternoon, only a few other people are visible in the distance.

I ignore the path and cut straight through the long grass, heading toward the pond and the ducks I used to feed as a child. There is a low wooden bridge over the water, and I cross halfway and lower myself to sitting, my legs dangling above the water, my arms folded on the bottom of the wooden rail. I rest my chin on my hands and watch the ducks splash around below my feet, wishing I'd thought to bring some bread to throw for them.

I don't look up when I hear steps on the bridge, but then a pair of legs slots in to place beside mine and a voice as familiar as my own cuts the silence. "Tell me everything," says Callie, her shoulder pushing into mine.

I suppose I should be surprised to see her here, but I'm not. My entire life she's always been one step ahead of me—of most people, for that matter. She always says she has eyes everywhere, and it's wise to take Callie at her word. Besides, I'm too relieved to see her to care how she knew where to find me.

"Callie," I say, smiling. "I went to the market yesterday, but there wasn't a message. I'm glad you're here."

"Me, too," she says, her eyes raking my face. "Are you okay?"

"Yes. But we're not living in President Lattimer's house. Did you know that?"

She nods. "I found out yesterday. From what I've heard, that was Bishop's idea. He didn't want to live with his parents." She shrugs. "Makes sense, I guess. But it definitely complicates things." She pins me with her gaze. "You're going to have to figure out a way to get what we need. You'll be in and out of that house, I'm sure. It may take a little longer, that's all."

"Okay," I say. The thought of snooping around President Lattimer's house while I lived there and might be able to think of a valid excuse if caught was bad enough. Doing it this way will be even worse.

One of the ducks below us dives for food, splashing cool water onto my foot. It tickles as it runs over my instep.

"So," Callie says, her voice quiet. "Was it bad? Did he hurt you?"

I glance at her. She is staring down at the water, her jaw clenched. "No," I say. "We didn't…you know."

She twists her head in my direction. "Why not?"

"I don't know, really. I think he could tell I was scared, that I didn't want to." I kick my feet back and forth. "Maybe he didn't want to, either."

Callie snorts. "The guy has self-control, I'll give him that. I didn't think he'd be able to resist…all that," she says, flapping a hand in my direction.

"Stop it," I say, but I can't help the little laugh that escapes me. It is good to laugh, even over something that's not really funny.

"And he's clever," Callie says. "Not forcing anything makes him seem like a nicer guy than he actually is. How's the rest of it going? Are you getting him to trust you?"

"It's been *two* days."

"I know that, Ivy. But we don't have the luxury of endless time. Three months, that's what you've got. The clock is already ticking."

Three months. I don't know if it's too long or not long enough. But it's the amount of time I have to complete the steps in my father's plan, the last one being to kill Bishop. President Lattimer's death will follow, and Callie's told me that plan is already in motion, cannot be slowed down or stopped. But Bishop has to die first. I don't know all the details. My father thinks it's safer if I only have pieces, in case I'm caught. But what I do know is that if I screw up, our plans will be ruined.

"So, are you doing what we told you, getting him to trust you?" Callie repeats.

"I guess so," I say finally. "I mean, we're talking." I think about the conversation we had last night. "I said something negative about his father, though. I probably shouldn't have done that."

"Oh my God, Ivy," Callie says, voice raised. "You are supposed to play *nice*. How many times did we go over this?"

"I don't think he was mad. He didn't seem upset by it."

Callie rolls her eyes. "Oh, yeah, I'm sure he doesn't care at all that his brand-new wife is criticizing the man he wants to turn into when he grows up!"

"It wasn't like that," I say, my own voice rising. "I mean, maybe he's acting. But it seems like he just wants to get to know me."

"Of course he's acting," Callie says, like I'm the dumbest person alive. "All he cares about is keeping his dad in power and you giving him a bunch of sons to continue the line. He's not interested in *you*."

I shift away from her, fix my gaze on the far side of the pond. I know what she's saying is true, but it doesn't exactly *feel* true, at least not completely, not when I remember the way Bishop asked me about myself, like he really cared about the answers.

"Remember what we talked about? How they'll try to muddle your thinking? Turn black to white and up to down? Try to make you believe he cares more about you than we do?"

I nod. I know she's right. I *know* what the truth is; I know my family wouldn't lead me astray and everything they ask me to do is for the good of us all. I have to be strong enough to remember their lessons. More than anything, I want to make them proud.

"Don't let him fool you," Callie says, and her voice is gentler now. "Don't forget what they're capable of." She pauses. "Remember what they did to Mom?"

I close my eyes. "Yes," I say, the familiar anger flowing through my veins. I have no memory of my mother, only a few stories passed down from Callie—how she sang us to sleep at night, how her hair always smelled like lavender. Stories I've relived so often in my mind that now they are worn and threadbare. But for everything I don't know about my mother, the one thing I'm sure of is that my life would have been different if she'd lived. My father quicker with a smile, less instructor and more parent. Callie less bitter and more joyful. All of us whole, instead of forever missing a vital piece. When President Lattimer killed my mother he did more than take her life. He took the lives we should have had as well.

"Keep your eyes on the goal, Ivy," Callie says. "Don't let your temper or your mouth get the best of you. You need to manipulate, not confront. That's how you'll get to him." She scoots closer to me, rests her hand on my back.

"Remember the dog?" she asks. I don't bother nodding because I know she's going to tell me the story anyway. "We'd walk to the market past that stupid, mangy dog Mrs. Paulson always had tied to her fence. And every day it would lunge at us and bark and go crazy. I told you a hundred times to ignore it, keep walking. I told you I'd figure out a way to handle that dog. But it made you so mad, that we had to be scared whenever we walked down the street." Callie removes her hand from my back and lays it on my arm. "Then one day you'd had enough, and you marched over there and swung your bag at it." Her voice sounds amused, but her eyes are serious. "And this is what you got in return." She rolls my forearm to the side, revealing the shiny, almost silvery scar tissue, traces her finger over the bite marks, the ripped and remade flesh. "All because you couldn't bide your time." She lets go of my arm. "Who won that day, Ivy? You or the dog?"

I glare at her, hating her just a little bit. "The dog," I finally say.

"But who won in the end?" she asks. The look in her eyes, a kind of wicked triumph, sends a sliver of unease down my spine.

"You did," I whisper, remembering the morning, not long after I was bitten, when we walked to the market and the dog lay dead, his chain wrapped around his neck, his tongue black where it lolled out of his half-open mouth.

"Don't bait him, Ivy," she says, standing up. "Don't ruin everything just to make a point." She brushes off the seat of her shorts with both hands. "We're not in this to win a few battles. We're in it to win the war."

5

Bishop returns home at five, exactly as he said he would. I didn't bother making dinner because I wasn't sure he'd be true to his word. He finds me lounging on one of the wicker couches on the screened porch, my bare legs hanging over the arm, feet dangling.

"Hi," he says. "How was your day?" He's got a small sack of groceries in one arm. There is a container of strawberries resting at the top.

"Boring," I tell him. There's a pause that goes on too long. "How was yours?"

He shrugs, turns to set the bag down on the kitchen table behind him before joining me on the porch. "Fine. Uneventful." He takes a seat on the sofa opposite me. "You're too smart to sit around here all day staring at the walls," he says.

"How do you know I'm smart?"

He just stares at me. In moments like this, it's easy to see how he was born to be a leader. His is the kind of face that intimidates simply by existing, so handsome it's almost scary. He has a strong jaw, with just the barest hint of his father's cleft chin, high cheekbones, those clear green eyes under straight dark brows. But he doesn't give the impression he's affected by his own beauty. It's impossible he's unaware of his looks; I'm sure enough people have told him over the years. Or stopped and stared. It's more that he seems unconcerned with how he looks, the image he sees in the mirror the last thing he's worried about.

"Okay, so...yeah," I say, shifting uncomfortably. "I agree. I need something to do." Most wives don't work. It's not forbidden, exactly, but it's certainly not encouraged. If they're lucky, babies start coming right away and that keeps them busy. A few work as teachers or train as nurses, set up small stands at the market if they can't have children. But reproducing, keeping families healthy and happy, that's what we're really expected to do. My father always told stories of the way it was before the war, stories he'd heard from his own father. About women judges and doctors, women running for president, even. Not every woman did that, of course. Some still stayed home and raised their families. But it was their decision, not one made for them. Women had choices back then—who to marry, what to be, free to pick whatever path they wanted to travel. It seems like a distant dream to me.

"You could work in the hospital," Bishop says. "Or

one of the schools. They always need teachers, I know." I glance at him, surprised. He doesn't seem fazed at all by the thought of my working, of trying to forge an identity separate from that of the wife of Bishop Lattimer. Is he as skillful at manipulation as Callie wants me to become?

Step two, find a way into the courthouse. But be subtle, wait for the right moment, don't push. But don't wait too long, either. Without even knowing it, Bishop has given me the opening I need. "What about something in the courthouse?" I ask. "I like the idea of working with the judges." I shrug, going for casual. "It seems like it would be interesting."

"Okay," Bishop says. "Let me talk to my dad, see what's available. I'm sure he can pull some strings."

I hate the idea of owing President Lattimer anything, but I need access to the courthouse. I give a quick, closed-mouth smile. "Thanks."

We sit in silence for a minute, the only sound the slight rustle of leaves in the big oak in the backyard. I wonder if we'll ever be able to have a normal conversation or if, at least, this silence between us will someday feel less strained.

"Come on," Bishop says, standing. "Let's get out of here."

I push myself upright. "Where are we going?"

"You'll see."

hesitate when I see where he's headed, my footsteps slowing until I'm barely moving at all. Bishop pauses, one hand on the gate outside his parents' house. The early evening light catches his eyes, and I notice for the first time that he has a darker green rim around each iris, the edges more emerald than lime.

"Why are we here?" I ask. I shove my hands into my back pockets. I'm trying to remain calm, like my heart isn't thumping out of my chest, but I don't think it's working. "They might not like us dropping by unannounced."

"They're not even home," Bishop says. "But they wouldn't mind." He pushes the gate, and it swings open on silent hinges. I don't have any choice but to follow him.

Bishop punches a code into a keypad by the front door and lets us inside. The foyer is cool and quiet, our footsteps muffled by the thick rug that runs almost the full length and width of the space. In the center is an ornate round table, a huge arrangement of flowers in its center. The smell is cloying, as if the flowers are on the edge of rotting. Dust motes hang in the still air, lit up by the late afternoon sun flowing in from a window above the front door.

"What are we doing?" I ask, my voice a whisper.

Bishop gives me a quick grin. "It's okay to talk," he says at normal volume. "Trust me, I didn't whisper my way through childhood."

I look at the sweeping staircase leading upstairs, which is already bathed in shadows. A hallway unfurls on either side of the base of the stairs, leading to the back of the house. Everything is hushed and perfect, and I can't imagine a child running through these halls with muddy hands or thundering feet. The house feels lonely to me, and it's not because we are the only ones here. It has an emptiness at its heart. Growing up here an only child can't have been easy.

"This way," Bishop says, pointing to the right side of the staircase and leading me down the hall. As we walk, I glance to my left and catch a glimpse of a study through an open doorway—big wooden desk, a couple of chairs, the president's seal framed on the wall. At the end of the hall, Bishop pushes open a thick walnut door and flips on the light switch with the flat of his hand.

It's a library. Books fill three walls, floor to ceiling, and a small ladder leans against the far wall so the highest shelves can be reached. There are lamps positioned on two end tables near a pair of wide, cushioned armchairs. I don't want to be impressed, I don't want to be awed, but I can't help it. We have a public library in town, but with too many people and not enough books, it can take months for something worth reading to become available. Often, when I am able to check out a book, I read it a dozen times before returning it, desperate to remain lost in the magic of someone else's story.

"Why aren't these in the library?" I ask, torn between anger that the president hoards these books for himself and selfish gratitude that I may be allowed to read them.

Bishop runs his hand along the spines of the books closest to him. "He did give a lot to the library. But he likes to have his own collection." He turns to me. "You can take anything you want, for as long as you want. And I don't need to be with you. I'll write down the front door code for you. My father won't mind you being here."

I can't imagine coming here alone, walking that hallway and spending time in this room knowing President Lattimer is somewhere in this house with me. But having the code will come in handy. And I'm not surprised Bishop offered it to me. No one worries too much about the president's safety nowadays. The majority of Westfall is far too happy to have food on the table, medicine in the hospital, and peace outside their front door. No one is in a hurry to upset the status quo, and hurting the president would definitely do that. All the same, goose bumps break out on my arms at the thought of being alone in this house with President Lattimer.

"You don't need to be afraid of him," Bishop says, taking a step closer. "He's not a monster."

It is on the tip of my tongue to say, *Maybe not, but he's done monstrous things*, until I remember Callie's words, warning me not to bait him, and I force the words back down, where they burn in my throat. I spin away, pretending to be engrossed with the books in front of me.

"You said you liked to read," Bishop says from right behind me. I never heard him move. "I thought this place might make you happy."

I take a deep breath and turn to face him, my hands curled around the bottom edge of the shelf behind me. He is close to me, close enough to touch, although he keeps his hands at his sides. His eyes roam over my face.

"Thank you," I manage. My fingers tighten on the shelf. I try to remember Callie's words, *manipulate don't confront*, but I am having trouble putting those words into practice. My way has always been straight through, even if the wiser course is the path around.

"Why are you being nice to me?" I ask him. Although *nice* isn't really the word I want to use. He's not *nice* the way boys in stories are, with poetic words and worshipful eyes, everything about them reverent and soft. There's nothing soft about Bishop. But these books, the strawberries in the bag, the offer of a job, the way he hasn't touched me—there is a kindness in those actions that makes no sense to me.

His head jerks back a little, his forehead furrowing. "Why wouldn't I be?"

I think about our new neighbors, Dylan and Meredith, his hand on her arm squeezing too tight, the soft menace in his voice. Already I can't imagine Bishop treating me that way, but that doesn't mean he isn't capable of it. It doesn't mean he won't. I shrug, look down, trying to find a way to answer his question without sounding angry. "It's just…a lot of times…with these arranged marriages, it doesn't work that way." I glance back up at him.

He doesn't respond, looks at me like he's waiting for me to finish my thought. He leans forward and I press back against the bookcase, but he only puts one arm above my head and leans sideways next to me, giving me his full attention. Already he's upset my balance. I can't remember the last time someone really listened to me. I'm usually the one doing the listening.

"When boys believe they've been given something, even if it's another person, it's easy to view the girl as a possession," I say. "Something that belongs to them. If something belongs to you, you think you're allowed to treat it any way you want."

"But couldn't you say that of any marriage?" Bishop asks. "Doesn't it depend more on the people involved and not how the marriage came to be?" He's not barking at me, doesn't seem upset by my opinions. His brow is still furrowed, like he's genuinely interested in the conversation, trying hard to understand my point of view.

"Well, yeah, I guess," I say. "But here, with us..." I pause. It's awkward to refer to our status as married. It doesn't seem real. I don't feel like his wife. "Or with any of the other couples, everyone knows the wife is less valuable because of who we are. We're marrying up." I can't keep the bitterness from my voice. "And when you marry up, someone is always looking down at you."

Bishop stares at me for so long and with such intensity that a blush blooms on my cheeks. I want to lay a hand along my face, use my palm to cool the heat, but my fingers won't uncurl from the shelf behind me.

"Obviously I can't speak for everyone," he says eventually. "But I don't see it that way." He pauses. "I don't see *you* that way."

I try to breathe Callie into my body, become the instrument of her words. This is where I smile and look at him from under my eyelashes. This is where I let him know how grateful I am for his view of me, where I say I'm such a lucky girl. But I open my mouth and say instead, "So you agree with this, the arranged marriages?"

"I didn't say that." He shifts and leans his back against the shelves, mimicking my pose. The heat from his body warms my side across the small space between us. "But in the course of history, there are a lot worse ways to try and keep the peace."

I laugh, short and sharp. "Spoken like a man."

He looks at me again, but I keep my eyes forward, staring at a random point across the room. "You're not the only one this happened to, Ivy," he says. "No one asked me if I wanted to get married, either."

"I know that," I say, defensive. But he's right, I don't think about the boys as often as the girls. Not even the boys from my side of town, who marry the girls from here. Because even then, the girls get the worst of it. Their new husbands are already angry that they're marrying girls who everyone thinks are better than them, and who better to take those feelings of inadequacy out on than their new wives?

And I especially didn't think about Bishop. I guess I assumed his father's arrogance passed seamlessly on to him, that he never cared much about our marriage one way or the other except as something he was entitled to take without earning.

"Doesn't it bother you?" I ask. "That all our choices are made for us?"

Bishop shrugs, and I want to scream. I don't understand how he can be so calm about everything, like nothing affects him. "It doesn't do any good to be angry about something you can't change."

"I don't think there's anything that can't be changed, if people want it badly enough," I say, while my mind whispers, *Careful...careful.*

"That may be true, in the abstract," Bishops says. "But right now and right here, the bottom line is, we're married. Whether we want to be or not. We have to figure out how to make this work. We don't have another choice."

I know what the other choice is and it ends with him dead and my father in charge. "Okay," I say. "I'll try." I don't sound very convincing, even to myself.

"Okay," Bishop says, pushing away from the bookcase. "Now, let's find you something to read."

I turn to look at the rows of books behind me, let my fingers trace across their spines. I'm not even searching for anything in particular yet, just enjoying the smell and sight.

"What about this one?" Bishop says. He's holding up a thin, black leather volume, the writing on the cover too small for me to read from where I stand. "*Romeo and Juliet.*" He waves the book in my direction. "Rival families. Star-crossed teenage lovers." His face is deadpan, but his eyes are laughing.

"Very funny."

"Call me crazy," he says. "But it sounds pretty intriguing."

I turn back to the bookcase before he can see my grin.

True to his word, Bishop talked to his father about my working at the courthouse. I imagine President Lattimer objected to the idea initially, but apparently Bishop is persuasive because I start tomorrow. I'm in the bedroom, trying to figure out what to wear for my first day on the job, when Bishop calls my name.

"What?" I ask, walking into the living room. He's standing there with a pile of dirty clothes at his feet. I point at the laundry. "What's that about?"

"I figure it's not going to do itself," Bishop says. "The longer we wait, the more we'll have, right?"

"Yes," I say, "that's generally how it works. But I don't have time to do it today. Maybe this weekend?"

"I'll do it," Bishop says, surprising me. Laundry is usually the wife's job. "But would you mind showing me how?" He palms the back of his neck with one hand. "I've never done it before."

"Really?" I ask, eyebrows going up. "Never?" Most boys on my side of town at least know how to wash clothes, even if they rarely perform the chore.

"Nope. There are maids in my dad's house. It's just not something I ever learned."

Of course it isn't. He's probably never had to do a lot of things the rest of us do daily. The spoiled president's son. I want to be annoyed with him, but at least he's making an attempt. And I remember what Callie told me at the park: to play nice, to not let my mouth run away from me. I've already ignored her advice too many times, so I manage to bite back my thoughts.

I eye the pile of clothes. "Grab the laundry and meet me outside."

In the backyard is a metal trough, similar to the one we used growing up. I pull the hose from the side of the house and begin filling the trough with water. Bishop's dropped the clothes on the cement patio and holds a bag of soap flakes in his hand. "Okay," I say, "sprinkle some of those in here. You want to put them in while the water's still running, otherwise they just sit on top and don't lather up." Bishop nods and proceeds to dump half the bag into the water. "Not so much!" I tell him. "I said sprinkle! Sprinkle!"

"Sorry," Bishops says. "What do I do? Take some out?"

"You can try."

He uses both hands to scoop half-dissolved soap flakes out of the water, flinging them onto the lawn. "I don't think this is working," he says. "I am clearly not meant for a life of laundry."

"Well, don't worry. It's probably the only time you'll have to do it."

Bishop frowns. "Why would you say that?"

"Because I'm the wife," I say slowly, "and you're the husband. And that's how things are done here."

"I don't care about that," Bishop says. "I mean, you have a job now, right? So it seems fair we should both help out around the house."

I sit back on my heels, turning his words over in my head, searching for the trap. "Okay," I say finally.

Bishop gives me a quick nod. "Okay." He turns his

attention back to the trough. "Now I just have to get the rest of this soap out of here."

A giggle bursts out of me, totally unexpected, and Bishop glances over. "What?" he asks.

"You look ridiculous," I tell him. His sleeves are rolled up and he's covered in water and soap flakes from fingertip to elbow, a handful of slimy soap still cupped in his hands. Another giggle escapes, and I cover my mouth with the back of my hand. "Sorry," I choke out.

He flings the soap away and wipes his hands on his shorts. "Yeah, laugh it up," he says, smiling. "What now?"

"Now you put a couple pieces of clothes in. Two or three!" I say when he grabs the whole pile. "Not everything!"

"This is going to take forever when we have a full load," he mutters as he throws two shirts and a pair of pants into the sudsy water.

"Then you take the washboard." I point to the wooden and metal washboard next to the trough. "And you scrub the clothes on it. Like this." I take one of the shirts and run it up and down the washboard, move it around until I've gotten it scrubbed and then pull it from the water. "Then you rinse it and hang it and you're done."

"Got it," Bishop says.

I rinse the shirt I've already washed and pin it to the line while Bishop gets to work on the rest of the clothes. When I turn back around, he's washing a pair of pants, scrubbing them like he means to wear a hole through the cloth.

"Umm…you're trying to get them clean," I tell him. "Not beat them into submission."

Bishop looks up at me. His dark hair is falling onto his forehead, and his nose crinkles up when he laughs. It makes him look younger, carefree. For the first time, I can clearly picture him as a boy. We stare at each other for a long moment, and then he begins washing again, gentler this time.

I take a deep breath, ignore the heat rushing to my cheeks. "That's better," I say, walking toward the house. "I'll just be here, on the screened porch relaxing, while you finish up. You obviously need the practice."

He flings a handful of soap in my direction and I dodge it with a yelp. Once I'm safely out of range, I realize this is the first time I've spent more than five minutes with him where I wasn't thinking about the plan or what to do next. Which is exactly what my father and Callie want, for me to act natural, to make it seem real. I should be happy. But I remember Bishop's laugh, his crinkly nose, the warmth in my cheeks, and can't help feeling I've done something wrong.

The courthouse is limestone like City Hall, and they sit directly across the town square from one another. My eyes slide over to City Hall as I climb the courthouse steps. Inside I'm sure they've dismantled the stage, put all the chairs back in storage until next year. The lives of dozens of children changed in the course of a day and the evidence already whisked away.

The courthouse entryway is smaller than the City Hall rotunda, but it has the same tile floors, the same chill in the air from the limestone walls. Two uniformed guards stand inside the door, guns in holsters on their hips. It's rare to see a gun these days. They are illegal to own and even the police don't carry them routinely, making do with batons and martial arts if situations get out of hand, which isn't very often. I remind myself not to stare. My flats make a loud clacking noise on the floor and already a blister is forming on my heel, making me long for my sandals.

There is an overweight man with glasses that seem too small for his face sitting at the reception desk. He watches me approach but doesn't speak, even once I reach the desk.

"Hi," I say. "I'm supposed to meet with Victoria Jameson."

"And you are?" he drawls.

"Ivy Lattimer."

For a split second, I relish the look of surprise on his face, the nervous recognition that accompanies his suddenly bright smile. But just as swiftly, I remember the day in the market when the woman gave me the pastry because of my name. I don't want people to like me or be afraid of me because of who I am. Lattimer doesn't even really belong to me anyway. It's just something I put on, like a dress or a pair of shoes.

"Mrs. Lattimer," he says, standing. "I didn't realize you were coming here today. If I'd known…"

I give him a strained smile. "I need to know where I can find Mrs. Jameson."

After a little more fumbling, some of it coming dangerously close to bowing and scraping, the man points me toward the stairs, tells me to go up to the third floor and take a left.

The door to Victoria Jameson's office is open and I can hear voices coming from inside. I stop outside the doorway and wait for someone to notice me, hesitant to interrupt. There is a man and woman in the room, the woman standing

THE BOOK OF IVY

behind the desk and the man sitting in the chair facing her.

"No," the woman is saying, "she was put out last time. But her parents won't stop shouting about it. President Lattimer wants it taken care of."

"Okay," the man says. "So one more warning?" He shifts forward. "If that doesn't work, then we charge them with disturbing the peace and—" He breaks off when he catches sight of me in the doorway.

"Can we help you?" he asks, voice brisk.

"Ivy?" the woman asks. I nod. "Is it okay if I call you Ivy?"

"Sure." It's a relief to escape from being Mrs. Lattimer.

She comes around the desk, hand extended. "I'm Victoria Jameson." She motions to the man. "And this is Jack Stewart."

As we all exchange handshakes, I take the chance to study Victoria. She's in her mid-thirties, I'd guess, with cocoa-colored skin and curly hair that falls to the middle of her neck. A pair of glasses is perched on top of her head, and gold hoops swing from her ears. She has a no-nonsense air about her, but her smile is friendly.

"We can continue this discussion later," Jack tells Victoria. He gives me a nod and closes the door on his way out.

"So," Victoria says, taking her chair again behind the desk and pointing me to the one Jack vacated, "you're Bishop's wife."

"Yes."

"And you want a job."

"Yes."

I wait for her to purse her lips or give me a disapproving look, but she grins. "I think that's great! I've never been a big fan of the sit-at-home-and-pop-out-babies route. Especially when you're only sixteen."

"Me neither," I say, and she laughs. "What about you?" I ask. "How did you end up working here?" It's unusual for a woman of child-bearing age to work, especially in the courthouse.

"My father used to be a judge," Victoria says. "I grew up wanting to roam these halls."

"Do you have kids?" She probably doesn't, if she's working here.

A shadow crosses Victoria's face and she looks away, out the window overlooking the street. "I never had children," she says quietly. There is something more than sadness, than disappointment, in her voice. Shame, maybe? Which makes me doubt her earlier easy words about popping out babies.

"Okay," Victoria says, back to business. "I'm in charge of the judges' schedules, calendars, dockets, pretty much anything they need to keep both courtrooms running. Plus all the filing and paperwork. There's always too much work for one person, which is where you'll come in."

I still don't have a good idea of what I'll actually be doing day-to-day, but it hardly matters. I remember the guards by the front doors, the guns in their holsters, and know I'm in the right place. My father will be pleased.

On Friday of my first week of work, I wake early and hop in the shower while Bishop eats breakfast. Victoria asked me to come in before nine so we could get a courtroom set up for trial, and I don't want to be late. As I'm getting dressed, I hear Bishop starting his own shower, and I wait impatiently until he's finished before heading back to the bathroom to brush my teeth. "Oh, sorry," I say, brought up short in the doorway. "I thought you were done."

Bishop looks at me, the lower half of his face covered in lather, a razor in his hand. He is wrapped in a towel at his waist and nothing else, showing off the lean muscles of his stomach. His dark hair is slicked back with water, his bare chest as smooth and golden as the rest of him. He has a tiny, pale brown birthmark just beneath his ribs. I don't know what to do with my eyes, can't find any safe spot for them to settle. "It's fine," he says. "There's room."

There's really not, but I sidle in next to him and he moves back a step to make space for me in front of the small mirror. It's so quiet as I put toothpaste on my toothbrush that I can hear the drag of his razor against his skin. The bathroom smells of soap and mint and something fundamentally male that makes my neck flush with heat.

I keep my eyes on my toothbrush and then on the sink as I brush. But after I wipe my mouth and straighten up, my gaze catches Bishop's in the mirror. We stare at each other, and my whole body tingles with awareness. I try to think what a wife would do in this situation, but I don't have a lot to go on considering I grew up in a house without a mother.

Before I can second-guess myself, I turn and plant a quick kiss on his bare shoulder. "Thanks for sharing," I tell him. My heart is trying to beat its way out of my body and my lips burn where they met his warm skin.

I risk a look up at Bishop, preparing myself for what might come next. He is my husband and there are only a few strips of cloth separating us. This may be the moment when he is no longer content to wait. The thought sends both fear and a strange buzzing heat through my chest. But Bishop only stares at me, then barks out a laugh—not a very nice one. He wipes the last remnant of shaving cream off his face with a hand towel.

"What?" I demand, humiliation painting my cheeks red. "Why are you laughing?"

He pushes out of the bathroom ahead of me, and I follow behind him to the bedroom. His hand falls to his waist and he glances at me over his shoulder. "Fair warning," he says, "I'm about to drop this towel."

I whirl around and step out into the hall. Behind me, I hear the towel hit the floor, the sound of clothes rustling. When Bishop emerges, he's wearing shorts and pulling a T-shirt down over his flat stomach. "You didn't answer me," I remind him. "What was so funny?"

He pauses and runs a hand through his still-damp hair. "Don't fake it on my account, Ivy," he says, his words clipped. "That's not what I want. And it shouldn't be what you want, either."

Frustration ripples through me. "I'm sorry we can't all be as perfect as you are," I say. "I'm sorry I don't always know the exact right thing to do or say at the exact right time!"

Bishop's jaw tightens. "I'm not perfect."

"Well, it's kind of hard for us mere mortals to tell," I say. "Don't you ever get upset or angry or embarrassed? Do you feel anything?"

He blows out a breath, takes a step toward me. The hallway is so narrow that I'm pinned between the wall and his body, heat rolling off him in waves. "Yeah," he says, voice low. "I feel things." His green eyes burn. It's the most emotion I've seen from him so far, and I have trouble taking a full breath, my lungs compressed with tension. "That's the whole point, Ivy. I want you to feel them, too."

I open my mouth, close it again, not sure how to respond.

"Forget it," Bishop says. The last thing I hear is the front door slamming behind him.

What do you wear for a dinner with your enemy? I stand in the middle of the bedroom, every article of clothing I own forming a pitifully small mountain on the bed. The only real dress I have is the one I wore on my wedding day, and I never want to put it on again. Just the slide of the material against my skin makes me wince. But somehow I think Mrs. Lattimer would not appreciate me showing up in shorts and a T-shirt. What I want is to curl up with one of the books I borrowed from President Lattimer's library.

But I have to face the Lattimers sometime. It won't do me any good to pretend they don't exist.

President and Mrs. Lattimer summoned us for dinner yesterday, more than two weeks after the wedding. Perhaps they couldn't stomach the thought of me in their home before that. We were told to be there at eight, and Bishop said they always dined late, even when he was a boy. There is something unsettlingly pretentious about it.

I finally decide on a black skirt, short but loose, with flat black sandals and a pale purple tank top. I leave my hair down, where it falls to the middle of my back in crazy waves I long ago gave up trying to tame. It will have to be good enough. I'm not interested in spending any more time trying to impress them.

Bishop is waiting for me in the living room, wearing jeans and a black dress shirt, the collar unbuttoned and sleeves rolled up.

"You look nice," he says to me.

"Thank you," I say. My eyes are drawn to his bare forearms, and against my will I remember how he looked without his shirt, all smooth skin and lean muscle. A tiny pulse beats low in my belly. I raise my gaze up to his face, find him watching me.

"I'm sorry about this morning," he says. "I shouldn't have laughed."

"I'm sorry, too," I say. "I'm trying. I just…I don't always know what I'm supposed to do." The understatement of my life.

"There's no *supposed t*o, Ivy," he says. "I don't have a

checklist."

Ah, but I do, I think. And the fact that this boy knows when I'm faking affection, trying to force a connection, makes everything so much more difficult. Why can't he be like a normal eighteen-year-old? The kind who would take a kiss from a girl no matter why it was offered? Instead, Bishop wants authenticity, which is the one thing I cannot give him.

It is still light out when we leave the house, although the sun is starting to sink in the sky as we walk, our footsteps keeping time with each other on the empty sidewalk.

"How was your first week on the job?" Bishop asks.

"Good. I mean, so far I'm not doing anything too exciting. Mainly organizing files. But it's nice to have somewhere to go every day, something to do."

"I'm glad," he says. "I know the days can get long if you don't have a purpose."

Is he talking about himself? He leaves the house every morning, but I never have any idea where he's going. And most days he comes home smelling like sunshine, which is probably in short supply inside council meetings. Maybe he's been going to the river, while I've been at the courthouse. He hasn't told me and I haven't asked.

As we get closer to his parents' house, my heart begins to pick up speed, thumping twice as hard as it needs to, sweat beading along my hairline even though the night air isn't particularly hot.

"Want something to hold on to?" Bishop asks. I'm not sure what he's talking about until I glance down. His hand—tan skin, long fingers—is held out. My eyes fly back to his face and he's giving me a half smile, waiting to see what I'll do. Not forcing, just asking. My first instinct is to say no, although this feels less orchestrated than the kiss in the bathroom, more natural somehow. But I've never held hands with a boy before and while it's hardly intimate, my stomach is still sick with nervous butterflies. I know I should accept; Callie would want me to.

I slide my hand into Bishop's, and he laces our fingers together. The warm pressure of his palm steadies me, spreading heat from my hand up my arm where it seems to pool in my chest, calming the mad pounding of my heart.

He holds my hand all the way up the long drive to his parents' house and only releases it once we've stepped inside the door. My bare palm feels naked, and I have to resist the urge to scramble for his fingers when his father approaches.

"Bishop, Ivy!" President Lattimer calls out. He comes toward us with both arms outstretched and pulls us into hugs before I can deflect him. "We're happy you could join us. We wanted to have you over earlier, but you know your mother," he says with a grin at Bishop, "she has to make sure everything's perfect." Which sounds like an excuse to me. It must to Bishop, too, because he raises his eyebrows at me over his father's shoulder.

Erin Lattimer appears behind her husband, a pained smile on her face, like someone is pulling on her cheeks at the same time she's gritting her teeth. She is wearing a cherry red skirt and long-sleeve blouse, too hot for the weather, but she doesn't have a hair out of place. I doubt she even knows how to sweat. She reminds me of the Barbie dolls that are found every once in a while—plastic to the point of perfection. I know that Erin was originally from my side of town, born Erin Bishop and a classmate of my father's. But it hardly seems possible, her refined elegance so at odds with most of the women I knew growing up. She's cultivated a new persona for herself, and she wears her chilly mantle like a queen.

She embraces Bishop, who gives her a stiff kiss on the cheek, but she only nods at me. I'm glad she's not faking affection. It's more honest than what her husband is doing, at least. Dislike is an emotion I can respect.

Dinner is served in the formal dining room, the four of us spread out at a table much too big for our small party even with the table not fully extended. The Lattimers are seated at each end, and Bishop and I are to sit across from each other. It's like being marooned on my own small island, surrounded on both sides by hostile waters.

Bishop pulls out my seat, then grabs an extra chair from against the wall behind us and sits down next to me. "It's too far away, across the table," he says to his mother. I try not to feel ridiculously grateful for this small act of defiance, this solidarity he's shown me.

Mrs. Lattimer is not happy with the change, but she doesn't make it an issue. She nods curtly to the maid waiting by the doorway, who scurries over to move Bishop's place setting across the table.

"They are still newlyweds, after all," President Lattimer

says with a smile. Whatever President Lattimer envisions, I doubt Bishop sleeping on the sofa every night is part of it.

We make it through the salad course and warm rosemary bread with small talk and only a few awkward silences. I'm starting to think I may survive the evening unscathed when President Lattimer turns toward me with a smile. "How are you enjoying your job at the courthouse?"

"I like it," I say. "I'm working with Victoria Jameson."

President Lattimer nods. "We know Victoria well, and her father, of course. That will keep you busy until babies come along."

My heart skips a beat. "Yes," I say.

President Lattimer cuts into his chicken. "Are you learning anything interesting?"

I take a sip of ice water. "Mostly I'm helping with case work," I say carefully. "Keeping the judges organized." I pause. "Victoria did say that next week we may be doing some work with the prisoners."

Mrs. Lattimer's hand rises to her throat before falling back to her lap. "Oh," she says. "I'm not sure that's appropriate, Ivy. Not for you."

"Why not?" I ask, the words coming out even more defensive than I intended them.

"You're only a girl," Mrs. Lattimer says. "There are some things that are too adult for you."

I focus on my plate. *Keep your mouth closed*, I tell myself. Just shut up. But I can't, and I now fully understand Callie's apprehension when Bishop asked for me instead of her. If I can make my father's plan work, it will be a miracle.

"I think if I'm old enough to be married off against my will, I'm old enough to work where I want," I say, raising my eyes to meet hers.

There's a long beat of silence. Mrs. Lattimer's fork clatters to her plate. "How *dare* you," she says, eyes wide. "How dare—"

"Erin," President Lattimer says, voice calm. "Ivy's allowed to have her own opinions. Especially here, at our dinner table." I look at him, taken by surprise. "I encourage debate," he tells me, no irony in his tone.

"As long as it's within the confines of your beliefs, right?" I ask. I put down my fork so no one can see my hand shaking. "Out on the streets, people aren't allowed to talk about democracy, are they? About having a voice in how things are run?"

President Lattimer's face tightens. "Democracy was what your grandfather espoused, Ivy. And he lost. He lost because he didn't have enough supporters behind him."

"No, he lost because your father got to the guns first." I need to stop. I take a breath, bringing myself back under control. Bishop's hand brushes against mine on the table-top. Just his pinky shifting against my fingers. I glance at him, startled, and his eyes hold mine. Encouraging me, or at least not trying to stop me.

"What's wrong with letting people decide the kind of government they want?" I ask. "What are you afraid of?" They are my father's words, and it makes me feel closer to him to speak them.

"People need certainty," President Lattimer says. "They

need peace. We've had enough war and unrest."

"Putting people outside the fence, that's a kind of unrest, though, isn't it?" I say,

"The people put out have done horrible things. The punishment fits the crime," Mrs. Lattimer interjects.

"Maybe for some of them," I concede. "But it's not just murderers who are put out. It's people who steal or upset the status quo. How does leaving them to die bring peace?"

Mrs. Lattimer opens her mouth to speak, but I cut her off before she can get a word out. "And what about forcing girls to marry, not letting them have any say in their own lives?"

"Our priority is not personal happiness, Ivy," President Lattimer says. "It can't be. We are all still trying to survive, increase our population, and when people have too many choices, they often make the wrong ones. So it's up to me to guide them."

I choke out a laugh. "So you know what's best for every single person in Westfall?"

"Yes," Mrs. Lattimer says. "He does." She glares at me, little wrinkles forming around her lips where her mouth is drawn tight.

"You know," President Lattimer says, pulling my attention away from Mrs. Lattimer, "you remind me of your mother. Of course, you look like her. She could be…impassioned, too."

"What?" My voice comes out as a whisper I can barely hear over the screaming in my head. "You knew my mother?"

"Yes." His smile is sad. "I knew her well."

I have so many questions that they form a ball in my throat and not a single one can escape. I want to scream at him, rake my fingers down his cheeks and ask how he can talk about her with such fondness in his voice when *he* was the one who had her killed? But a bigger part of me doesn't care, right in this moment, who he is or what he's done. If he can tell me about my mother, then I'm willing to listen.

My family often uses the memory of what happened to my mother to invoke my wrath, but no one's ever talked to me about her life. About who she was before she became a symbol of my family's rage. All my life, the most I've gotten are whispers passed back and forth above my head like a hot potato no one wanted to be caught holding— fragments of sentences I craved like a drug: *tragic, disgrace, heartbroken, gone, never coming back.*

"How did you know her?" I ask, voice raw.

A chair scrapes back, making me jump. "I've had enough of this," Mrs. Lattimer says, throwing her napkin down on the table as she stands. "It's not bad enough that *she's* the one he marries? But then she comes into my home and spews her father's delusions and we're expected to sit and listen?" She points at me. "I won't—"

"Enough," Bishop says. He doesn't raise his voice, but his word is a warning just the same.

Mrs. Lattimer stares at her son, her lower lip trembling. "*Two weeks?*" she hisses. "That's all it takes for her to turn you against us? Two weeks."

"No one's against you, Mom." Bishop sounds weary,

like he's had some version of this conversation a thousand times before. Did he spend his childhood having to constantly prove his devotion to his mother instead of being the recipient of hers? Maybe he and I have something in common after all.

"Erin, please," President Lattimer says, "sit down. There's no need to make a scene."

But Mrs. Lattimer is not going to be easily consoled. "I'm not the one who made a scene," she shoots back, eyes on me. She turns and leaves the room, her heels tapping a fading staccato rhythm on the wood floor of the hallway.

"Excuse me," President Lattimer says. He doesn't seem particularly ruffled by his wife's behavior. He follows her from the room, and Bishop and I are left alone. I stare down at the chicken congealing on my plate. The candles in the middle of the table flicker and glow, casting shadows across my hands. The only sound is the ticking of the grandfather clock in the hall.

"I'm sorry," I manage to say. And I am. Sorry I couldn't keep my mouth shut. Sorry I'm not the girl my sister and father need me to be.

"No need to apologize," Bishop says. I turn to look at him, half his face in shadow. "I told you before, I want you to be yourself. That includes speaking your mind, even if it makes people uncomfortable."

I nod. "There was a man on our side of town. He lived a few houses down from us." I have no idea why I'm telling him this, maybe testing to see if he means what he says. Which is stupid and risky, but I can't stop the flow of words.

"A couple of winters ago, his son got sick. And the hospital wouldn't give him medicine."

"There are protocols for the medicine," Bishop says. "They don't just hand it out." He is speaking like his father now, always with an answer for everything. I yank my hand off the table where it lays close to his. Bishop draws his hand back, too.

"I know that. But this man's son was really sick, about-to-die sick. And they still put his name at the bottom of the list. So my neighbor stole some medicine, saved his son's life. And your father had him put out for the crime. He froze to death on the other side of the fence, didn't even make it one day." I hold Bishop's gaze. "That's your father's idea of justice. Those are the kinds of choices he makes."

Bishop stares at me. "What do you want me to say, Ivy?" he asks finally. "That I agree with what my father did? That I don't? What's the answer you're looking for?"

"I'm not looking for a specific answer," I tell him, although the part of me that's been coached to kill him hopes he agrees with his father. "I want to know what you think."

"I think," Bishop says, "that we can love our families without trusting everything they tell us. Without championing everything they stand for." He delivers the words matter-of-factly, but his eyes are locked on mine. "I think that sometimes things aren't as simple as our fathers want us to believe."

7

have a pile of new books on my bedside table, but no
matter which one I pick, I can't seem to turn off my brain
and settle down. It's long past the time I usually turn out
the light, and I will be cursing my inability to sleep come
morning when it's time for me to get up for work. Finally, I
give up and climb out of bed. The hallway and living room
are dark, and I tiptoe into the kitchen and grab a glass of
water as quietly as I can. I'm sneaking back to the bedroom
when Bishop shifts on the couch. "Can't sleep?" he asks.

"No," I say. "You can't, either?"

The room is dark, but a sliver of moonlight shines in
through the not-quite-closed front window curtains. Bishop
shakes his head, the light glinting off his cheekbones.

"I was just getting some water," I say.

"Yeah." He smiles. "I can see that." He has one arm

hooked behind his head, his sheet tangled at his feet. His pale T-shirt glows in the dim light. "Want to keep me company while you drink it?"

"Okay," I say, starting toward one of the chairs across from him, but he bends his legs at the knee, making room for me on the end of the couch. "Thanks," I say, sitting down, curling my legs up next to me.

"It's weird, isn't it?" Bishop says, breaking the silence before my mind can spin away from me, worrying about all the things I should be saying and doing.

"What?"

He gestures broadly. "This. Us. How only a couple of weeks ago we were just teenagers living with our parents and now we're…here."

"Yes," I say. "Very weird."

There's a long pause where I can feel him watching me. I turn my head and look at him. "Remember the day we went to my house," he says, "and got the books from my father's library?"

"Yes. What about it?"

"You were right, Ivy," he says quietly. "It does bother me. The way our choices are taken away from us."

I'm almost scared to breathe. He is confiding in me, opening up to me exactly the way my father and Callie wanted. "Why didn't you say something right then?"

Bishop sighs. "I'm not…I'm never going to be the guy who lays it all out there. That's not me. Until I really know someone, not much gets out. It's just the way I'm built."

"Okay," I say, waiting. If nothing else, I understand

what it's like to have a part of your personality that's not easy to change.

"But it doesn't mean I don't have feelings," he says. "That things don't matter to me."

I take a sip of water. "I shouldn't have said that, the morning we fought, about you not feeling anything. That wasn't fair."

"I understand why you might think that," Bishop says. "But it's not true." He pauses. "I wanted something else, too. Something more than being your husband."

"Like what?" I ask.

His eyes drop away from mine. "Nothing that matters now. This is what we have. This life. Each other. This house." His hand thumps downward. "This couch."

My heart jumps. Was all this a prelude to getting me into bed? I'm already kicking myself for sitting down on this stupid sofa.

"Relax, Ivy," he says, a smile in his voice. "I'm not asking for anything."

But someday he will. As far as he knows, this relationship is forever, and I can't imagine he'll want to sleep on the couch for the next fifty years. I'm not sure what I'll say if he does ask. For the sake of my father's plan, I know my answer has to be yes.

"Well, I'd better get to bed. Work in the morning." I stand, set my cup down on the coffee table.

Bishop's voice stops me before I get to the hallway. "You told me you were trying, remember?"

I glance back at him. "Yes," I say, cautious.

"I'm trying, too."

"I know," I say, watching the way his eyes shine in the moonlight. I turn and go back to bed.

try not to be nervous as Victoria leads the way into the basement of the courthouse. It's not as if I'm going to be left alone in a room with any of the prisoners. I don't want Erin Lattimer's words—*there are some things that are too adult for you*—to be a prophecy. I'm determined to do this, and do it well, if for no other reason than to prove her wrong.

"What are we doing with them?" I ask Victoria, trotting to keep up with her. Even though I'm taller, she walks fast everywhere she goes, like she's rushing to catch something that's always disappearing around the farthest corner.

"These are prisoners who are already convicted," she tells me. "We need to get some final information from them. Next of kin, that sort of thing. We should have it already, if the screenings were done correctly the first time around." Her tone of voice tells me that's unlikely. "But we have to double check, before…"

"Before we put them out," I say, because she seems reluctant to finish the sentence.

"Yes," she says, glancing at me and then back to the hall in front of us. "I know that must be hard for you to understand, with your father being who he is."

She says it with no malice in her tone, but I'm wary

anyway. I don't have any trouble speaking when my temper gets ahead of my good sense, but being drawn out on the subject is a danger even I should be able to avoid.

"Well, he's not a big fan of putting people out," I say, choosing every word with care. It's no secret my father opposes Westfall's method of punishment. My family always has, since my grandfather's time. But my father is careful not to be too vocal. He makes our position clear without being strident. He is smart, with one eye always on the long-term goal.

Victoria uses her shoulder to push through the door at the end of the hall. "But does he have a better solution?" she asks, eyebrows raised. She doesn't give me a chance to respond, just leaves me to follow or risk getting hit by the door swinging back in my face.

We're in another hall, this one short and with a single door at the end. The door has a small window at the top and there's a guard standing outside it, hands crossed in front of him, gun at his waist.

"Hey, David," Victoria says. "We're here to do the final interviews."

"We're ready for you," David says. He barely glances in my direction. "They told me you'd be down this morning, so I went ahead and brought the first one in. Laird, Mark."

Victoria holds out her hand, and I shuffle through the stack of manila folders in my arms until I find the one labeled with Laird's name and pass it to her. I've gotten used to Victoria's efficiency, which can sometimes border on rudeness.

"Okay," she says to me. "This time, watch and learn. You'll be doing these on your own soon enough."

"I'll be right here," David says, "if you need me."

Victoria nods and twists the silver door handle with her free hand. The room beyond is tiny, barely enough space for the three folding chairs inside, only one of which is occupied. The one bolted to the floor.

I couldn't have said exactly what I expected to find, some evil creature from a storybook in human form, maybe, but the boy in the chair doesn't look much older than me. I would guess he's younger than Bishop, in fact, but I glance at the file over Victoria's shoulder and see he's twenty-two.

He smiles at us and waves with his free hand, the other handcuffed to the side of the chair. "Hi. I was starting to think you'd forgotten about me." He has sandy blond hair and round blue eyes. His cheeks are smooth with bright pink patches on the apples. He reminds me of the baby dolls my sister and I played with as children. I imagine a different type of girl might find him attractive.

Victoria takes a seat across from him, and I slide into the empty chair beside her. Mark's eyes follow the line of my bare leg peeking out from my skirt as I sit, but when he raises his gaze to mine, his look is carefully polite.

"Mark," Victoria says, capturing his attention. "You know why you're here, I assume."

"You need to get everything finalized before you put me out."

"Yes." Victoria draws a sheaf of papers from his file and uncaps a pen. As she goes over his address and next of kin, I take the chance to study him. He is answering her easily enough, but his foot jumps against the floor and he's swallowing too fast, like he has to keep wetting his mouth or the words will dry up.

"Will I...will I have a chance to say good-bye to my family?" he asks.

"You will," Victoria says. "We'll be notifying them of a day and time when they are allowed to visit."

Mark nods, his head bobbing on his neck like a spring. "I wish there was someone I could talk to," he says. "Someone in charge. I'm sure if I just *explained*—"

"You had a trial, Mr. Laird," Victoria says. "And the judge found you guilty. There's nothing left to discuss."

"But you can't just put me out!" he says, voice rising. His handcuffs rattle against the chair. My whole body tenses, but Victoria remains unfazed. She probably hears these pleas, and ignores them, every time she enters this room. The thought of it makes me want to vomit.

"If you'll calm down," she says, "I'll go over the procedure for your release with you."

"My release?" Mark's voice breaks and he chokes out a high, hysterical laugh. "It's not a release. It's a death sentence. Why don't you call it what it is?"

"Well," Victoria says, shutting the folder with a snap. "If you're not going to be reasonable, it looks like we're done here. We can try again tomorrow."

She moves toward the door. I stand to follow her, and Mark leans forward, his body stretching out of his chair, and snags my wrist. "Please," he says. "Please help me."

I twist out of his grasp, the tiny hairs on my arm standing at attention. I know I should be reacting to the pain in his voice, but there's something swimming in the depths of his eyes—a calculating slyness at odds with his boyish face—that makes my skin crawl.

Victoria holds the door open and I go out, breathing fast.

"Everything okay?" David asks.

"He grabbed her," Victoria says. "But no harm done, right?"

I nod, crossing my arms across my chest and holding my elbows to still my shaking fingers. David goes into the room with Mark, and Victoria starts down the hall away from me. "Let's take a quick break before the next one," she says as she walks.

"He was right, you know," I call after her. She turns and looks at me over her shoulder. "You were playing word games with him. It is a death sentence."

Victoria stares at me, runs her tongue over her front teeth. Her footsteps are fast and loud as she walks back to where I stand. "No, I wasn't," she says. "He'll be alive when we release him. And if he's half as smart as he thinks he is, he can figure out how to stay that way."

I shake my head. "You know that's not true. He'll die out there. No one deserves—"

"Do you know what he did?" Victoria asks me. Her voice is quiet but deadly sharp and accurate, each word like an arrow pointed home. "He raped a nine-year-old girl. Carved his name into her belly so she'd have a souvenir for the rest of her life."

My stomach flips, bile rising up in my throat. I turn my face away from her, toward the wall, remembering the look in his eyes when he touched my arm. I want to scrub my skin with hot water, rid myself of him so there's no evidence left behind. I don't let myself think of the little girl who will never be able to do the same.

Victoria leans closer. "What do you suggest we do with him, Ivy? Should we let him loose? Keep him here forever, feeding him during winters we can barely feed ourselves? Give him medicine that could go to innocent children instead?" She shoves Mark Laird's folder against my chest. I take it with numb fingers. "Personally, I think he deserves worse."

I don't look up, even after the door at the end of the hall swings shut behind her.

I walk home angry and don't even know why. It's not as if my father didn't admit that a lot of the people put outside the fence have done horrible things. And Victoria's right, maybe Mark does deserve worse than he's getting. But I still feel lied to, like all the speeches my father gave me were supposed to end in easy answers, not more questions. *It means sometimes things aren't as simple as our fathers want us to believe.* I hear Bishop's words in my head and have to resist punching at nothing, screaming at the humid air pressing against the back of my neck. My throat feels raw and tight and I stalk along the deserted sidewalk with my fingernails biting into my palms, leaving the sounds of downtown behind me in the distance.

Bishop is in the kitchen when I get home, forming hamburger into patties at the counter. "Hi," he calls as I throw my bag on the sofa. "How were the prisoners?"

I stand in the kitchen doorway, the same way he did on the second night after our wedding. In most of the ways that count, nothing has changed since then. We haven't slept together or shared secrets together or done much of anything together, really. But in perhaps the most important way of all, everything's altered since those first hesitant nights. Because by being the person I come home to, the person who asks me about my day and listens to my answers, Bishop's become the constant my life revolves around. Even if most of the time we navigate so carefully we might as well be bombs trying not to explode, we are still always there, in each other's paths. Just waiting for the moments we intersect.

"Awful," I say. "We met with one who is going to be put out. A guy who hurt a little girl." Using euphemism to disguise horror. "But he still begged me to save him." My voice is high and tight. "He begged."

Bishop snorts. "I bet he did."

"That's all you have to say? Don't you care about what's happening to people?"

Bishop flips on the faucet with his forearm, soaping up his hands. "To this guy?" he says. "Not really. The better question is, why do you?" He turns off the water and grabs a dishtowel from the oven door handle.

I huff out air. "I don't. I mean, not him specifically. But we can't put people out every time they do something wrong. It's…barbaric."

"Look around, Ivy. The world we live in is barbaric. We just try to hide it with"—he flaps the dish towel toward the counter—"hamburgers on the grill and cute houses. And what's the alternative? Would it be better to kill them in the electric chair, like they used to? Use up resources we don't have keeping them alive?"

I roll my eyes. "Now you sound like Victoria."

"Victoria has a good point, then." Bishop steps closer to me, leans one hip against the counter. "Last winter we lost more than two hundred people, Ivy. Two hundred. Would you rather keep the guy you talked to today alive or one of those people?"

"That's an unfair question and you know it! Not everyone who is put out has done something like what this guy did. Some people steal bread from the market or refuse to get married. I don't think it's a waste of resources to feed those people. We managed to feed them before they committed a crime. We should be able to feed them afterward."

"Okay," Bishop says. "But what about the murderers and rapists? What do we do with them? Saying you want something different isn't going to cut it." His face is as calm as ever, his eyes a thoughtful, liquid green.

"So what are you saying? If someone doesn't have every

single possible answer, it's stupid to ask the question?" I wish he'd raise his voice so I'd have an excuse to raise mine, release some of this frustration that's boiling at the base of my spine. I don't worry any more about offending him or making him mad. He seems able to handle my recklessness with a level of composure my family never mastered.

Bishop doesn't miss a beat. "No, of course not. But it's not enough to want things to change without asking what they're going to change into."

"That's easy for you to say. The president's son," I taunt. "Did you ever even think about this stuff before I came along, or did you spend your days splashing around in the river, letting other people worry about justice and what's right?"

His eyes flash, so fast I think I might have imagined it, because his face stays impassive. "You don't have a monopoly on worrying about the future, no matter what you might think." He throws down the dishtowel. "And at least I don't need my father to tell me what I believe."

I spin away from him and walk down the hall to the bedroom, slamming the door behind me. I cross to the bed and punch a pillow as hard as I can, lift it to my face and scream out my frustration, the cotton dry and bitter in my mouth.

8

hide out in a bathroom stall in the basement of the court-house until my watch says six. I usually leave around five, but I know David, the guard who let Victoria and me in to see Mark Laird, is on duty until six, and I want to find out where he takes his gun at the end of the day. Step three, find out where they keep the guns. That's one of the facts my father needs to know if he's going to make a successful bid for power. He's always said he doesn't want anyone to get hurt—other than the obvious people, of course—but having control of our government's limited supply of weapons is going to be vital to his success.

After last night's argument with Bishop, which left me awake half the night with scathing retorts burning unsaid on my tongue, I woke up determined to take a step forward on the path toward my father's goal. I refuse to allow

Bishop's words to knock me off course. Callie always says that there's family, and there's everyone else. My father is family. And Bishop is everyone else.

I hear a door slam outside the bathroom and a set of heavy footsteps passes in the hall. I uncurl from where I've been crouching on the toilet seat, wincing at the tightness in my legs. I peek out the bathroom door and David is turning the corner at the far end of the hall, an area of the basement I've never been in before. I tiptoe after him barefoot, my sandals in my hand. It's eerily quiet down here this time of day, the only sound a faint buzzing from lights above my head and the click of David's receding footsteps.

I turn the corner cautiously and see David punching in numbers on a keypad set into the wall. When he's done, he opens the door next to the keypad and goes inside, but he doesn't let the door close behind him. I can hear his voice and the voice of another man coming from the room.

"Thank God it's Friday, right?" the unknown man says. He sounds older, his voice gruff.

"You're telling me," David says. "Next week is going to be a long one."

"Putting them out?"

"On Wednesday."

The older man clucks his tongue, but without seeing his face I can't tell what the noise indicates. Approval? Criticism? I hear the rustling of leather and the clank of metal followed by a heavy thud. David taking off his holster and setting it down. My heart rate picks up, a thin line of sweat beading at my brow. I clutch the folder I'm carrying tighter in my hand—my insurance policy in case I get caught.

"Go ahead and sign it back in," the older man says.

I hear the scratch of pen on paper and I know I should leave, race down the hall the way I came, but I want more information. There's a sound I can't immediately identify, like the whir of a wheel. The turn mechanism on a safe maybe? Against my better judgment, I slide all the way over to the doorway and lean in a fraction of an inch, holding my breath. Both men have their backs to me and stand in front of an open walk-in safe. From where I stand, I can see rows of guns stretching back, floor to ceiling, at least twenty feet. There are handguns, like the one David is turning in and bigger guns, too. All sizes. Shotguns, and even a few assault rifles. These days guns are a theory for most people, not a reality, so they don't know much about them. But my father taught us to identify the basic types of weapons. Although I've never shot a gun, I have no trouble imagining the heft of one in my hand. The older man goes into the safe and sets David's gun on a metal rack with dozens of guns of the same type.

I move out of the doorway and race-walk away, back down the hall. Once I turn the corner, I take a second to slip my shoes back on and catch my breath. I memorize where I am and where the room is, close my eyes and picture every detail in my mind, try to burn the images of the guns I saw into my closed eyelids.

"Hey, Mrs. Lattimer," David says, right over my shoulder. "What are you doing here?"

I jump, a startled squawk escaping. "Oh, hi, David," I say, one hand on my chest where my heart is slamming against my ribs. "This case is closed, so I was just bringing the file down for storage, but I couldn't find the right room. It's so confusing." I give him a smile that feels more like a grimace. "Everything's so white."

He cocks his head at me, points at the file. "What's the case number?"

I hold it up for him to see. "That goes in Records Room B," he says. "I don't mind taking it for you. Technically only the guards are allowed down here unaccompanied. Next time just let us know and we'll be happy to take any closed case files off your hands."

"Thank you," I say, give a breathless little laugh as I hand over the file. "Sorry I didn't follow protocol. Still learning."

"No problem," David says.

"Now can you point me in the right direction for the stairwell? Otherwise I'll be wandering around here for days."

David smiles, points down the hall. "Stairwell is right there."

"Thanks. Have a nice weekend." I practically run to the stairs and push through the door, resting my head against it once it's closed behind me. There is one benefit of being a Lattimer—most people are easily fooled. They think because I've changed my name, they know where my allegiance lies. As if a few weeks can overcome a lifetime.

I hurry through the streets, anxious to reach the market before all the stalls shut down for the evening. It's less crowded than the last time I was here, so even though there are fewer people, more of them notice my presence. Murmurs follow in the wake of my passing, like that childhood game where the whisper starts at the beginning of the line and by the time it reaches the end it's transformed into something new and undecipherable. I was well-known on my side of town but not talked about. I was part of the fabric of people's lives, the founder's daughter. Here I am only a curiosity, and I hate it.

The man at the jam stall is beginning to pack up as I reach his table. I grab a jar of jam, not even looking at what type, and thrust it toward him. "I'd like to get this."

He glances up at me. "It's three vouchers."

We don't have cash anymore, after the war. People are paid for their employment with vouchers. Women who don't work—the vast majority of females in Westfall—and children are given a certain number of vouchers per month as well.

"Okay." I dig into the messenger bag slung across my chest for some vouchers.

"Do you need a sack?"

"No. I can put it in here." I nestle the jar into the bottom of my bag.

"Anything else?" the man asks.

I glance around. There's no one nearby. "Tell her I found where they're kept," I say, voice low. I walk away without looking back.

Euphoria sings through my blood as I walk home, my steps bouncing against the pavement. I imagine Callie's face when my message is delivered. It means next to nothing to the jam man, but to Callie it will mean everything. She will tell my father and they'll both be pleased with what I've accomplished so far. They'll stop worrying that they've given me an assignment I'm not capable of completing.

But the closer I get to home, the faster the euphoria fades. Because in my haste to prove myself to my father, to prove something to Bishop, I forgot what finding the guns means. It means my father is one step closer to the final step of the plan, to killing Bishop and President Lattimer. I believe in my father's cause, I do. But I'm beginning to realize there is a difference between letting someone die and being the one who pulls the trigger.

The living room and kitchen are empty when I get home, a pan of chicken resting on top of the stove. The door to the screened porch is open and Bishop is stretched out on one of the wicker sofas, his long legs taking up the entire cushion.

"Hi," I say. I put my bag on the floor and sit cross-legged on the sofa across from him. My fingers tie nervous knots in my lap.

Bishop's gaze takes me in. "Hard day?" he asks.

"Yeah."

"That's two in a row."

I nod. I'm poised right on the edge of tears, for no reason I can name. I have a sudden fierce wish that the man at the jam stall had been gone for the day, that my message was not already on its way to Callie.

"I wish we hadn't had a fight," I find myself saying. "Last night." I didn't know it was true until the words left my mouth.

Bishop raises his eyebrows, gives me an easy grin. It's the opposite of the presidential smile he gave Callie on our wedding day. This one is the real Bishop, less perfection, more warmth. "That wasn't a fight. It's not a fight unless we give each other the silent treatment for at least a week." His mouth is still smiling, but his eyes are sad. I think of his mother's impersonal gaze, her stiff embrace. I'm guessing Bishop knows firsthand the pain of growing up in a house where an icy wind is blowing. "But I am sorry for what I said about listening to your father," he continues.

"I'm not a complete idiot, you know," I tell him. "I do think about alternatives if things were to change in West-fall."

Bishop swings his legs off the sofa and sits forward, facing me. "I have never, not for a single second, thought you were an idiot, Ivy."

"You listen to your father, too, don't you?" I ask him.

Bishop looks down at his clasped hands, then back up at me. "Sometimes. I just think that because of who we are… the president's son and the founder's daughter…" He rolls his eyes, making me smile. "It's doubly important that we think for ourselves. We're not our parents. We don't have to agree with everything they stand for."

"But what if I do agree with my father?" I ask, because

it seems like I should, like it is important I reaffirm my belief in my family's cause.

"Then great. More power to you," Bishop says. "But I think it's easy to fall into the trap of thinking that because of who we are, because of who *they* are, we owe them more than we do. We're still free to choose who we want to be."

"Really?" I ask. "Because I didn't get to choose much of anything." All my life, my father and Callie made my decisions for me. Any dissent on my part was taken as disloyalty. Then Bishop's father determined who and when I would marry, setting the course for the rest of my life.

Bishop takes my sarcasm in stride. "Well, obviously a lot of things are out of our control." He wiggles his ring finger, and the early evening light catches the gold band, making it gleam. "But no one controls who we turn into but us."

"And who do you want to turn into?" I mean the question to be mocking, but that's not how it comes out. I sound interested. I reach down and scratch my leg, trying to hide my embarrassment.

Bishop looks at me. "Someone honest. Someone who tries to do the right thing. Someone who follows his own heart, even if it disappoints people." He pauses. "Someone brave enough to be all those things."

A boy who doesn't want to lie, married to a girl who can't tell the truth. If there is a God, he has a sick sense of humor. "What about you?" Bishop asks. "Who does Ivy Westfall Lattimer want to be?"

This is all new to me. The back and forth, the give and take. I would suspect it was a trap, but no matter what Callie warned me about, I can tell Bishop is genuinely interested in me and what I have to say. It's scary and thrilling at the same time. "I don't know," I say quietly. My throat aches. "I've never really had the chance to think about it."

"Well, now you do," he says simply. As if figuring out who I want to be is as easy as deciding to do it. Maybe for him it is. He stands and holds out his hand to me. "Let's have dinner. And tomorrow we're going to do something fun."

I put my hand in his and let him pull me to my feet.

9

"Saturdays are for sleeping in," I inform Bishop at eight o'clock the next morning as he makes sandwiches at the kitchen counter.

"Sleep is for wimps," he replies.

"At least tell me what we're doing. Does it involve a nap?"

Bishop laughs, a rich, warm sound. "No naps," he says. "But you won't want one. Trust me."

He grabs two small jugs of water from the icebox and puts them into his backpack, along with the sandwiches, a couple of apples, and some cookies from the market. "Ready?" he asks.

"As I'll ever be," I say with a long-suffering sigh, which nets me only a grin in response.

"You've got a swimsuit under there, right?" he says,

pointing at my tank top and shorts.

"Yes." I ignore the heat in my cheeks. Ridiculous to be embarrassed by such a mundane question.

"All right, then." He swings the backpack onto his back. "Let's go."

I follow him out the front door and as we head side by side down the front walk, our neighbors' door opens and Dylan comes out. We make eye contact across the lawns, and it seems rude not to stop.

"Hi, Dylan," I say. Bishop slows next to me.

Dylan crosses his lawn into ours, his hand already outstretched. "Hey, Bishop," he says. His voice has a false heartiness that grates on my nerves. "Don't know if you remember me. I was a couple years behind you in school."

"Refresh my memory," Bishop says as they shake hands, and I have to bite back a smile as some of the enthusiasm dies in Dylan's eyes.

"Dylan Cox." Behind him, their front door opens again and Meredith comes out. I inhale sharply at the sight of her, and Bishop looks from me to her. Her left eye is blackened and she's walking with a slight limp.

I dart around Dylan toward her. "Meredith," I say. "Are you all right? What happened?" Although I'm sure I already know what happened. My hands ball into fists.

Her gaze flits to mine and then away. "Oh." She gives a breathy laugh. "I'm such a klutz. I fell down the basement stairs and hit my face on the railing."

Dylan comes from behind me and wraps an arm around her shoulders, pulling her against him tightly. "She went down there at night without turning on the light. Can you believe that?"

"So stupid of me," Meredith says. She keeps her eyes on the ground.

Bishop is beside me, his bare arm brushing against mine. "You should have let us know," he says. "We would have been happy to come over and help."

"We had it covered," Dylan says. We all stand there for a minute, an awkward little group. I wish Meredith would give me some sign she wants me to interfere, but she keeps her face averted, making eye contact with no one.

"Well, it was nice to meet you," Bishop says, voice flat.

"You too," Dylan says, although he seems annoyed all over again that Bishop didn't remember him. I hope Meredith doesn't suffer for that, too.

Bishop and I walk in silence to the north side of town, where the main road peters out into gravel. The sun is already high in the sky and sweat trickles down the back of my neck. Only June and already so humid it's like breathing through a wet washcloth. I imagine this is the closest you can get to drowning on dry land.

Bishop veers off the gravel road and into the thick stand of trees. I try not to think about ticks as we crash through the brush. I'm about to complain when a narrow path opens up in front of us. The trees overhead bring some welcome relief from the sun. I keep waiting for Bishop to bring up Meredith, but he doesn't. So I do.

"He did that to her," I say to Bishop's back.

He doesn't stop or turn around. "I know."

His lack of reaction only fuels my irritation. "That's the kind of stuff I was talking about when I said I didn't like arranged marriages. He thinks he owns her."

"That can happen whether the marriage is arranged or not. It depends more on whether the guy's a piece of shit than on how they ended up married."

I allow myself a quick grin only because he can't see me. "Still, somebody needs to do something to help her. Because your father's laws aren't going to cut it." Under the law, as it stands, there is no easy path to divorce. A marriage can only be dissolved if both parties sign a joint petition and President Lattimer approves it, something I've only ever heard rumors of happening. And, even then, only when the parties involved were personal friends of President Lattimer's. "Something tells me Dylan's not going to agree to sign away his marriage." The path is sloping upward and I stop to catch my breath. "He's finally got his very own punching bag, one that makes him dinner and has sex with him, too. He's not going to be in any hurry to give her up."

Bishop stops just ahead of me. He slides the backpack off his back and digs inside. "Can we not do this right now?" he asks. He hands me the water jug.

"Do what?"

"Argue."

I take a gulp of water, backhanding the excess that dribbles down my chin. "We're not fighting, according to you," I point out. "No silent treatment."

Bishop gives me a closed-mouth smile and shakes his head, holding out his hand for the jug. "At this point, I'd consider the silent treatment a blessing."

I slap the jug into his palm. He tilts it to his mouth and takes a long swallow, his Adam's apple bobbing in the tanned column of his neck. There's a sheen of sweat on his skin, darkening the neck of his T-shirt. I jerk my eyes away.

He gives the jug back to me to carry and takes off again. I sigh and hike after him, waving my hand through a small army of gnats that circle my head. "How much farther?"

"Not far," he says. He's not even slightly out of breath.

"Are you taking me to some stupid clubhouse where you hang out with your friends? Will I have to learn the super-secret handshake to get inside?"

He huffs out a laugh. "I don't have friends. I'm the president's son, remember? I have sycophants."

"Wow," I say. "Fancy word."

He glances at me over his shoulder but doesn't slow his pace. "Don't even pretend that you don't know what it means. Anyone who reads *Anna Karenina* as a bedtime story is familiar with fancy words."

Okay, he's got me there. I wonder if he's serious about not having friends. Since we've been married I haven't met any. Maybe that's why he doesn't mind me saying exactly what I think; maybe no one has ever done that with him before. I suppose being a leader's child doesn't lend itself to genuine friendships. It certainly never has for me.

After ten more minutes of hiking, I begin to hear the sounds of water to our right. I try to visualize the town map in my head, but I'm not that great with directions. "We're near the fence, aren't we?" I say. I've rarely been close to the fence in my life.

"Yes," Bishop says, unconcerned. "But we're not going there."

The tightness in my shoulders relaxes at his words. I don't know why the very thought of the fence makes me anxious. It's not as if it's a living thing that can harm me. But my entire life, safety has been inside that fence, and everything beyond is unknown and unknowable.

"My dad said people used to try and get in, back when Westfall was first founded," I say.

"That's what I've heard, too," Bishop says. "Sometimes we would let them in, sometimes not. I think it depended on whether they seemed sick and how much food we had. But nowadays that doesn't happen very often."

"Didn't some just breach the fence?" I remember my father's stories about groups coming right over the top when he was a boy, heedless of the razor wire.

"Yeah, but we have the constant patrols now, just to make sure it's in good shape, that no one's tunneling underneath it or ripping it apart." He glances back at me. "But there's hardly ever any activity outside the fence these days, at least close by. Only the people we put out, and they rarely try to get back into Westfall. I guess they figure it's better to take your chances out there than be guaranteed a death sentence in here."

"Either option sound pretty horrible to me."

Bishop shrugs. "I don't know, sometimes I think we should just tear down the fence. Towns didn't have fences around them before the war and everything was fine. I think it was supposed to keep us safe, but instead it's made us scared."

Before I can respond, we emerge from the trees next to the river and my thoughts fly right out of my head. These are not the wild, raging waters I've seen before. Here it is lazy and shallow, bubbling quietly over huge flat rocks that lie half submerged. Trees bend over the water like they're straining to touch it with their leaves and small white flowers grow along the banks, nodding their heads in the breeze. There's a steep limestone cliff on the far side, which adds to the feeling that this is a secret, secluded place. Its tranquility is catching. Standing at the edge of this water makes me calm.

"Nice, huh?" Bishop says.

"It's beautiful," I breathe.

"Follow me." He steps out onto one of the flat rocks in the water, moving across to the far bank in seconds. It takes me a little longer to find my footing, but I make it across without getting my shoes wet.

Bishop drops the backpack at the base of the cliff and kicks off his tennis shoes. "Leave everything here," he says. "Except your swimsuit." He reaches behind him with one hand and yanks off his T-shirt.

I feel self-conscious as I step out of my shorts and remove my tank top. I take the time to fold both items of clothing, keeping my eyes on my task. My black bikini is more sporty than sexy, but I am still closer to naked than I've ever been with anyone other than my sister.

When I turn, Bishop is watching me. I stare back at him,

telling myself I am not embarrassed.

"Ready?" he asks.

"For what?"

Bishop heads toward the limestone cliff and begins to scale it as if it's a ladder, barely looking at where he puts his hands and feet. "Put your feet where I put mine," he says. He doesn't seem at all concerned about my safety, as if he's sure I can handle the task. Strangely, his confidence in me erases any questions I had about making the climb.

I clamber onto the rock below him and start up, watching to see where he moves. The muscles in my shoulders burn as I pull myself upward, but it's a good kind of pain. The cliff isn't so high that I'd inevitably die if I fell, but I'd break something, maybe many somethings, so I don't look down. I keep my focus on Bishop climbing above me, the muscles in his back shifting and hunching as he moves. His body works with a kind of lazy grace, making every move seem effortless.

"Almost there," he calls down to me as he heaves himself over the top lip of the cliff. I curl my fingers into a handhold in the rock and use my legs to help propel me upward the last few feet. Bishop leans over and I grasp his forearm, and together we get me over the top.

"So I'm guessing we're going to jump?" I say, sucking in air. My heart is pounding and sweat stings my eyes. I haven't felt this alive in a long time. "Unless there's an elevator I'm unaware of."

"No elevator," Bishop says with a grin.

I walk to the far edge of the cliff and look down. There's a pool on this side, the greenish water still and flat in the midday heat. It's impossible to tell from looking how far down it goes, but it must be deep because we have to be at least three stories high.

I cross back to where Bishop is standing. "Run and jump?" I ask.

He nods. "Don't think about it—"

But his words of advice are lost to me because I'm already running, flinging myself off the edge with a scream of delight. Hot air rushes against my skin, the water rising up to meet me until all I see are its green depths. I plunge in feet first, the shock of cold forcing a yell from my mouth. Bubbles tickle against my closed eyelids and the underwater silence envelops me. I let myself sink, down, down, down, until the need to breathe takes over and I kick my way upward.

I break the surface just in time to witness Bishop make the leap above me, his body plummeting like an arrow. He barely makes a splash, disappears with a slight ripple into the water beside me. He takes so long to come up that I start to worry, until his fingers clamp around my ankle, dragging me under.

I rise with a splutter and a squeal, splashing him in the face when he bobs up next to me. He grins, shaking the water off his face. "I can't believe you jumped like that," he says. "What if there were rocks down here?"

I shrug. "You would have warned me beforehand if there were."

"Again?" Bishop asks. I nod in agreement, and he cuts through the water to the bank with long, sure strokes.

We climb and jump until my fingertips burn from pulling

myself up the rock face and my stomach is cramping with hunger. I swim over to one of the flat rocks poking partially out of the water near the base of the cliff and rest my arms on its heated surface. Bishop joins me and mimics my pose on the opposite side of the rock.

"Having fun?" he asks.

"Yes," I say with a smile. I tip my head up and close my eyes, let the sun burn into my closed eyelids. I didn't have a bad childhood, but there was no magic in it. No one hit me, no one neglected me, but there wasn't much that was childlike about it. Even fun involved barely disguised lessons about my future and my father's plans. It is only now, away from the presence of my family, that I can admit that to myself. This has been one of the most carefree afternoons of my life.

"When you smile," Bishop says, "it gives you a dimple." I feel his finger press gently against my cheek. "Right here."

I open my eyes and look at him. His hair is wet and unruly, his eyes glowing. He's at home here, outdoors, in the water. I wish I had never mocked his love of the river. He may be the president's son, but his rightful place will never be at a stuffy council table.

My stomach gives a huge growl and Bishop laughs. "Guess I don't need to ask if you're ready for lunch."

We eat sitting on the flat rock, letting our feet dangle in the water. I can't remember the last time a simple sandwich tasted this good. I'm glad he packed extras, because I down two in a matter of minutes, along with an apple and three cookies.

"Where'd you learn to cook?" I ask him.

Bishop glances at the remains of our lunch. "This wasn't exactly cooking."

"You know what I mean. You make dinner more often than I do." Boys don't usually cook, not anymore. It's the wife's job to get food on the table. Not a law or anything, but an unspoken rule, just like with the laundry. But Bishop not only cooks without complaint, he's good at it. His food always tastes better than mine.

"We had a maid when I was growing up. Charlotte. She used to let me sit with her in the kitchen while she cooked, and I guess I learned by osmosis. She always smelled like cookie dough." He smiles at the memory. "I spent most of my time with her."

As opposed to his mom, I imagine. I can't picture Erin Lattimer as the cookie-baking type. I stretch out on my stomach on the rock and rest my head on my folded arms. "I'm thinking that nap I mentioned earlier might be in order," I mumble against my skin. The heat of the sun is like a warm blanket on my back, the only sound the slight gurgle of the water, the drone of bees flitting among the flowers along the bank, lulling me to sleep.

"Go for it." Bishop lies down on his back next to me, one arm bent behind his head.

I fall asleep almost instantly and wake, disoriented, to his hand on my back, resting right between my shoulder blades. The outline of it burns into my skin. "Ivy," he whispers. "Wake up."

I open my eyes by degrees, my limbs heavy and sleep-drunk. "How long was I out?" I ask, my voice husky.

"A while. Long enough that you're starting to turn a little pink."

Bishop is still lying next to me, but he's turned on his side, his head propped up on his hand. I have no idea how long he's been watching me sleep. We're close enough that I can see the faint shadow of stubble on his cheeks, a single dark freckle nestled on the edge of his cheekbone. We look at each other without speaking, the silence between us stretching on and on, as thick and cloying as the humid summer air. Bishop moves his hand from my back, his fingers trailing across my skin, and I shiver, goose bumps breaking out along my arms and neck. I have to struggle for air, my heart and lungs seizing up like they're being squeezed in a vise. He lifts a lock of my damp hair, lets it slide through his fingers. He reaches for it again, curling it around his fingers.

"Thank you for today," I whisper. The movement of his hand in my hair is hypnotic, the unexpected warmth in his eyes as drugging as the sun on my back.

"You're welcome," he says, voice low.

This is exactly what Callie warned me about, letting my guard down and a Lattimer worming his way under my defenses. But she told me to play nice, too. Act like a content wife so he won't suspect I'm actually something much more lethal. Maybe with some other boy, some boy without thoughtful green eyes and a calmness at his core, performing those two opposing actions would be easy.

But not with Bishop. I don't know how to let him touch me without welcoming the heat of his hand.

10

My father is not a fan of surprises, so I know I've done something either very good or very bad when I see him coming toward me on the sidewalk, Callie trailing in his wake. I stop dead, my messenger bag slamming into my hip, and wait for him to approach. I haven't seen him since the wedding, and if anyone is watching, they might find my reaction strange, so I stretch a smile across my face. His presence is a relief, but it's a burden, too. I've missed him, but I don't want to be reminded of what he expects me to do.

"Hi, Dad," I say, when he's a few feet away. "What are you doing here?"

"Can't a father visit his favorite daughter?"

Callie socks him on the arm and flashes a grin. "Hey, standing right here."

My father smiles at us both, and I recognize this whole strained interaction as a performance, put on for the benefit of any curious eyes and ears. It makes me sad that we have to pretend to be comfortable with each other.

I allow myself to be folded into a hug, a quick kiss pressed against my cheek. "We'll walk you home," my dad says.

"Okay."

I lead the way, the two of them walking on either side of me, the same way they did the day of the wedding. Boxing me in.

"We got your message," Callie says, once we're past the semi-crowded streets near the courthouse and on an empty sidewalk.

My father puts his arm around my shoulder and gives it a gentle squeeze. "Good work, Ivy." He withdraws his arm. "Where are they exactly?"

"In a room in the basement of the courthouse. There's a keypad on the door and inside the room there's a safe."

"How many?"

I shake my head. "I couldn't get a close look. But I'd guess several hundred. Different types. Handguns, shotguns, rifles."

"We're going to need the codes," Callie says. "Knowing where the guns are doesn't do us any good without those."

"They don't leave them lying around," I snap, irritated for no good reason. I knew when I found the room that the next step would be finding the codes; it's not a surprise.

"I'm aware of that," Callie says. "That's why you're going to have to figure out where they are. And you can't take too long. Three months is coming up fast."

"I have the code to get into President Lattimer's house," I tell them. "Bishop gave it to me." My father beams at me and I flush with pride. "I can use that to get in and search for the code to the gun room and safe."

"Once we have the codes, we'll be close to putting the final phase into action," my father says. He stops walking, and Callie and I do the same.

The street is very quiet. In the distance, I hear children's laughter. I scuff the toe of my shoe against the sidewalk. "You mean the phase where we start killing people?"

From the corner of my eye, I see Callie give my father a look, her eyebrows slightly raised. But when she speaks, it's to me. "You've known all along what's involved, Ivy. No revolutions are won without sacrifices."

I take a step toward her. "Thanks for patronizing me, Callie. You've made everything so much clearer."

Callie jerks her head back like I slapped her. But before she can respond, my father puts a finger under my chin and turns my face until I'm looking into his brown eyes. The same eyes he passed on to Callie. Eyes so dark you can never figure out exactly what's happening behind them.

"Yes, Ivy, the phase where we start killing people," he says. "The same way they killed your mother. The same way they showed her no mercy."

The familiar anger swirls in my gut, so automatic now at the mention of my mother's name I wonder if I even really feel it anymore or if it's just a reflex. "President Lattimer told me he knew her," I say. "Is that true?"

My father pauses, shrugs. "Probably. They grew up on the same side of town, so I'm sure their paths crossed at some point."

"But he made it sound like—"

"Does it matter?" my father asks. "It doesn't change anything. The facts are still the facts. And you know what needs to be done." His voice is gentle but firm. "Not everyone who dies in a war is guilty. Sometimes they're just on the wrong side." He gives my chin a little chuck as he moves his hand away. "Do you understand?"

"Yes," I say. And the hell of it is, I do understand. They are both right. But it's easy to talk about what's right when the sacrifices for a cause are abstract…a president's son, a distant stranger, a symbol. It used to be easy for me, too. But now I know the color of Bishop's eyes in the sunlight, the way his hair stands up in the morning before he showers, the warmth of his palm on my back.

My father smiles. "Find the codes, Ivy," he says. It's not a request.

Callie squeezes my hand. "We're counting on you."

I bite back a swell of disappointment that Bishop isn't sprawled on the couch when I get home, his long legs resting on the coffee table, or out in the kitchen whipping up something for dinner. Already, I'm not sure how to define what we are to each other. Certainly not husband and wife, although that may be true on paper, and not exactly friends, either. But whatever it is, whatever we are, it will only make it harder in the end, because I am incapable of faking a relationship with him in order to make it through. For better or worse, my feelings for Bishop are real, whether they're anger or frustration or something else entirely. I'm different from Callie. I can't base my whole life on a lie, even if it's only temporary. So it's better if Bishop sleeps out here, with the safety of a wall between us.

I leave my messenger bag on the end of the couch and go into the bedroom. My neck and left shoulder have been sore since climbing the cliff at the river, and I rub the muscles with my right hand as I walk. Once in the bedroom, I kick off my shoes and one goes flying under the bed, disappearing beneath the bed skirt. I bend down and reach for it, my hand finding something hard instead of my shoe. Frowning, I get down on my hands and knees and lift up the bed skirt to peer under the bed. I pull out my shoe and toss it aside. Next to where it landed is a large photo album. I slide it out. Its cover is glossy red leather with gold leaf scrolling up the side.

I shift to sitting, my back leaning against the bed, and balance the heavy album across my legs. When I open it, the pages stick together slightly, making a faint ripping sound as I pull them apart. The first pages are dedicated to newspaper articles about the beginning of the war, the newsprint yellow with age. It's all information I learned from my father—how the bombs fell first on the east coast of the United States, then the west, how we retaliated, how more bombs were dropped, both here and on our allies, the ever-escalating futility of war, like the world's most deadly game of chicken. But the articles end before the war did, simply because the destruction was too vast. There was no one left to report on the damage. Everyone was too busy trying to survive it. And most of them didn't. Those who did were then cast into nuclear winter and their ranks further culled by disease and exposure. It's a miracle anyone survived, really.

After the articles, there are old photographs stuck to the pages, descriptions written below them in faded ink. Some I know from pictures I've seen in books, Mount Rushmore, the Grand Canyon. Others I've never seen before, the sequoias in California, the Northern Lights, the Great Barrier Reef. I run my fingers over the images, trying to imagine a world large enough to encompass endless treasures.

"So," Bishop's voice says from the doorway, "find something interesting?"

I jump, the album sliding off my lap onto the floor. "Oh my God," I breathe. "You scared me!" I glance from him to the album. There's no way to hide what I was doing. "I'm sorry. I didn't mean—"

But he only smiles, walks in to the room, and lowers himself to the floor next to me. "It's all right. I don't mind."

He reaches over me and pulls the album back onto my lap. "It was my grandfather's. He started it after the war so we wouldn't forget the way the world used to be. I've added to it over the years."

I flip to the next page, which is covered with pictures and ragged-edged postcards, all with images of the ocean. The next page is the same. And the one after that. I look up at Bishop, who keeps his eyes on the album. "You want to go beyond the fence," I say quietly. "Don't you?"

He nods. "I want to see the ocean."

I pause, remembering the conversation we had on the couch the night we both couldn't sleep. "That's what you wanted, isn't it? What you gave up when you married me." It's not even really a question, I already know the answer from the look on his face.

"Hey," he says, "it's okay. Maybe in a few years I can convince you to take a very long hike with me."

"But…" I trace the edge of a shoreline with my fingertip. "The bombs hit the coasts hardest. Would it be safe? Even now?"

Bishop shrugs. "Maybe not. Probably not." His face tightens. "But I don't think we're doing ourselves any favors staying isolated this way. Who knows what's out there? We may find other people. Whole societies like ours. And even if we don't, I'd get to hear the waves on the shore." He gives me a sad smile. "That would probably be enough to make it worth it."

I stare at him, this landlocked boy who dreams of water. It might have been an easily attained dream before the war. But now, when our knowledge of the world is limited to this small parcel of earth, when safety can be counted in square miles, yearning for the ocean seems like a form of bravery most people will never come close to attaining. It feels like reaching for the stars.

I bump my shoulder gently against his. "My grandfather saw the ocean, before the war. The Pacific. He told my dad it was loud and cold and beautiful, and that the water was so salty it made your eyes burn." I glance down at the album. "Do you think we ruined it?"

"Probably." Bishop sighs. "We ruined everything else. But I'd still like to know for sure."

I've never given much thought to going beyond the fence. My world has always been confined to the boundaries established by my father. But hearing Bishop's words, I try to imagine what it would be like to simply leave, strike out into unknown land, free from expectation, free of judgment. A whole world in front of me where I could be whoever I wanted to be.

"So what stopped you from going earlier?" I ask. "Before the wedding?"

He's quiet for a moment. "My father's sent surveying parties out. Did you know that?"

"No." I doubt my father knows, either. I've never heard a word about it. It surprises me. President Lattimer doesn't strike me as a leader who cares much about what's happening beyond his borders.

"Not many people do," Bishop says. "He sent one group of three volunteers when I was ten. And another group just a few years ago."

"Did they find anything?" I ask.

"No. Only one man ever came back. They didn't even make it twenty miles beyond the fence before they were attacked, all their food and weapons stolen. The man who returned to Westfall died a few days later from his injuries." He gives me a quick sideways glance. "That's why I didn't go, I guess. Fear."

I stare at his profile, the sharp line of his jaw. I remember his ease in the woods and the water. I remember his words about wanting to follow his heart. "I don't think you were scared to go," I say. "I think you were scared to leave."

"Aren't they the same thing?" he asks with a crooked smile.

"No." I shake my head. "You're not scared of what's out there. But you don't want to disappoint your father."

Bishop doesn't say anything, but the somber look in his eyes gives him away.

"You're going to be president someday," I say. "You'd really turn your back on that?" It's hard to imagine someone giving up the presidency willingly when my own father is fighting so hard to claim it.

Bishop huffs out a laugh. "I'm not cut out to be president. I've known it since I was young. But my father doesn't see it or doesn't want to see it."

"I think you'd be good at it," I say, and I mean it. I think he would be more thoughtful about balancing the needs of the group with the desires of individuals. I can't imagine Bishop continuing the arranged marriages or forcing couples to stay married, although he's never come right out and condemned his father's practices.

"No, I wouldn't be," he says. "I'd rather find out what's beyond the fence than protect what's inside it. I don't care enough about the power."

The polar opposite of his own father. And of mine. "That's exactly why you'd be good at it," I tell him. "Because the power doesn't matter to you."

"Maybe." He doesn't sound convinced.

"Would you govern like your father?" I ask, eyes back on the photo album. I already know he doesn't like the fact that we don't have choices anymore, but I've never asked him this question directly.

Bishop hesitates. "No," he says finally, and my heart leaps as my stomach falls. "I think my father's done a good job of keeping us alive. I think in his own mind, he means well." Bishop sighs, runs a hand through his hair. "But part of being a human being is making your own choices, having freedom. I think my father's forgotten that."

"See?" I say quietly. "You would be good at it."

Bishop smiles, shakes his head. "I'd still rather explore than govern." He takes the album from my lap and slides it back under the bed. "Dinner?" he asks.

"Sure." I push myself to standing. I grab a rubber band from the top of the dresser and reach up to gather my hair into a ponytail, wincing as I tweak my sore shoulder.

"What's wrong?"

"Just sore from all the climbing."

"Here." He holds out his hand. "Let me."

I raise my eyebrows at him in the mirror above the dresser. "You can do hair?"

He smiles. "I can try." He gathers my thick hair with both hands, making me laugh as he tries to pull it back and push it up at the same time. He finally manages to twist the band around it a few times, although it's a long way from smooth. "There," he says. He rests both hands on my shoulders and meets my eyes in the mirror. As I watch, his thumbs come up and run down the sides of my neck, slow and gentle.

A curl of heat unfurls inside me, starting deep in my belly and spreading outward. I feel it in my toes and fingers and the heated flesh of my cheeks.

I feel it everywhere.

"Will that work?" he asks quietly.

"Yes," I say. I'm having a hard time finding my voice. "It's fine." The skin under his thumbs burns like it's been painted with fire.

His eyes are still on mine in the mirror, like he's waiting for something. Some signal I'm too scared to give him. Bishop lifts his hands and steps away from me. "I'll go start dinner."

I nod. "Okay, I'll be right there."

Once Bishop is gone, I walk to the bed on shaky legs and sink to sitting. I press my palms hard against my closed eyelids. I can still feel the weight of Bishop's hands on my shoulders, the memory of his thumbs against my neck. I remind myself what his father's done. What he is still doing. But Bishop's touch is gentle, his intentions good. No matter how hard I look, I cannot find the blood on his hands.

11

Trying to find the right time to approach Victoria is an art I'm still mastering. She is not mean or spiteful, but she can be curt if she's preoccupied or believes that her time is being wasted. It doesn't generally bother me because Callie is the same way. Most of the time I manage to not take it personally.

We're grabbing a quick lunch in the small courthouse cafeteria, when I think I may have an opening. I'm picking at a slightly stale turkey and cheese sandwich, while Victoria speeds her way through a chicken salad. Her selection looks better than mine.

"So," I ask, "has David worked here long?"

Victoria shrugs. "I don't know exactly. He's been here as long as I have."

I pinch off a tiny piece of turkey but don't eat it. "Do

you think it's weird for him, having a gun and everything?"

"And everything?" Victoria asks with raised eyebrows.

"I just mean, most people aren't comfortable with weapons, since there aren't many around."

Victoria takes a bite of salad and chews it before answering. "He seems pretty comfortable to me."

I give what I hope sounds like a normal laugh and not some crazed cackle. "Yeah, I guess so." My sandwich is hopeless, so I wad it up along with the paper it's wrapped in. "Is that his gun or does he get it here?" I am sure she can see my heartbeat pulsing through my shirt.

"He gets it here. Work issue," Victoria says. She is answering my questions easily enough, but her eyes are sharp on mine.

"What, do they have a stockpile hidden away somewhere?" Again with the laugh that's not quite my own.

"Why so curious?" Victoria asks, putting down her fork. "I didn't know you were interested in guns."

I shake my head. "I'm not. Well, I mean, maybe I am a little. I've read about them in books, but I haven't ever really seen one. You know…forbidden fruit and all that."

My answer must make sense to Victoria because she picks her fork up again and stabs at a chunk of chicken. "You're not the only one who feels that way. Half the men who work here are constantly begging David for a chance to hold it." She snorts. "I could make an inappropriate joke about over-compensating, but you're too young, so I won't."

I laugh, and this time it's genuine.

"But David's careful with his gun. As he should be.

Only a select few people are trusted with them. And Ray...I don't think you've met him yet?"

I shake my head.

"His job, for as long as anybody can remember, has been to keep the weapons safe and in the right hands." Ray must have been the older man I saw in the gun room with David.

"So I'm guessing Ray and David aren't going to be taking me out for target practice anytime soon?" I ask.

Victoria smiles. "Doubtful. The person you should be talking to, if you're really serious, is your father-in-law." She points at me with her fork. "Ray's in charge of the guns, but President Lattimer's in charge of Ray."

"That's a good idea," I say, my heart rate picking up. "Maybe I'll ask him." I'm not sure exactly where to go from here. I can't think of a way to get the code from David or Ray that won't give everything away, and I have no idea where, or even if, they keep a record of it in the courthouse. But Victoria is probably right. The person who would undoubtedly have the information is my father-in-law. I think of his study and his big walnut desk. I'm sure it holds plenty of secrets.

"Ready?" Victoria asks me. She is already standing, her empty salad bowl in hand.

"Sure." I scramble to my feet, tossing my sandwich into the trash can.

"They're being put out this afternoon," Victoria tells me as we leave the cafeteria. "We need to get everything ready."

My footsteps slow. It reminds me of being a little girl when I didn't want to go wherever my father was taking me and I dragged my feet until he was forced to pull me.

"What?" Victoria asks over her shoulder. She sounds aggravated.

I speed up. "Are we actually there when they're put out?"

"No," Victoria says, and I breathe a sigh of relief. I know what Mark Laird did, but I still don't want to watch his punishment, have to listen to him beg for mercy he doesn't deserve and definitely won't receive.

"How many are there?"

"Three today," Victoria says. "All men."

"Is that typical? The number, I mean?" President Lattimer never gives us details about who is being put out. There is always gossip in the market and I've heard my father talking about it with neighbors, but no official accounting is ever released. Probably because while the threat of being put out serves to keep us in line, knowing actual names and numbers might cause people to question what's happening.

"It varies," Victoria says. We start up the stairs, turning sideways against the flow of people heading to the cafeteria. "We do this every month, and a lot of times there's no one. The most I can remember is five at one time, but that's unusual. That was a bad winter." She glances at me. "Generally, all men, but not always."

"Does President Lattimer come?"

"No."

"Of course not," I mutter. "That would be getting too

close to the dirty work."

Victoria stops in her tracks, and I almost slam into her back. "Watch yourself, Ivy," she says. She doesn't sound angry, so much as concerned. "You're his family now, but you can still overstep your boundaries."

My throat is instantly bone dry. I manage to give her a tiny nod. I don't think President Lattimer would hurt me. It wouldn't be good for public relations to punish his newly minted daughter-in-law, especially after the speech he gave me about valuing my opinion, and the way he always tries to come across as benevolent. He's more the type to hurt other people in my stead—Callie, my father—people whose punishment would be even more painful to witness than my own, the same way he killed my mother as a way to hurt my father.

Victoria pauses in her office to grab a stack of files from the edge of her desk. Then it's back down the stairs to the basement. On days like this, I wish for the elevator, but it's considered an unnecessary use of electricity.

"Do we give them anything?" I ask, skipping down the steps at Victoria's break neck pace. "Before we put them out?"

"Like a going away present?" Victoria asks with a humorless laugh.

"No, of course not. But water, maybe? Or a map?" Even as I ask the question, I know the answer.

"Nope." Victoria yanks open the basement door and holds it for me to pass through ahead of her. "Besides, a map would be only a guess on our part. We have no idea what's out there, either." She points toward the corridor where the gun room is located. "This way."

I manage to pass by the closed door without glancing at it, although the urge is strong. We take another right and, huddled at the end of the hall, are three men in shackles. David and another guard lean against the wall.

David sees us coming and pushes himself away from the wall. "Hey, Victoria," he says. "Mrs. Lattimer."

"Ivy," I tell him. From the expression on his face, I know it will be a cold day in hell before he ever brings himself to call me anything other than Mrs. Lattimer.

"Hello," Victoria says. "Everything going according to procedure?" Her voice is brisk and businesslike. She doesn't look at any of the prisoners.

"Yes," David says. "Just waiting for you to bring the paperwork so we can get them out of here."

"Sorry we're a little late."

"That's okay." David flaps a hand behind him at the men. "They're not going anywhere. But it's a long walk. Sooner we get started, the better."

"Absolutely," Victoria says. She flips open the first file in her hands. "You know the drill." She hands David a pen and holds the file steady while he signs the paperwork inside. I tune them out and turn my attention to the prisoners.

The oldest one is probably in his fifties, with a hard paunch of belly and downcast eyes. Sweat stains the armpits of his shirt and moistens his forehead. Next to him is a small, wiry man who reminds me of a rodent, all his features pinched toward the middle of his face and sharp front teeth resting on his bottom lip. He's not sweating, but he's breathing fast. I can hear his labored inhales from where I stand. The final man is Mark Laird. I glance at him and he gives me a tentative, sad smile, looking for all the world like a wronged man valiantly accepting his fate. But that cunning, calculating gleam in his blue eyes gives him away. He's already sizing up his situation, figuring out what can be used to his advantage. He's obviously done with begging.

I don't want to look at him. His eyes on mine make my skin crawl. I can hear the voice of the little girl he hurt crying inside my head. But if I look away, he'll know he's scared me. And that is worse than meeting his gaze.

"All set," David says from behind me, and the second guard straightens up from his relaxed slouch against the wall. It seems like there should be more formality, something more dramatic to mark the moment, but David simply moves past the prisoners and pushes open the door in front of them. It opens directly to the outside and the bright sunlight streaming in makes us all squint. I put up a hand to shield my eyes.

"Come on," David says gruffly to the first prisoner in line, the older man, "get moving." The man hesitates for only a second before shuffling forward, following David out into daylight. The other two have no choice but to do the same, as they are all chained together. The second guard brings up the rear, the door swinging shut with a hollow bang behind him. I lower my hand, sun spots still shifting before my eyes. The hallway is eerily quiet. I think I can still hear the men's chains jangling from outside, but I know it's only my imagination.

Victoria moves up next to me, her eyes on the door. "Well, that's that," she says. "Let's get back to work."

"Okay," I say, my voice small but steady. For all intents and purposes, I've just watched three men die. It was not as difficult as it should have been.

I'm passing the secluded edge of the park on my way home when Callie steps out from behind a tree and loops her arm through mine. I'm not even that surprised, but I pull away all the same.

"What is the deal with you and Dad lately?" I say. "Always lurking."

"Calm down," Callie says, rolling her eyes. "Dad doesn't even know I'm here."

"Why *are* you here?"

"You seemed a little off the other day," Callie says, falling into step beside me. "I wanted to make sure you're okay."

I snort. Callie has been a lot of things to me over the years—confidante, teacher, torturer, but nurturer has rarely been on the list. "What do you really want?"

"God, you're prickly," Callie says, probably annoyed that I'm stepping into territory she usually occupies.

I stop and stare at her, arms folded across my chest.

"Okay," Callie says, mimicking my pose. "I want to know what's going on with you and Bishop Lattimer."

"What do you mean?" I ignore the way my pulse increases at her words, my palms suddenly slick with sweat.

"You were acting weird the other day," Callie shrugs. "Reluctant or something."

"You mean reluctant to kill someone?" I ask. "Pardon me if I'm not jumping for joy." My voice has an edge to it, one Callie must hear, too, because she takes a step closer to me.

"Oh, grow up, Ivy. Did you actually think any of this would be *easy?*" Her voice cracks against me like a whip. "Anything worth fighting for...worth having...is difficult. There are always going to be casualties of war." She studies my face for a long moment. I try to keep my expression blank, but just like it's been since we were children, she reads me in an instant.

She points at me, her finger coming millimeters away from stabbing me in the middle of the chest. "Do you... do you *like* him?" She sounds horrified, disgusted, like I've eaten a handful of worms or slept in my own vomit.

I look away, willing my heart to calm down. A warm breeze rustles the trees above our heads, blowing a tangle of hair into my eyes. I push it back impatiently. "I don't have to like someone to not be okay with killing him."

"You know how important his death is to our success," Callie says. "If his father dies, Bishop steps right into power. Nothing changes. They *both* have to go. You *know* that."

"I don't think he's like his father. He—"

"I don't care," Callie says, voice ice cold. "I don't care what he's like. And you shouldn't, either. You're selfish if you do. You're going to put what you feel, what you want, before what's best for our family? Before what's best for everyone?" She grabs my forearm, her fingers digging trenches between the tendons. "After all these years, our family is finally close to being in control. Do you not get that?"

"Yes, I get that." I pry her hand off my arm, bending her fingers back as I do. "I saw three men put out today," I say through clenched teeth. "Do you even care? Isn't that the sort of thing we're supposed to be fighting against?"

Callie's eyebrows snap together. "What are you talking about?"

I shake my head at her, all the anger draining out of me. I shrug, my whole body lifeless and so tired. "Forget it."

"Whatever's going on with you," Callie says, "you need to remember who you are. Fast. It's us against them." She grabs my hand, but this time her grip is gentle. Her voice is soft as she says, "We're your family. We love you. We're the ones who would do anything for you. Don't forget it."

"I never do," I say. It's hard to speak around the burning knot of tears in my throat.

Callie gives my hand one final squeeze. "You have to do this, Ivy, or everything falls apart. Think how proud Dad will be when it's over." She gives me a little smile and takes a few steps backward, eyes still on mine. "Don't make Bishop Lattimer more important than he is. He wouldn't do the same for you."

I stay on the sidewalk for a long time after she's gone. Is it still manipulation if you know it's happening, but it works anyway?

12

I wake when it's dark outside. I lay on my back, my eyes cloudy with sleep, and try to figure out what woke me. At first there's nothing, only the faint sound of birds outside the window, the whir of the ceiling fan above my head. I'm about to roll over and try to get a little more sleep when I hear it again, the sound of a kitchen cabinet closing. It's earlier than Bishop is usually up and he's trying hard to be quiet. I can tell because the sounds coming from the kitchen are careful, the tread of his feet light.

I startle him when I appear in the kitchen doorway, still rubbing sleep from my eyes. Belatedly, I realize I'm dressed only in a tank top and my underpants, but I guess it's nothing he hasn't seen before, given the bikini I wore to the river. "What are you doing?" I ask.

He is wearing a T-shirt and shorts, his hair unruly from

sleep. His eyes skim over my bare legs then rise to my face. I manage not to blush. "Nothing," he says. He's not trying to hide the open backpack on the counter, but I can tell he doesn't want me to notice it, either. "It's early. You can go back to bed if you want."

"Okay." I turn and pad back to the bedroom but don't crawl into bed. Instead, I throw on clothes and shoes, pull my hair up into a bun on the top of my head, and wait until I hear the front door close softly behind him. Then I sprint to the kitchen for a jug of water and slip out after him.

I don't really think through why I'm following him, but I want to know what he's up to, why he's keeping something secret from me. Which is ridiculous, given the number of secrets I have from him. But I want to discover what he's doing and I'm not above sneaking around in order to find out.

Following him without being seen or heard is difficult. He walks the same route as we took to the river, at least at first, but he navigates fast and sure through the woods, barely slowing for downed tree limbs or branches that effortlessly reach out and find places on me to scratch. I'm hoping the sound of his footfalls drown mine out because I'm hardly quiet, practically having to run to keep sight of him in spots.

I begin to hear the river to our right and know the pool is close, but he veers left, off the path, and straight into the tangled undergrowth. I lean against a tree trunk for a second to catch my breath before heading after him. Vines tangle around my ankles and foliage snatches at my bare arms. I manage to sidestep a large rock half buried in the ground, but my foot snags on a tree root and I go down hard, landing on my right shoulder.

I lay there for a minute, breathing through gritted teeth. I'm not hurt so much as stunned, although a tiny rivulet of blood runs down my arm. This was such a bad idea, but it's too late to turn back now. I have to know what he's doing. I push myself to my knees and then to my feet and head after him. I've completely lost sight of him and I cock my head, hoping to hear something. Nothing but silence. Risking the noise, I run in the direction Bishop was last headed, leaping over obstacles and straining for any glimpse of his blue T-shirt.

I stop again, listening. There's the faint sound of voices coming from ahead and slightly to my right. They are difficult to hear over the leaves whispering in the early morning breeze. I can't hear what the voices are saying, but I'm positive the deeper one is Bishop's. I move slowly now, careful to set each foot down quietly as I move in the direction of the sound.

I'm not sure exactly where I am. I can no longer hear the river, but up ahead and through the trees I see sunlight glinting off metal. The fence. What is Bishop doing at the fence? Maybe he's talking to one of the patrol guards? My breathing is labored and not only from running. I inch closer, stopping right on the edge of the tree line and hiding myself behind a wide trunk.

The fence stretches in either direction, a large gate set into it about ten yards to my left. Is this where the prisoners are put out? There is a patch of grass and weeds about twelve feet wide between the tree line and the fence. Directly in front of me, Bishop is crouched next to the fence, talking to a figure laying on the ground on the other side. I press myself against the trunk and crane my neck to try and get a closer look. It's a girl on the ground, her long hair tangled around her face like a dirty cloud. The only skin visible is one mud-encrusted foot. It looks more bone than flesh.

"Come on," Bishop says. "Take the water. Please." He shoves a slim container of water through a gap in the fence, but it falls to the ground on the other side. The girl makes no move to reach for it. She looks dead, but I know she must not be if Bishop is talking to her.

"Hey, I already told you, stop wasting your time with her," a man's voice calls, and my head whips to the side, scanning the fence line. It takes me a minute to locate the source of the voice. There's a man sitting outside the fence, most of him camouflaged by long grass. I catch a flicker of shrewd blue eyes. Mark Laird. My blood freezes in my veins. There's no sign of the two men put out with him. Maybe they've moved on, looking for shelter, food, water. Maybe he killed them. Either possibility seems likely.

Bishop ignores him, doesn't even turn his head. He pushes some bread through the fence. It meets the same fate as the water, landing untouched on the ground.

"Don't give her that!" Mark protests as he pulls himself to standing using the chain-link fence for leverage. He's favoring his right leg. He was walking fine yesterday. "She's practically dead anyway! You're feeding a corpse."

"Shut up," Bishop says, still not looking at Mark. I've never heard him sound so cold. He bends his head down, says something else to the girl that I can't hear, but she doesn't respond. After a minute, he stands with a sigh. I shrink back into the shadows of the tree.

Bishop walks over to Mark and shoves another container of water and more bread through the fence. Unlike the girl, Mark doesn't waste any time before grabbing them, groping on the ground like the food and water might disappear if he's not quick enough. Bishop watches, his face a blank mask I do not recognize.

"You need to find water," Bishop says. "The river is that way." He points to the east with his head. "Food may be more difficult, but I'm sure you'll figure something out."

"Is it safe to drink the water?"

"Do you have a choice?"

Mark shrugs at that, biting off a huge hunk of bread. He speaks with his mouth full. "Will you be back?"

"Don't count on it," Bishop says. He reaches a hand out lightning fast and pins Mark's fingers against the fence where they're hooked through the metal. "Leave her alone," he says, voice quiet. I have to strain to make out his words. "Don't take her food. Don't touch her." He twists his hand and Mark cries out, the bread falling from his free hand.

"Okay," he whines. "Okay! Let go!"

Bishop removes his hand and backs away from the fence, not taking his eyes off Mark. He finally turns and looks at the girl one last time before heading in my direction. I shift my body to the side of the tree, hoping he'll pass right by without noticing I'm there. I press my spine into the tree and close my eyes, willing him not to see me.

I hear his footsteps approaching and a hand closes around my arm like a manacle, dragging me forward, away from the fence and into the woods. I gasp and stumble after Bishop, who doesn't say a word, just keeps hauling me along.

"You're hurting me," I say to his back, keeping my voice low. It seems important that Mark not know I'm here. I never want him to look at me or even think about me again.

Bishop lets go instantly, but when he turns to face me, his usually placid eyes blaze, his jaw muscle bunched like a fist. "What are you doing here?" he demands. I've never seen him truly angry before. It's almost a relief to know he's capable of it, that he isn't always in perfect control of his own emotions.

I massage my arm. "I followed you."

"Yeah, I got that part," he says. "I figured it out about a block from the house."

So much for my stealth. "Why didn't you say something?"

Bishop takes a step closer to me. "I wanted to see how far you'd come."

"Well," I say, tipping my head up to meet his eyes. I ignore my heartbeat in my throat. "I came all the way."

Bishop blows out a breath and, with it, the anger appears to leave him, dissipating on his exhale. "It's dangerous out here, Ivy."

Now it's my turn to set my jaw. "You're out here. Besides, it's not like they can get back over." From where we stand, I can still see a glimpse of razor wire along the top of the fence.

"That's not what I meant." He runs a hand through his hair. "It's against the law to help them."

"Then why are you doing it?" I demand. "That guy out there"—I hook my thumb toward the fence—"he was the one I met the other day. The one who raped a little girl." Bishop winces at my words but doesn't shift his gaze. "You said you didn't have any sympathy for him. So what are you doing?" My voice drops. "Do you know the girl?"

Bishop shakes his head. "No, I don't know her. She was put out last time. She's given up." He holds out his hands like he's searching the air for the right words, then lets them fall back to his sides. "This isn't sympathy. It's basic humanity. I just…" He scrubs at his face with one hand. "I want to give them a chance, I guess. The ones who deserve it, at least."

"How can you tell the difference?"

Bishop gives me a rueful little smile. "I can't."

I stare at him. His father imposes the sentence, without even the guts to watch it carried out. And my father's no better, not really, although it pains me to admit it. He rails against the president's policies, but never once has he bothered to come out here and hand out water or comfort. Of all the people I know, on both sides of the equation, only Bishop has the heart and the will to do that. Only he is strong enough to show a little mercy.

I know Callie is right. Liking him, feeling anything for him, is the most dangerous act of all. Worse than being found out or making a mistake. But even as I know I cannot like this boy, I know it is too late.

I already do.

"I'll help you," I find myself saying. "From now on." I take a step closer, bridging the space between us. I hesitate, torn between what I want and what is wise. I reach out and take his hand. Something sharp and electric sizzles up my arm when our skin meets, a bittersweet ache. "We can do it together." Even Callie can't argue if she discovers what I'm doing, not when putting people out is one of the things my father stands against. She doesn't need to know family loyalty is not why I'm doing it.

I expect him to argue, but he only nods, his green eyes on mine. They look darker out here, surrounded by woods, as if their color was stolen from the very trees above us. He doesn't let go of my hand as we begin the long walk home.

13

"Dylan and Meredith invited us to dinner." Bishop sets a sack of food from the market on the table where I'm finishing a late morning bowl of oatmeal, enjoying a lazy Saturday.

"When?" The reluctance in my voice matches his.

"Tonight. Dylan cornered me on my way in." Bishop sighs. "I didn't feel like I could say no."

"Because he'd take it out on her." I put down my spoon, no longer hungry.

"Yeah," Bishop says with another sigh. He slides into the chair opposite me. "They invited the couple two doors down, too. I know the husband, Jason, from school. We're the same age. He's a nice guy. Haven't met his wife, though."

"Well, this ought to be fun," I say with fake brightness.

Bishop gives me an exaggerated wink. "Don't say I

never show you a good time."

I snort out a laugh, my eyes finding his across the table. He leans forward and snags one of the strawberries from my oatmeal. I thump the back of his hand with my spoon and he grins around the mouthful of fruit. He looks relaxed, slouching back in his chair, his dark hair ruffled from his fingers, a trace of stubble on his cheeks. I'm staring, but I can't figure out a way to stop.

"Are you happy, Ivy?" he asks, surprising me.

In my whole life, I don't think anyone's ever asked me that question. I take the time to really consider my answer, give it the weight it deserves. I know what I'm supposed to say. I know what I'm not supposed to feel. And the truth lies somewhere in between. "I'm a work in progress," I tell him finally. "But I'm getting there."

Bishop smiles, slow and easy, and warmth spills into my blood, heating me from the inside out.

I smile back and duck my head to hide my flushed cheeks.

Meredith is setting the picnic table in the backyard when we come through the gate. She smiles at us, hurrying over to take the bowl of fruit salad from my hands. "We're so glad you could come," she says.

"Thanks for inviting us," I say.

She points us toward the table and a collection of

lawn chairs. "Make yourselves comfortable. I'll get you something to drink."

Bishop sits down in one of the lawn chairs, and I perch on the picnic table bench. Meredith returns with two glasses of lemonade and Dylan, who is carrying a platter of meat.

"Hello, there," he says, all smiles. "How does steak sound?"

"Great," I force myself to say. My voice is as falsely cheerful as his, and Bishop raises his eyebrows at me, amused.

"Figured only the best for the president's son," Dylan says, slapping Bishop on the shoulder with his free hand. Bishop smiles, but it's not a real one. His eyes are like flint.

We manage to make stilted small talk for a few minutes until Jacob and his wife, Stephanie, arrive. They are both small and dark-haired and could easily pass for siblings. Jacob is as friendly as Bishop predicted, giving me a wide smile as we're introduced. Stephanie is pregnant, her belly so swollen she looks in danger of toppling forward at any moment. She sinks into a lawn chair with an audible sigh of relief. She flashes me an apologetic smile. "No one told me how exhausting this was going to be."

"I can imagine," I murmur, although I really can't.

She rubs her hand over her belly. "Only a few more weeks, thank goodness. We're getting anxious to meet this little guy. Or girl."

Jacob takes the seat next to hers and rests a hand on her shoulder. "Do you need anything?" he asks.

She smiles up at him, her whole face glowing. "No, I'm fine." She seems happy, but I wonder how much of her joy is real and how much is tied up in the idea that she's successfully fulfilled her role as a wife and soon-to-be mother.

Meredith joins us, standing with her hands clasped in front of her, a wistful expression on her face. "I can't wait to have a baby," she says.

I look down at the ground and tell myself to keep quiet. And for once I'm able to heed my own advice. I can't believe she would want to have a child with Dylan. Has she been so brainwashed that she actually thinks it will improve her situation, that a boy like Dylan will ever change? And does she not understand how a child will trap her? No matter what happens to her relationship with Dylan, she will love their child, and that maternal bond will lock her in for the rest of her life. Babies at sixteen serve more than one purpose for a clever government.

It strikes me suddenly how ridiculous all of this is. The group of us still children in many ways, playing at being grown-ups. Throwing barbecues and talking about babies. Even at eighteen, Jacob and Stephanie seem young, too young to be embarking on parenthood, surely. My father told me that before the war, a lot of people didn't marry or have children until they were in their thirties. Sometimes even their forties. It had been shocking to contemplate. Now, the younger you are when you reproduce, the better the chance your baby will be born with the right number of fingers and toes, the better the chance you'll be able to have a child at all.

But I envy the women who came before me, the ones

who had the option of waiting or of not having children at all. Nowadays, children are the most valuable currency there is, and if you're able, you have them. It's not a question of what you want, it's only a question of how many and how healthy. I know that Bishop and I aren't destined to raise a family together, but I wonder if he is envious of Stephanie's growing belly, if he wishes he had his own child on the way. I catch his eye across the yard, and he gives me a small, secret smile. Something in his face tells me I'm not the only one who recognizes the ridiculousness of this life we're living.

"Steaks are ready!" Dylan calls, and Meredith rushes over to his side with a platter. Her constant vigilance to his needs has to be exhausting, always trying to anticipate what he'll want before he even wants it.

We line up for plates, Jacob urging Stephanie to stay seated while he gets her food. I sit at the edge of the picnic table with Dylan and Meredith across from me. Bishop sits in the same lawn chair he vacated earlier, Stephanie and Jacob to his left.

I'm halfway through my dinner when I notice the cozy way Stephanie and Jacob are sitting, their knees touching, laughing under their breath at some private joke. Even Dylan and Meredith are having a conflict-free evening. She is holding out a forkful of watermelon for him, smiling as he slides it into his mouth. I have to resist the urge to vomit. I'd be more tempted to stab him in the eye. But there's no denying that the closeness of the other couples makes the distance between Bishop and me more awkward, noticeable to everyone. I can't afford to have people speculating about our relationship, questioning my commitment to my husband. Especially after…when suspicion is sure to swirl around me.

I take a deep breath and push myself up, plate in hand. I walk to where Bishop is sitting. When he looks up at me, I smile. "Is there room for me?" I ask. I don't give him a chance to answer. I lower myself to sit sideways across his lap, resting my weight gingerly on his thighs. I hope he can't feel my body quaking.

He studies me for a long moment. "I won't break," he says finally. He puts a hand on my lower back, supporting me.

"I'm tall," I say by way of apology as I let him take my full weight.

"I've noticed." Bishop's voice is quiet. "I like it."

The heat in my chest threatens to engulf me, like a fire's been set inside my rib cage and is raging out of control, tearing its way through my body, burning up all the available oxygen. Out of the corner of my eye, I can tell Stephanie and Jacob are watching us, but I can't shift my gaze from Bishop's.

"How's…" I have to clear my throat. "How's your steak?"

"Good." Bishop glances down at my plate. "Yours?"

"Same," I say. I don't trust myself to lift my fork.

A wisp of Bishop's hair falls over his forehead, blown by the breeze. I don't give myself time to think about it, just reach up and smooth it back, the strands so much softer than I thought they would be, thick and silky against my fingers. My head knows what a horrible idea this is, screaming at me to *stop*, that I'm taking things too far, but the rest of me has no such reservations. I have the fleeting thought that perhaps self-preservation isn't my strongest character trait.

Bishop turns his head slightly as I ease my hand away so that I touch his cheek, his skin warm and stubble-rough under my palm. His hand remains on the small of my back. His thumb rubs in a slow up-and-down motion, my entire body centered right there at the point of contact.

"I thought you were making strawberry shortcake," Dylan says behind me. "That's what I said I wanted."

Bishop's thumb stills on my back, and I turn my head, following his gaze to where Dylan and Meredith stand near their back door. She's carrying a pie in her hands, her happy smile dying on her face as I watch.

"The strawberries at the market didn't look good today. But they had fresh blueberries, and I thought—"

Dylan's hand moves so fast I don't even see it until it cracks across her cheek. The contact creates a sharp popping sound, and Meredith's eyes widen, tears blossoming along her lids. Stephanie gives a quick, startled inhale before quiet descends again.

Meredith raises a hand to her cheek, her eyes on the pie. "I'm sorry," she whispers.

Bishop's whole body has gone rigid, his hand forming a fist in my shirt.

"Blueberry will be fine," Dylan says, like he's granting her an official pardon. "But next time, do what I say."

"All right," Meredith says with a wobbly smile. She sets the pie on the table, and Dylan turns to all of us, clapping his hands. "Who's ready for dessert?" he calls. He doesn't appear to notice the awful tension in the yard, or maybe he doesn't care—the casual violence he inflicted simply part of the everyday fabric of their lives.

"I'm not feeling well," I say, my voice loud in the silence that meets Dylan's dessert announcement. "I want to go home." I stand and put my plate down on the picnic table.

"Don't you want some pie?" Meredith asks, her brow furrowed.

"No." I can barely meet her eyes. I know I should stay, for her sake, that Dylan will blame the party breaking up on her, but I can't. If I stay, I will say something that will only make things a thousand times worse for her. Better to go now, before I do even more damage.

Bishop is behind me, making our apologies and saying good-bye, but I walk away, out the gate and through to our yard. Once inside, I lean against the kitchen counter, my hands shaking with rage.

"We have to do something," I say as soon as Bishop is inside, the back door shut behind him.

"I know," he says. "But you need to stay away from him."

I blow out an exasperated breath. "I can handle him."

"I have no doubt you could kick his ass from here to next Tuesday," Bishop says, voice calm. "In a fair fight. But guys like him never fight fair." He pulls out a kitchen chair and straddles it, his hands resting on the back. "He's unpredictable, and that makes him dangerous."

"He seems pretty predictable to me. He hits her

whenever he wants."

"I'm serious, Ivy. Don't try to deal with him on your own."

I stare down at the floor, still hearing the crack of Dylan's palm against Meredith's cheek. I hate President Lattimer all over again for putting girls like Meredith in a position they can never get out of, left with absolutely no power over their own lives.

"What was that, by the way?" Bishop asks. I look up and he's staring at me.

"What are you talking about?"

"Sitting on my lap." He pauses. "Touching my hair."

I have no idea how to respond to his question. Which answer is the truth and which is a lie, which one will make things temporarily better and which will make things permanently worse?

"If you touch me, I want it to be because you want to, not because people are watching," he says. "I don't care what other people think. What does, or doesn't, go on between us isn't anyone's business but ours."

I didn't know he could read me so well. I don't know why I'm surprised. He's been watching me since the moment we met, learning me like he's learned the river and woods. I want to tell him that I may have started out touching him because I was worried about other people, but that's not what I was thinking about by the end. Everyone else in that backyard had ceased to exist for me.

I want to be honest with him. But I've already made so many mistakes today. I can't afford to make another one.

14

We return to the fence a week after the barbecue, but this time, although we walk in tandem, we do not hold hands. There's been a distance between us since that night in the kitchen, a tension that simmers on the surface of every painfully polite interaction. I hate it, but I tell myself it's better this way. I pretend I don't miss the sound of his voice and the touch of his hand.

The walk seems to take longer today, maybe because I'm not running after him like a crazed maniac, maybe because of the silence between us and the oppressive heat. The sun is high in an electric blue sky, not a cloud to be seen, the air so hot it practically sizzles on the inhale.

When we reach the tree line, I approach the fence warily, not wanting Mark Laird to surprise me. It would be foolish for him to have remained here, but that hasn't stopped the girl, whose crumpled form still lies at the base of the fence. The spot where I last saw Mark is empty, and no one else is in sight. The only sound is the breeze sighing through the long grass beyond the fence.

But the breeze brings something besides sound. It brings the smell of death, burning the delicate lining of my nostrils and coating my throat so that I can barely swallow past its foulness.

"Oh, God," I manage to choke out, my eyes watering.

Bishop is already crouching down beside the girl, one hand covering his nose and mouth. I take a cautious step closer and wish I hadn't. Her face is a dark purple horror. She's been strangled, her head lolling on a snapped neck. Her long skirt is hiked up around her waist and I turn my head away, press my cheek against the hot metal of the fence and close my eyes. I know I will never be able to unsee the livid bruises on the insides of her thighs, her milky, sightless eyes.

"He killed her," I say. I'm breathing like I just ran a race, gulping down air contaminated with the remains of the dead. I dry heave, gritting my teeth until I gain control over my stomach.

I feel, rather than see, Bishop stand up beside me. I can hear him breathing hard, too, a harsh, ragged sound.

"What did she do?" I ask, although I don't really want to know.

"Does it matter?" he asks. He sounds so tired. "Will it make it better if she deserved it?"

I shake my head, the fence pressing harder into my

cheekbone. "No. I just want to know."

"She wouldn't agree to an arranged marriage, refused to even take the personality tests," he says. I squeeze my eyes shut even tighter. She is the girl I heard Victoria talking about with Jack Stewart my first day at the courthouse, the girl whose family was making too much noise about her punishment. For the first time, it sinks in that the horrors beyond the fence are the same as those inside it.

People. And the brutal things we do to one another.

The fence shakes against my cheek and I turn, careful to keep my gaze lifted. I don't have it in me to look at her again. Bishop is grasping the chain-link with both hands, knuckles white, his eyes closed. His whole body is wound tight as a spring, like if I reached for him he would simply break apart at the joints, splinter into a hundred pieces. I don't try to touch him.

He lets out a yell and then another and another, loud and wild and out of control. He shakes the fence hard with both hands. His anger and frustration are more potent somehow because they are unexpected. When his scream fades into silence, he rests his forehead against the metal. "Sometimes," he says, voice raw, "I hate this place." He twists his neck and looks at me, hands still hooked in the fence above his head.

"I know," I say, barely a whisper. "Me, too."

It takes every ounce of energy I have to make the return walk home. The day has taken something from me that I know a shower or a nap or a good meal will never replace. I haven't felt innocent in years, but maybe there was still some left down deep inside of me that is now forever gone. The space it left behind filled with the image of a dead girl I never even knew.

As we are dragging up the walk to our front door, Dylan appears from the side of his house. He has a tool belt around his waist that is threatening to pull down his pants, and he looks so ridiculous I want to laugh. "Hey," he says, giving us a wave. "I was just looking for you, Bishop."

"Yeah?" Bishop asks. He runs a hand through his hair, exhaustion written on every inch of him.

"I've got some loose shingles." Dylan looks over his shoulder at their second-floor dormer. "Thought maybe you could give me a hand."

Bishop glances at me, then back to Dylan. "Sure. Give me a minute, okay?"

"Yeah, yeah, no problem," Dylan says with a smile. Every time he smiles it's disconcerting. His open grin doesn't fit at all with what I know lurks underneath.

We go inside and I kick off my shoes, harder than I intended because one hits the living room wall with a clatter. Bishop raises his eyebrows at me.

"I can't believe you're helping him," I say.

"It's just some shingles."

I hate how casual he's being, like he's already forgotten

what Dylan did to Meredith. "So what?" I fire back. "We shouldn't be helping him at all."

Bishop doesn't respond other than to grab a jug of water from the icebox. I glare at his back for a second, then stomp to the bathroom, slamming the door behind me.

I take a long, cool shower, water stained brown with dust swirling over my toes and down the drain. When I step out, the house is quiet and I can hear the faint sound of hammering from next door. Maybe the universe will dispense some justice for once and Dylan will hammer a nail through his hand.

I wrap myself in a towel and stand in front of the mirror. My face is sunburned, freckles popping out on my nose and along my cheekbones. I still look like the same girl I've always been, but I don't feel like her anymore or at least not entirely. I am my father's daughter. And Callie's sister. And I always will be. The biggest parts of me are theirs. But as much as I don't want it to be true, I know there's a space inside me, however small, that belongs to Bishop now. I'm not even sure how it happened or what I could have done to stop it.

I slide down the bathroom wall and rest my forehead on my upturned knees. If Callie had been the one to marry him, she would never have let this happen. Her loyalty to the cause would have been unwavering. I don't know what it is about me that is so easily bent. Why when I look at Bishop's face I see a boy who gives water to the dying and encourages me to think my own thoughts instead of all the ways his father has wronged us and how his death can help set us free.

I sit until my skin grows cold, my back aching from being pressed into the unforgiving wall. My damp hair leaves a wet streak on the paint when I stand, and I wipe it away with my towel. I throw on clean shorts and a T-shirt and pile my wet hair on top of my head. I'm not sure what we have to eat, but I figure it's probably my turn to make dinner. From the kitchen I can still hear hammering, the muffled sound of Bishop's and Dylan's voices through the open back door.

As I lean in to the icebox to peruse my options, there is a crash from outside, followed by a scream. The sound is piercing, the kind of scream that means pain and blood and torn flesh. I leave the icebox door swinging and run out through the screened porch, pushing the screen door open with both palms as I pound down the steps.

Dylan is on the ground in his backyard, upper body on the grass, his legs lying twisted on the concrete patio. He is not moving. I glance up at Bishop, who is standing on the edge of the roof, looking down at Dylan. The sun is behind him, and I cannot see the expression on his face, but something in his stance stops my forward movement. I stand at the fence, not sure what's happening, and watch as Bishop swings himself onto the ladder, moves down to the ground in seconds. Dylan has blood on his face and one of his legs is bent in a way nature never intended, a flash of white bone peeking through a rip in his pants.

"I need to get help," I call to Bishop. Meredith is nowhere in sight.

"Wait," Bishop says, eyes on Dylan, who is beginning to stir on the ground. Bishop sounds as calm as I've ever heard him. Too calm for the situation, and my blood turns to ice in my veins.

Dylan lifts his head and pushes himself up on one bloody elbow. He's groaning, his free hand hovering over his shattered leg. Bishop takes a step toward him, and Dylan looks up, then tries to scoot backward on his elbows, making frantic mewing sounds in his throat. Bishop ignores him, squats down near his head, and puts a hand on Dylan's chest to keep him in place. I can't hear what Bishop says, only the low murmur of his voice, but Dylan's eyes go wide. He shakes his head and Bishop's hand pushes harder against his chest. There's a breathless moment where no one speaks, even the birds in the trees go silent, and then Dylan nods.

"I think Dylan needs help, Ivy," Bishop says without turning around. "His leg is broken."

"Okay," I say. I turn and run, through the gate, out onto the sidewalk and down the street. My bare feet slap against the hot pavement, but I don't feel the sting. I don't slow down and I don't stop until I'm at the hospital and have paramedics on their way back to Dylan's house with a bicycle-pulled stretcher cart.

By the time we return, Meredith is sitting next to Dylan in the grass, his head cradled on her lap. His face is as white as the bone protruding from his leg, and Meredith is weeping without sound, murmuring nonsense as she runs a hand over his hair. Bishop is sitting on the picnic table, his long legs balanced on the bench in front of him. His face is carefully blank.

I stand next to him while the paramedics work to stabilize Dylan's leg. He screams as he's lifted onto the stretcher, and Meredith's hands flutter uselessly above him like injured birds.

"It might be easier on him if he passed out," Bishop says flatly.

"Maybe he will," I say. "It's bound to be a bumpy ride." I surprise myself with how little sympathy I have, even knowing how much pain Dylan is in.

The paramedics walk out of the yard with Dylan, Meredith trailing behind them. I don't say anything until they are out of sight.

"What happened?" I ask.

Bishop hops off the table and stands next to me. "He fell."

I tilt my head up and look at him. "Did you push him?"

Bishop doesn't answer for so long I think he isn't going to. "We were discussing the way he treats Meredith. He got agitated," he says finally. "A roof is a dangerous place to be if you're not focused."

"Which doesn't answer my question," I say, voice quiet.

"No, I guess it doesn't."

"What did you say to him, after?" I can't get the image of Bishop pushing his hand into Dylan's chest out of my head. It wasn't a violent gesture, but there was menace behind it, a warning Dylan would be a fool to ignore.

Bishop's mouth tightens. "He's not going to hurt

Meredith anymore. That's all that matters."

"But how—"

"I'm gonna go inside and get cleaned up," he says, cutting me off. He walks away from me and I watch the long, lean line of his body as he goes. He's strong, I know that. I felt it when he pulled me up the cliff at the river, when he shook the fence in frustration. And now I know he can be ruthless, too. If he had been the first night, it would not have surprised me. But now, after all these weeks, it comes as a shock, a side of him I didn't know existed. I wonder whether the other parts of Bishop he's never shown me are as dark and dangerous as the current I sensed today pulsing beneath his calm exterior.

Although it should make me wary, I admire him for his ruthlessness. He isn't afraid to act, when action is necessary. When we first met, I thought he was apathetic, as if he didn't care at all about what went on beyond his small, privileged world. But now I realize he feels things just as deeply as I do; he simply approaches them differently, less headlong dive and more deliberate thought.

From the very beginning he has wrong-footed me, upended all my simple, pre-formed ideas about who he is. This is just one more piece of the Bishop puzzle, a piece with jagged edges and no simple place where it slots into the bigger picture. I like that he is complex, that the final result of all his pieces will be something unique and hard to solve. I have no right to wish it, and no hope the wish can ever be granted, but I still long to be the one to decipher him.

15

We eat a quiet dinner and I don't ask Bishop where he's going when I hear the front door open and close softly while I'm clearing the table. Out of the kitchen window, I see Meredith going into her house, and I knock on the window to catch her attention. The face she turns toward me is tear-swollen, her eyes red-rimmed and exhausted. I hurry out the back door before she can disappear inside.

"Hey, Meredith," I call. "How is he doing?"

Her hands are clutched around the iron railing on her steps as if it's the only thing keeping her upright. Her hair looks dirty, hanging in lank clumps around her shoulders. "He's out of surgery. It went well."

I stand awkwardly on her bottom step. "Well, that's good," I say. I'm not sure what the protocol is, when I'm not sorry her husband was hurt and don't understand why she is.

"He said…" A tear slips down her cheek and she brushes it away impatiently. "He said as soon as he's able, he's going to sign a petition to end the marriage and I need to sign it, too. He said President Lattimer will approve it." Her voice breaks. "He said we're not a good match. He didn't even ask me what I wanted."

So that must have been what Bishop said to him when he was lying on the ground, putting the final nail in the marriage's coffin. "Isn't it what you want?" I ask. "He hits you, Meredith."

She gives me a look of such withering contempt that I back up a step. "Don't you think I know that?" she says. "But how is this any better? Our marriage is over. I move back across town with my parents and then what? No one's going to want me. They say they'll put me back in the pool for next year, but you know they won't."

"If they don't, there are bound to be some boys on our side of town who are looking for wives."

"Not wives who've already been passed over once before."

"You don't know that. Besides, you don't have to get married," I tell her. "You can get a job and make a life for yourself where someone isn't beating on you all the time."

She laughs, a harsh, bitter sound that doesn't match her sweet, heart-shaped face. "I want a family, Ivy. I want children. I don't want to live with my parents and watch people pity me because I couldn't keep a husband."

"That won't happen," I say, although I have no real

conviction that it won't. There are plenty of girls who are never picked and who live their lives alone, not shunned but always regarded as less than, as having been not quite good enough. "And even if it did, if you never have children or get married again, it still has to be better than him hitting you every day."

Meredith bites her lip, tears streaming down her cheeks now. "Maybe," she says. She shrugs. "I guess now I'll never know."

"Oh, Meredith," I say, torn between frustration and sorrow. "You don't mean that."

"Don't tell me what I mean. It should have been my choice." She pushes open her front door. "I know you meant well, both of you." She doesn't look at me as she speaks. "But it wasn't for you to decide." The door latching behind her is very quiet, and very final.

I'm not sure how we got to this place, where a girl's only value is in what kind of marriage she has, how capable she is of keeping a man happy. Maybe Bishop is right and it depends on the couple. Stephanie and Jacob appear to love each other. But there's something fundamentally wrong in a system where a girl like Meredith would even consider staying with a boy like Dylan if she has the chance to be free of him. Meredith doesn't know her own worth, and in this world we're living in, she never will. My father might not have held my hand or expressed his love openly, but he taught Callie and me that we had inherent value, that we were fully formed human beings without a boy by our side. For that, I will be forever grateful.

I return to the house and try to read on the screened porch, but the stifling heat and my own restlessness conspire against me. Bishop is still not home when I fall into bed at close to midnight, and I hope he isn't punishing himself for what happened earlier. Perhaps Meredith is right and it wasn't Bishop's decision, but I'm not sorry he made it. And I don't want him to be sorry, either. My only regret is that I didn't think of it first.

I don't remember falling asleep, but the sound of the shower wakes me. I push myself up on my elbows and listen to the rattle and spit of Bishop brushing his teeth. The bathroom door opens, and the dark outline of his body moves down the moonlit hallway.

"Did you just get home?" I call to him.

He stops in the doorway. The pale towel around his waist glows in the darkness. "A few minutes ago. Did I wake you?" he asks quietly.

"It's okay." I scoot up to sitting. "Where were you?"

He runs a hand through his hair and sighs. "Out walking. I'm sorry I left without telling you. I needed to be alone for a little while."

"I saw Meredith. She said Dylan had surgery and it went well."

Bishop doesn't answer, shifting slightly in the doorway. I can smell the fresh scent of soap as he moves, tangy and sharp.

"He told her he's signing the petition to end the marriage."

Bishop nods. I can tell he's watching me, though I can't

see his eyes.

"You did a good thing," I say. I hesitate, but he deserves to know all of it. "Even if Meredith doesn't believe it yet."

"Did I?" His voice sounds ancient. "Can hurting someone ever be a good thing?" He blows out a breath. "I'm not that different from Dylan, really, in the end."

I push myself forward so I'm kneeling on the edge of the bed. I wish I were closer so I could touch him, although it's a horrible idea. "Don't say that. Sometimes pain is the only language certain people understand. And you are different than him." My voice is strained. "You wouldn't hurt me that way, Bishop. I know you never would."

For a long time, there is only the ticking of the clock on my bedside table, the muted melody of water dripping from the showerhead across the hall. His eyes are on me and mine are on him and the tension swirling around us is so strong it's like another person in the room, a living thing breathing heat into the space between us.

"You never say my name," he says finally. His voice is low and rough.

"What?" I'm so confused that for a split second I think maybe I'm dreaming. I don't know what I expected him to say, but it wasn't that.

"Just now. You called me Bishop. You've never said it before." He pauses. "I like the way it sounds."

He's right, and I never even realized it. I haven't said his name, as if by subconsciously keeping that tiny bit of distance I can make what's happening between us less real. Like that might be the omission that saves me.

I am a fool.

"I'm sorry," I say, willing myself to speak past the tears gathering in my throat.

"Don't be sorry." I see the outline of his smile in the moonlight. "Just say it again sometime."

I nod. I will not allow myself to cry. "Good night, Bishop," I whisper.

"Good night, Ivy," he whispers back.

I stay kneeling on the bed long after he's gone, until my legs are numb and my eyes are dry and I can't feel anything at all.

16

President Lattimer looks genuinely pleased to see me. "Ivy," he says with a crinkle-eyed smile. "To what do I owe the pleasure?" It's possible he's mocking me, but I don't think so. He opens the front door wider. "Come in, come in." The air wafting out of the house is chilly and smells, as always, of flowers. Too sweet for my taste.

"Can we sit out here?" I ask, pointing to the front porch. "It's such a nice day." It isn't really. It's hot and muggy, and I think I acquired a dozen new mosquito bites on the walk over, but I can't stand the thought of being shut up inside the house with him. I need to be able to at least have the illusion of freedom, if not the reality.

President Lattimer glances at the front porch. The wrought-iron furniture arranged along its perimeter looks like it was picked for style, rather than comfort. But he nods and ushers me in front of him, closing the heavy door behind us.

"I don't know if I've ever sat out here," he says, confirming my earlier assumption. But he gamely takes a seat in one of the chairs and I sit down next to him, a small table edged with dust positioned between us.

"How are you, Ivy?" he asks.

"I'm fine." Ever since Bishop and I had dinner here and President Lattimer mentioned knowing my mother, I've wanted to come back and talk to him. Especially after I asked my father about it and it was clear he was keeping something from me. But fear kept me away. Fear that I would ruin the plan, say something in anger that would give away the game. Fear of President Lattimer himself. Fear of what I would find out. But the need to know has gnawed at me, not going away no matter how hard I tried to ignore it. I'm not sure where to begin, though, so I blurt out the question. "How did you know my mother?"

President Lattimer sighs and pinches the bridge of his nose. "I had a feeling you wouldn't let that go." He lowers his hand and looks at me. "It probably would have been better if I hadn't said anything."

"But you did say something," I remind him.

He gives me a quick smile. "So I did." He points across the street to the large house sitting kitty-corner to his. It is gray clapboard and is hard to see, hidden behind a screen of old oaks, half of them dead, half still thriving. "I grew up in this house, Ivy. And your mother grew up right there."

My breath catches in my chest, like a splinter snagged

on cloth, a sharp, sudden twinge. Of course I knew my mother grew up on this side of town, but I've never known where. In my mind she's always existed in some in-between world. I could never quite picture her as a living, breathing person, let alone one who grew up across the street from Bishop's father.

President Lattimer leans forward, puts his elbows on his knees, and stares at his hands. In this moment, he looks very much like his son. "What do you know about your mother?" he asks me.

"I know you killed her," I tell him, my voice flat. Sometimes my capacity for self-destruction surprises even me.

He blows out a shaky breath and lowers his forehead to his clasped hands. "That's a cruel thing to say." After a long moment, he raises his head, keeping his eyes on the house where my mother grew up. "But I suppose, in all the ways that count, it's a true thing as well."

I'm glad he admitted it, that we aren't going to have to pretend. Dancing around the truth is exhausting. "Tell me about her?" I ask, and I half expect him to laugh in my face after what I just said to him. But he only nods.

"We loved each other," he says simply. "From the time we were very young."

I knew what he was going to say, had known since the moment I saw the look on his face as he showed me her house, but my stomach drops all the same, something solid and heavy as iron taking its place. The day is as hot as ever, but I am suddenly cold.

"She was headstrong, your mother. She had the same

eyes as you, the same beautiful hair." The corner of his mouth turns up at some ancient memory. "She did things without thinking, forever figuring out the consequences after the fact." He raises his eyebrows at me.

"That sounds familiar," I allow, and he laughs.

"But she was full of energy and life and warmth. She made me happy to be alive, even when the world was dark and frightening. I could tell her anything."

I can't help but like the picture he's painted of my mother, and hope that I am as similar to her as he believes me to be.

He glances at me. "There was never anyone else, for either of us."

I've always known my parents didn't marry for love. How could they, with their marriage arranged for them? But the way my father speaks of my mother, I know he did love her by the end. My heart aches to think that the affection may have only flowed one way.

"What happened?" I ask. "Between my mother and you?"

"She thought we would get married. Have children. She thought because I was the president's son, I could make that happen." He looks at me, his blue eyes full of sorrow. "And I suppose I could have. I wanted to, so much. But that wouldn't have been fair. I can't expect everyone else to enter into an arranged marriage and not do the same thing myself. Westfall has thrived because we put the needs of the group ahead of individual desire. We start making exceptions, and the whole structure falls apart." He sounds like he's still trying to convince himself, even after all this time.

"So you married Mrs. Lattimer instead?" I ask.

"Yes. I took all the personality tests and sat through the interviews and Erin is who fit me the best. So I married her. And despite what you might think, it hasn't been a bad match. We have an amazing son. We work well together. In some ways, it's been a much easier marriage than one to your mother would have been."

Which sounds a long way from love to me, but what do I know of love, anyway? I am hardly an expert.

"But I broke your mother's heart the day I married Erin," President Lattimer says. He leans back in his chair. "And in return, she broke mine."

"When she married my father?"

"No," he says, shaking his head. "I never blamed her for that. She was only doing what was right. What was expected. I was glad she made a life for herself. And Callie was born...and then you. I thought she was finally happy. Or at least that she'd found a way to move on and let go."

"Then how...how did she break your heart?" I don't want to know. I don't want to know.

He points again, this time with an unsteady finger, to the lone oak standing on his own front lawn. There are yellow roses blooming at its base. "She hanged herself right there." As I watch, he catches a sob between his teeth before it can escape. "More than fifteen years ago, and I still see her there every damn time I walk out the front door."

I look back at the tree, but I can't focus on it. The whole

world is a roaring blur around me. What he said cannot be true. It cannot be.

"You're lying," I whisper.

"No, I'm not," he says, and I hear the truth in his voice. "I wish I was." He stares at the tree. His voice is far away, gone back to a time when my mother was still alive. "Yellow was her favorite color."

I lower my head down between my knees and cover my ears with my hands. I fight off the black spots twirling in front of my eyes through sheer will. My father hardly ever spoke of my mother. When he did, it was as a whip to keep me on the path he wanted me to walk. And this man sitting next to me has flowers planted in her honor, even though the sight of them must torture him a little every day. I want to tear off my own skin to escape his words. I want to curl into a ball and die. I want to kill something and hear it scream.

President Lattimer puts his hand on my back and I buck it off, a high, keening cry bursting from my mouth. "Don't," I pant. "Don't touch me."

"I'm sorry, Ivy," he says. He sounds confused. "I thought you knew how she died."

I'm up and running before he can say another word. I scramble down the front steps, ignore him calling after me. My breath is coming in short, sharp gasps as I flee from the truth of my mother's death. I run through town like to stop means to die. People stare as I sprint past, a few call my name, but I don't slow down, weaving around obstacles. Thunder claps over my head, streaks of heat lightning rip jagged gashes in the sky. My legs ache and my lungs scream and I welcome every stab of pain like a long-lost friend.

My father and Callie are both sitting at the kitchen table when I burst in, the remains of dinner between them. They stare at me, my father half rising from his chair.

"Ivy?" he says. "Are you all right? What's happened?"

"I know…" My voice is ragged, like I've swallowed glass and I'm choking on the shards. "I know what happened to Mom. You lied to me." I cross to my father and push hard against his chest. He grabs my wrists before I can touch him again. "You *lied* to me!" I scream.

"Callie," he says, looking at my sister over my shoulder. His voice is steady.

From behind me, I hear Callie get up and the back door shut and lock. The curtains over the sink are yanked closed. I wrench my head around and catch Callie's eyes. One look and all the fight goes out of me. I sag in my father's grip. "You knew?" I say. "You knew and you never told me?"

"It was better that way," Callie says. "You couldn't handle it. Look at you now."

"Callie, stop it," my father says sharply. He rarely speaks to Callie that way. He lets go of my wrists and puts an arm around my shoulders. "Come sit down. We need to talk."

I follow him into the living room on numb legs. Callie trails behind us, but at the doorway, my father looks at her over my head and she turns back to the kitchen.

"Here," my father says, guiding me to the couch. I sink down into its familiar softness and he sits next to me, our knees touching. I've spent a thousand hours in this room, know its tan walls and wood floors by heart, but it feels like a stranger's house to me now.

"I don't know exactly what he told you," my father says. "It was President Lattimer who told you, wasn't it?"

I nod.

"That bastard," my father mutters.

"This isn't about him!" I practically shout. "You should have been honest with me a long time ago."

"You're right," my father says. "But you deserve to hear my version, too." He takes a deep, shuddering breath. "I wasn't happy about the arranged marriage. I didn't want to marry some girl I'd never met before. I thought about refusing, but I didn't see how that would get me anywhere except put outside the fence. So I went through with it. And your mother walked up to me at the ceremony..." He shakes his head. "It's such a cliché, Ivy, I almost couldn't believe it. But, for me, it was love at first sight." He laughs, but there's no humor in it.

"But it wasn't for her," I say, to save him from having to say it himself.

"No. Because her heart already belonged to him." My father looks away, his throat muscles working. "We got along, though. She *liked* me." He says the words with a bitterness that reveals how much it hurts to be merely liked by the person you love. "And I thought once you girls were born that things might change. Because whatever was lacking between her and me, she loved the two of you. Very much."

"Not enough to stay with us, though," I say, with some

bitterness of my own.

"Oh, Ivy." My father sighs. "Her heart was broken, and no matter how hard I tried, no matter how hard she tried, we couldn't fix it."

My own heart aches when I look at him. How much it must have hurt him to love a woman who could never love him back. And I think of Erin Lattimer who is in the same position. I know why President Lattimer thought he was doing the right thing by not marrying my mother, but he wasn't. Love isn't something you can legislate. Love is more than charts and graphs and matching interests. Love is messy and complicated and it is a mistake to deny its random magic.

"But why did you lie to me?" I ask him. "Why did you tell me he killed her?"

My father takes my rigid hands in his. His knuckles are big and scarred and I can't count the number of times as a child I'd wished he'd hold my hand. "We should have told you the truth, you're right. But the basic facts are still the same. He killed her." He must recognize the incredulous expression in my eyes because his hands tighten on mine. "*He did.*"

"She killed herself," I say flatly. "She swung from that tree because she wanted to be married to him, not to you." Some vindictive piece of me relishes the pain that flashes across his face.

"She killed herself because he let her believe they'd end up together. But in the end, he forced her to marry someone she didn't pick for herself. The same way he forced you to marry Bishop. The same way he's forced a hundred other girls." He ducks his head to find my eyes. "And he'll keep doing it until we stop him."

"Do you even really care about the arranged marriages? Or about the fence? Or any of it?" I ask him. "Or are they only convenient words you say to get what you want from me?"

"Of course they aren't," he says, squeezing my hands.

"Then why?" I ask, hating the break in my voice. "You still haven't said why you lied to me."

"It didn't feel like a lie," my father says. "I still believe he killed her. Maybe not with his own hands, but he gave her the rope."

"That's not—"

"And I lied because I was afraid to tell you the truth," my father continues. "You look so much like your mother. Half the time you act exactly like her. Plunging into things head first." He taps a finger against the scars on my arm and I want to scream. I will never outrun that dog bite as long as I live. "I didn't want you to think…I didn't want you to think you were destined to end up the same way."

A cold spot opens in my chest at his words and I can't speak, everything frozen inside of me. All my life I've felt a void inside myself, an empty place that never gets filled no matter how hard I try. Is that what my mother had inside her, too? Is that what my father is afraid of, that someday the world will be too much for me and I'll give up? Does he have such little faith in my strength?

"You think I'm weak," I say, voice dull.

"*No*," my father protests. "I've never thought that. You could have handled the truth and we should have trusted you with it. We know you're strong. If we didn't, we never would have asked you to do what you're doing."

But maybe I am weak, because the thought of ending Bishop's life is starting to become more than I can bear. "Daddy," I whisper, my voice breaking. "I don't want to kill him."

"Of course you don't," he says gently. "I'd worry about you if you did."

"He doesn't believe in the marriages, Dad. He wants to help people, make things better. He wants people to have choices too."

My father nods. "Is that really what he wants, Ivy, what he believes? Or is that only what he tells you? Remember, his father is playing this game, too." He pauses. "But if you can't do it, you can't do it."

I look up at him, hope bubbling in my blood.

"But how many more women have to end up like your mother before things change? Isn't freedom worth it? The chance to make our own choices?" He touches my cheek, smooths my hair behind my ear. My heart breaks a little at his tenderness. It's the most he's ever offered me and it's still too much for me to bear because I can no longer tell whether it's the truth or another lie.

"Don't make a decision yet. The clock hasn't run out," he says. "Take some time and really think about it. About who has your best interests at heart. We're your family. And none of this works without you. *We* don't work without you."

I'm slowly coming to understand that what he's asking of me is wrong and sick and ugly, yet the warmth of his words spreads throughout my body. They need me. They can't succeed without me. I have a place in this family that no one else can take.

"Callie," my father calls, and she enters the room so quickly she must have been lurking outside the doorway the entire time. She sits on my other side and kisses the top of my head like she used to when I was small and she tucked me in at night. I close my eyes and breathe past the swift knife of pain in my ribs. "I'm sorry for what I said earlier," she murmurs against my hair. "And I'm sorry about Mom. I wanted to tell you a hundred times. But I didn't want to hurt you." She pauses. "I didn't want you to doubt yourself."

"You hurt me more by lying to me." I twist away from her.

"I know that now," she says. "I was wrong." Her words are soft, but her gaze is hard. I have disappointed her. I find I don't care. She's disappointed me, too.

"We both were wrong," my father says. "But we won't keep things from you any more." He looks from Callie to me and his eyes blaze. "Just think of all the changes we can make. All the choices you girls will have. We can make peoples' lives so much better. Think about it, Ivy. Promise me that?"

"I promise." I don't have to think about it to know that no matter his reasons for wanting to overthrow President Lattimer, my father would be a better leader. He would never put someone out for a minor crime. He would give us back our free will. People would have a say in their own government. After everything, I still have full belief in my father's ultimate goal. It's his methods that are the stumbling block. If I kill Bishop, my family will be in power, but Bishop will be dead and what will I be? A murderer. A girl who killed a boy who had done nothing to deserve it. A boy who held my hand, and let me speak and not once tried to silence me. I will be the one with blood on my hands, and I don't know if that's something I can ever wash away.

It's raining in earnest when I leave my father's house, but I refuse the umbrella Callie holds out to me, along with her offer to walk me home. I want to be alone, and the rain is a relief against my overheated skin. I have no idea what time it is, but the sun has set and there is no one out on the rain-slick streets. My sneakers are soaked by the time I turn up the walk to our house, water running in rivulets from my hair and down my back.

I don't see Bishop until I'm almost to the porch. He is sitting on the front steps in the dark, the roof overhang protecting him from the rain. His face is solemn. I stop mid-step and watch as he stands, a towel clutched in his hands. One second I'm standing still and the next I'm running toward him and I don't know when my legs decided to move. I fly up the three shallow steps and wrap my arms around his neck. He is strong and warm and after only a second's hesitation, he clutches me against him. I am sobbing; all the tears I've wanted to cry for what feels like years are flooding out of me, mixing with rainwater on his neck.

He holds me and lets me cry. He doesn't try to talk me out of my sorrow, like my father did, or tell me to snap out of it, as Callie tried to, always impatient in the face of emotion. Bishop simply stands with his arms firm across my back, his breaths steady against my temple. I didn't realize until this moment how badly I wanted him to be the one to witness my tears. His left hand comes up and grips the back of my neck lightly, his thumb rubbing against my skin.

It takes longer than I would have expected for my grief to burn itself out, leaving me breathless and limp. I pull back a step, loosening my arms from his neck. "I didn't mean to…I shouldn't…" My breath hiccups out of me.

"Shhh," he says. "It's all right, Ivy. It's all right." He lifts his hands from my back and presses the towel against my head, runs the dry cotton over my forehead, under my still streaming eyes. "My father told me what happened," he says. "I've been worried about you." He gives me a rueful smile. "I thought I might have to sit out here all night."

"Did you…" I take a gulp of air. "Did you already know?"

"No. Or at least not all of it. I'd heard bits and pieces over the years, but I never knew it was your mother they were talking about." He gathers my hair to the side and dries the dripping ends with the towel. "Your father never told you anything about her?"

"Not really," I say. "He acted like it was too painful to talk about."

"Maybe it was," Bishop says.

But I'm not ready to hear words in my father's defense. "All he told me were lies." It is a betrayal of my father to say this to Bishop, but right now I don't care. "He told me your father killed my mother."

Bishop doesn't stop drying my hair, doesn't pull back in anger the way I thought he might. "And you believed him?" he asks, voice mild.

"He's my father!" I exclaim, almost choking on another sob. "Don't you trust your father?"

"Honestly?" Bishop shakes his head. "Not completely. I don't trust most people." He lets the towel drop. "Except for you."

A sharp burst of hysterical laughter threatens to escape me. Callie would be doing a victory dance if she could hear him, but all I feel is dismay. "Why me?" I ask.

"Because everyone needs someone to put their faith in," Bishop says. "Life's too lonely otherwise. And I'm putting mine in you." He lifts my wet hair off my neck, gathers it in his hands, and lets it fall down my back. The rain pounds on the pavement behind me, rushing off the eaves of the porch like a miniature waterfall. He skims his thumb across my cheekbone. "If I'd known about your mother," he says quietly, "I would have told you."

I believe him. He would have told me. He would have trusted me with the truth. He, of everyone, would have trusted me to be able to take it. "Bishop," I murmur. We are standing so close together that our chests touch, his shirt wet from mine. I slide one hand up to his chest, pressing the damp cotton against his skin. He sucks in a breath and his heartbeat stutters drunkenly under my palm. His skin is warm, even through the cold cloth.

I'm not a toucher by nature, so the contours of his body under my hand are foreign to me. I might have been more comfortable with touching if my mother had lived or my father were a different type of man. As it was, Callie was the only one who ever offered a kind caress, and that was usually when she wanted something from me. I'm guessing Bishop isn't a born toucher, either, considering the woman who raised him. But I think if we were given a chance, we might be able to learn it together, guiding each other over unfamiliar topography. But we aren't going to have that chance, not one based on honesty and trust. Our story was written long ago, and it does not have a happy ending. Bishop has put his faith in the wrong person.

I let my hand drop.

Maybe my father was right in suspecting I'm too delicate for this world. Because right now, I have never felt more fragile. I feel like a mouse being played with by a cat, batted around until I have lost all sense of direction. I still believe in my father's cause, but now, standing next to Bishop, I am no longer convinced of anything except how much I do not want him to die. I recognize I'm right on the edge of disaster, although I can't imagine there's anything left of me to break. A detached, coldly curious part of me wants to push over the precipice just to see how far I fall.

Bishop leans forward, and his breath stirs the tiny hairs on my neck. He smells of rainwater and soap and long-ago sunshine. "Ivy," he whispers. His mouth rests below my ear as he breathes my name, his lips brushing feather-light against the sensitive skin. The raw, hollow space inside me opens briefly, singing with need. I have never wanted anything in my life the way I want him at this moment— my father's approval, my sister's admiration, they are pale desires in comparison.

I wrench away before he can touch me again. "I'm sorry," I choke out. "I can't…"

I barrel past him as he reaches for my arm. I stumble inside and down the hallway until I'm safe in the cool white porcelain bathroom, back pressed against the locked door. He knocks and I count my breaths—in out, in out—until I hear his footsteps walking away. Until the only sound left is a sharp buzzing silence in my head.

17

"How come my lunch never looks as good as whatever you order?" I ask Victoria. I poke at a piece of chicken that more closely resembles a shriveled worm. "I'm not even sure this is food."

Victoria laughs, but her gaze skims over my face with too much interest. "Rough night?" she asks.

I touch a self-conscious hand to my eyes, which I know are still puffy and swollen from tears and too little sleep. "Allergies," I say.

"Uh-huh." Her tone lets me know she doesn't believe me, but she doesn't press, for which I'm thankful. It was difficult enough facing Bishop this morning across the breakfast table, his eyes worried and his jaw tight. I wanted to close the distance between us and put my arms around him again, feel his wrapped around me, but instead, I picked at my oatmeal in near silence and escaped to work as soon as I could.

"Well, it's your lucky day because we have a relatively light afternoon," Victoria says. "You can go home early if you aren't feeling up to being here."

"No," I say too quickly. "I'm fine."

Victoria gives me a sad smile. "Marriage can be hard work."

I open my mouth to protest, but deception takes more energy that I have today. "Yeah," I say. "I think Bishop would have been better off with a different girl." I didn't know I was going to say that until it was out of my mouth.

"Oh, I don't know." Victoria grins at me. "I think he's pretty happy with who he got."

"Why would you say that?" I ask, even as my stupid, self-destructive heart tap-dances in my chest.

"I've run into him a few times since you got married. Bishop's not an easy guy to read, but there's something in his face when he talks about you." Victoria shrugs. "I don't know, just an impression."

My cheeks are burning and I lower my head to study my salad. I want Victoria to be right at the same time I know I should be hoping she's wrong. I don't want to talk about Bishop and me anymore. It's a minefield with a million potential ways to ruin me.

"Are you married?" I ask Victoria. She doesn't wear a ring and she never mentions a husband, but that doesn't necessarily mean anything. Rings are hard to find; a lot of people don't have them. We don't have the resources to make jewelry, so the only rings available are those scavenged or passed down from before the war. And maybe her husband died, or she doesn't like him, or she wants to keep her relationship separate from work. There is a multitude of valid reasons why she might choose not to talk about him.

"I used to be," she says. "It didn't work out."

"What happened?" It is probably rude to ask, but Victoria won't answer if she doesn't want to. I'm imagining a marriage like Meredith's, although I can't picture Victoria taking a fist to the face without throwing one right back.

Victoria swallows a long drink of water, crunches an ice cube between her teeth before answering. "He was from your side of town. Kevin." She says the name like it hurts her to speak it. "We were married for ten years. But I could never get pregnant." She turns her head away to look out the smeared cafeteria window. "In the end, I let him go."

My brow furrows. "What do you mean?"

"He wanted children. And I couldn't give him that. I told him a hundred times I'd sign the petition to end the marriage. I knew President Lattimer would sign off on it if my father asked him to. But Kevin wouldn't do it. But the hundred and first time, he finally agreed." Her eyes are shiny with unshed tears.

"Did you love him?" I ask, although the answer is already clear on her face.

"Not right from the beginning. But they did their job well pairing us up. We were such good friends, almost from the start. And the love grew from there."

This is the side of the arranged marriages that Bishop was talking about when he said that sometimes they work. Victoria and Kevin. Stephanie and Jacob. They are the matches that end in love and have the potential to make it long term. It's probably about the same percentage of marriages that work when people decide for themselves. No better, no worse. But at least with the old-fashioned way, the decision was in the hands of the ones actually getting married. And they weren't still essentially children when they were joined for life.

"Did he get remarried?" I ask.

Victoria nods, eyes on her plate. "He married a girl from your side of town. One who didn't get a match when it was her year." She pauses. "They had twins a few years ago."

Twins are rare. A single live birth with all the requisite fingers and toes is cause enough for celebration, but twins? That's a whole other level of achievement entirely. And I know who she's talking about now. I never knew his name, but I saw him sometimes in the market with his wife, proudly pushing the double stroller. He was tall and gangly, with a shock of red hair and a goofy grin. Not who I would have pictured Victoria with in a thousand years.

"Do you ever see him anymore?"

"No." Victoria puts her trash onto her tray with brisk movements. "We did at first, but it was too difficult."

"I'm sorry," I say. "It's not fair."

Victoria laughs at that, a small, wounded sound. "No, it's not. But not much is these days." She pauses in her cleanup efforts and finds my eyes. "We're all doing the best we can. Bishop and his father included."

"Do you really believe that?" I ask. I lower my voice. "About President Lattimer?"

"There aren't any easy answers here, Ivy. Maybe your grandfather's vision would have been better. Maybe it would have been worse. There's no way to know that. And President Lattimer and his father have kept more of us alive than we ever dreamed possible. We're safe, we have enough to eat most of the time, our numbers are slowly growing, no one's standing over us with guns forcing us to do their bidding."

"What about the marriages?" I ask, my voice tight. "That felt pretty forced to me."

"Maybe it did to you," Victoria concedes. "But most of the people on that stage were happy to be there, saying vows and maintaining peace. For them it's a tradition, not a duty."

"I don't think everyone feels that way," I say quietly. "They're just scared. No one wants to rock the boat. But the way things are now, someone else is still making their choices for them. That's not freedom."

"Maybe freedom's overrated," Victoria says as she stands. "We had freedom before the war. And look where it got us."

There is no one I'm less prepared to deal with when I walk in my front door at the end of the day than Erin Lattimer.

She is perched on the edge of the couch, as if sinking back into the cushions and getting comfortable would be beneath her

I want to ask her how she even got in, but I push a smile onto my face. "Hello. What are you doing here?" I ask, one hand still on the doorknob.

She stands and smooths her dove gray skirt with both hands. As always, she's styled to within an inch of her life. "We have a key," she says.

I shut the door, drop my bag on the floor. I hate the thought of her being in this house without my permission. "Okay," I say. "Next time maybe you could wait outside? Or let us know you'll be dropping by?" I think I sound very reasonable, but Mrs. Lattimer purses her lips like I've insulted her.

"Fine," she says.

"Is there something you needed?"

Mrs. Lattimer steps around the coffee table, closer to me. "President Lattimer's birthday is coming up."

I stare at her blankly.

"And we always have a big party." She cocks her head at me. "I guess you haven't come in the past, but I thought you'd know about it."

I shrug. "I've heard about it before, but we've never been invited."

"Well, you'll need a dress," Mrs. Lattimer says, voice brisk.

"I have a dress," I tell her. "I wore it the day I married Bishop." I have no desire to wear it again, but I don't want her charity, either.

"Not that kind of dress, Ivy. Something fancier." She gives me the once over. "Something that fits."

"I like that dress," I say, stubborn in the face of her pushiness.

"No, you don't," she says. "I saw you fussing with it the entire time you had it on. It was too short." She walks to the front door and opens it, gesturing for me to step outside. "You represent the Lattimers now, and you are going to look the part." She doesn't need to say *whether you like it or not* for me to hear it. "Most girls would be thrilled to have the opportunity for a new dress."

"I'm not most girls," I mutter as she ushers me out the front door.

"Yes," she says from behind me, voice crisp. "I'm aware of that."

"Where are we going?" I ask her as we reach the sidewalk and she turns left toward the center of town.

"I have a dressmaker I use. She agreed to meet with us today." Mrs. Lattimer's heels click loudly on the pavement.

"Am I going to get any say in this?"

"Of course." Mrs. Lattimer looks me up and down. "As long as you have good taste." Her expression tells me she finds that possibility highly unlikely.

It turns out I've passed the storefront of the shop every day going to and from work but never really noticed it. There's no sign out front, nothing hanging in the windows. And Mrs. Lattimer has to press a buzzer before we are admitted.

"Very exclusive," I say as we go inside.

Mrs. Lattimer doesn't respond, but the tips of her fingers press a little harder than necessary into my back as she pushes me forward into the cool dimness of the shop. There are bolts of fabric leaning against the walls and two comfy-looking chairs near the front window. The back wall is all mirrored glass, other than a curtain-covered doorway on the far right. The woman who emerges from the doorway is younger than I expected. Given Mrs. Lattimer and her somewhat severe and formal style of dress, I pictured a wizened old woman with knobby fingers and a witch's cackle.

But this woman is in her forties, I'd guess, with short black hair and a friendly smile. It's only as she walks toward us that I notice the foot she drags behind her, giving her a rolling gait that makes me fear she's going to fall with every step.

"So this is your new daughter-in-law," she says, holding out both arms and giving me a hug. I stand rigid in her arms, not sure how to respond. "I'm Susan," the woman says, "it's nice to meet you."

"Hi," I say, trying to extricate myself as gingerly as I can.

Susan moves from me to Mrs. Lattimer and gives her the same warm welcome. Although Mrs. Lattimer smiles, I suspect she is as excited with the hug as I am.

"Like I told you, she's tall," Mrs. Lattimer says, and both women turn to look at me.

"Very," says Susan. She tilts her head and inspects me.

"She can get away with something dramatic," Mrs. Lattimer continues. "She has the body to carry it off. Maybe strapless?" She looks at Susan for confirmation.

"Not strapless," I interject. I would be pulling at the top all night, living in fear of it slipping down around my waist.

Mrs. Lattimer raises her eyebrows at me. "Any other contributions, Ivy?"

I figure staying silent won't gain me anything. I'm not very good at it anyway. "I like purple."

Mrs. Lattimer nods, as though my color preference needs her approval. Granted, it probably does. "Maybe a lilac, Susan?"

"Yes, I was thinking the same thing." Susan motions for me to follow her and, as I do, Mrs. Lattimer pulls the shades closed on the front window. "Take everything off but your bra and panties," Susan says matter-of-factly, "and stand right here." She positions me in front of the huge mirrored wall.

I've never considered myself a particularly shy person, but there's something about stripping down to my underpants in front of Bishop's mother that has me rattled. She must sense my hesitation because she snaps her fingers at me. "Oh, for heaven's sake. It's nothing we haven't seen before."

I kick off my shoes without another word, unzip my pants and step out of them, and pull my T-shirt over my head. My black bra and underwear look very dark against my pale skin. I face the mirror with my chin high and fight the hot blush working its way up my neck into my cheeks.

Susan holds up a finger, telling me to wait, and disappears behind the curtain to the back. I try not to fidget, but Mrs. Lattimer is watching me in the mirror and her gaze makes me nervous. I can't help feeling like she's sizing me up to see if I'm good enough for her son. Susan finally returns with a length of pale purple fabric in her arms. She holds it up against my chest and nods. Mrs. Lattimer moves closer, gathering my hair in her hands and pulling it back. "I think that color's perfect for her," she says.

"I agree," says Susan. "Maybe a full-length skirt and" — she shifts the fabric to drape over my shoulder — "one shoulder covered?"

"Where did you get this material?" I ask. It's richer and softer than the homespun material sold at the market.

"Leftover from before the war," Susan says. "Isn't it beautiful? We have dozens of bolts of different fabrics in back. I hate to think of the day when it's all gone. We barely have anything this nice anymore."

"It's very pretty," I say, because they are both looking at me. Once they go back to talking about the style of dress, I tune them out. Now that I know I'm safe from strapless, I don't care what they come up with. So it takes me a second to realize Mrs. Lattimer is speaking to me.

"You really are lovely," she tells me, her eyes on the fabric in the mirror.

I am? I've never bothered to think about it much. I mean, I know I'm not unattractive; enough boys have given me second looks for me to know that. But in my house, beauty was not prized. No one ever gave compliments about looks, other than Callie's teasing about my height and curves. The lack of focus on physical appearance was a good thing, in a lot of ways. But there's something sad about your own father never calling you pretty, about not even really knowing whether you are.

"Thank you," I say as Susan disappears back behind the curtain with the lilac fabric.

Mrs. Lattimer looks up at my face in the mirror. She runs her thin fingers over my hair, jerking my head as she tears through a stubborn tangle to send a drift of pale strands floating to the floor. "You've got your mother's hair. It looks just like hers. Color of fresh honey." From the tone of her voice, it is hard to tell whether she's bestowed me with a compliment or a curse.

I am growing tired of the constant comparisons to my mother lately. They make me doubly thankful for Bishop, who, when he looks at me, sees only me, not the shadow of some long-dead memory.

"You knew my mother, too?" I ask.

Mrs. Lattimer smiles, but it's mirthless. "A smart woman always knows her competition."

Well, that answers the question of exactly how much Mrs. Lattimer knew about the relationship between her husband and my mother. Did her heart sing the day they found my mother hanging from the tree because her rival was finally gone? Or did it break because she knew that from that day on, her husband would never, ever be truly free of my mother?

"You hate that I'm the one he married, don't you?" I

ask.

Mrs. Lattimer sighs. "I hate that every time I see you, I see her. But whatever you might think, I'm fair enough to know that's not your fault." She fingers the pearls at her throat, her eyes like chipped ice. "I want my son to be happy. And if you can do that for him, then we won't have a problem."

I notice my happiness does not enter into the equation. And I know that if Mrs. Lattimer had even the slightest inkling of my plans for her son, she would not hesitate one second to destroy me. She, I think, is probably the most ruthless of us all.

Susan returns with a box of beads, which she shows to Mrs. Lattimer. There is some discussion about making a chain with them to wind through my hair.

"Pull it all up?" Susan says, eyeing my mane.

"No, I don't think all of it up," Mrs. Lattimer says. "That's too severe for her. Having some down around her face suits her."

I look at her in the mirror and think I see a little give in her eyes as she looks at me, a very minor softening. But when I try to give her a tiny smile in return, her face turns stern. "Hold still, Ivy," she says. "We're a long way from done."

18

As mid-summer begins its long, slow descent into fall, my life takes on a newly familiar rhythm. I wake early and eat breakfast with Bishop before work. At night we reverse the routine, eating dinner together before Bishop begins tinkering with whatever needs fixing around the house. There's always some project requiring his attention. Some nights I retire to the screened porch and read. Others, I sit and watch him work; he's efficient but not in a hurry. Bishop never rushes, never seems like he has anything to do other than what he's doing at that moment. Just being near him calms my racing mind.

We are easier with each other than we were in the beginning. We talk about safe things—my job, the coming winter, the plans for his father's birthday celebration. We do not touch. The lack of contact does not feel like the relief that it should.

I know my days with him are running short. My father has given me the time he promised. Time to come to terms with what he's asking of me and what he expects. But he can't afford to wait forever and I can't keep dragging my feet. The three-month deadline is coming up fast. Whenever I picture Callie in my head, all I can see is her standing with her arms crossed, toe tapping impatiently. *Get on with it, Ivy.* Soon I will have to find a way into the gun safe, and then it will be too late to turn back.

But for tonight, I just long for something good to eat, some quiet conversation, to watch Bishop's eyes light up as he smiles. There are no dinner smells drifting from the kitchen when I come in the front door, though. No lamps are on in the house and the rooms have a shadowed twilight glow.

"I'm out here," Bishop's voice calls from the screened porch.

I step through from the kitchen and he's sitting on the floor, next to the squat table between the wicker couches. The table is covered in an old tablecloth that puddles onto the floor. On the table is an assortment of meats and cheeses, fresh fruit, cut vegetables, slices of bread. A cluster of unlit candles sits at one end, next to a pitcher of water.

"What's all this?" I ask.

"Ice didn't get delivered," Bishop says. "Figured we might as well stuff ourselves before the food goes bad." He looks around the ivy-shrouded porch. "Semi-indoor picnic."

I smile, slip off my shoes, and join him. I sit across from

him, the food-laden table between us.

"Dig in," he says with a grin. We don't bother with plates, creating little sandwiches, piles of meat and cheese, right on the tablecloth. Bishop pushes the entire carton of strawberries toward me and although I give a halfhearted protest, I end up eating them all. By the time we're done, most of the food is gone and what's left I couldn't fit in my stomach anyway.

"Oh, I'm stuffed," I say, leaning back against the couch behind me.

"That was the idea," Bishop says.

"What are the candles for?" I ask, nodding at the table.

"I figured we could light them and pretend we're at summer camp."

I can't tell from his face whether he's teasing me or not. "I never went to summer camp."

"Never?"

I shake my head. My father didn't like Callie and me being away from him for that long. A less generous person might say he didn't like it when we were out from under his influence. Either way, I was never allowed to attend the summer camp in the woods for kids aged ten to fourteen, not even for a single night.

"Well, now we have to light them," Bishop says. He kneels next to the table and lights the candles, three short, fat pillars and two tall, slender tapers. Once they're lit, he scoots back against the opposite sofa, his long legs breaching the space between us, so they lie almost against mine, his toes at my hip.

"What did you do at camp?" My voice sounds slightly breathless and I'm not sure why. I don't want to think about why.

"Stupid stuff, mostly. You know…" Bishop pauses, gives me a lopsided grin. "Well, I guess you don't."

I roll my eyes at him.

"At night we sat around the campfire and told ghost stories. Sometimes we'd try to get away with spin the bottle, but the counselors didn't like that. They weren't fans of all those pesky attachments." It's the first time I've heard Bishop speak of the lengths the adults go to in order to keep children from forming any kind of romantic bond with each other prior to the marriage ceremony. It makes arranged marriages a lot smoother if the participants aren't all in love with other people already. Bishop's father and my mother being prime examples of the chaos that can ensue.

I don't look at him as I ask, "Did you have an attachment to someone?"

"No," Bishop says. "I played the occasional game of spin the bottle. But there was never a particular girl I hoped the bottle would land on." The last of the sunlight is fading from the sky and the candles chase away only the edges of the gloom on the porch, putting half his face in shadow. We stare at each other and I know I should be asking another question or saying something, *anything*, to break the silence, but all my words are dead on my tongue, my heart galloping against my ribs.

"My favorite game was truth or dare, though," Bishop says finally.

"What's that?" I ask. I take a sip of water from my glass on the table to clear my throat.

"You've never played truth or dare?" Bishop's eyebrows are in danger of disappearing into his hair.

"I've never played a lot of things," I inform him. "My family wasn't big on games."

"It's easy," Bishop says. "If it's your turn, you say whether you want truth or a dare. If you pick dare, then I give you a dare and you have to do it or you lose. If you pick truth, I ask you a question and you have to answer truthfully or you lose." He grins at me, his eyes dancing. "Want to play?"

Oh, this is such a bad idea on so many levels, but when I open my mouth, "Yes," comes out instead of "no." "But you go first."

"Okay, then." Bishop looks up at the ceiling as if he's considering his options. "Truth."

Truth. I can ask him anything and, in theory, he's supposed to tell me the truth. There are a million things I want to know about him and a million ways those answers can hurt me. I should make an excuse and go inside, but I've tamped down my curiosity about him for too long. My longing to know him is trumping everything, even my good sense. I should, at least, stick with meaningless questions.

"How many girls did you kiss when you played spin the bottle?" I ask. I laugh like it's a joke, but the sound is forced.

"Not very many." He sounds amused. "Are we talking a real kiss? Or a peck?"

"A real kiss." I don't tell him that, for me, they are the

same thing, considering I've never kissed anything other than my father's and Callie's cheeks.

His face is serious, his eyes locked on mine like he's trying to figure out what's behind the question. "I've kissed three girls in my life. One when I was thirteen, a spin-the-bottle encounter. Another at camp when I was fourteen, which involved the overzealous use of tongue."

I laugh, and this time it's genuine. "Yours or hers?"

Bishop holds up both hands in mock surrender. "I plead the Fifth."

Now I'm laughing hard, and Bishop has the strangest look on his face. Like he's heard the best news in the world, a huge smile spreading across his face like sunshine.

"What?" I ask between fading giggles.

He's still smiling. "Nothing."

"You didn't say anything about the third kiss," I remind him.

"That was two years ago. Right before I was supposed to marry your sister. It was a girl from school. And it was more than one kiss."

"Did those involve too much tongue?"

"No. Those were much better."

His words slice at me, although I know they shouldn't. He didn't even know me then and even if he had, it shouldn't matter to me what he felt for some other girl. "Did you like her?" I ask and immediately want to kick myself.

Bishop hesitates for only a moment before he says, "Not the way that I like you," his voice deep and even, gaze steady. Not embarrassed. Not nervous. Sure and simple.

And there it is. The thing I've wanted him to say for weeks now and the one thing I absolutely cannot bear to hear.

"Bishop…"

"You're only supposed to get one question and you've asked me about a hundred," he says, cutting me off. "It's your turn on the hot seat. Truth or dare?"

"Truth," I say, when I know I should say dare. The reckless side of me pulling out a chair and taking a seat at this party.

I brace myself for a question I will not be able to answer truthfully. Something about my father or how my family really feels about his. But instead he grins and asks me how many boys I've kissed.

It's an easy question, given the alternatives, but it's surprisingly difficult to make myself answer. I consider lying, but with all the other lies and omissions swirling between us, it seems only right I should be honest when it's possible. "None," I say. I keep my head up, but my cheeks wear a pink stain I'm hoping the candlelight hides.

Bishop doesn't laugh or tease me. He just nods. "Was it lack of opportunity or lack of desire?"

"Both, I guess." There's no way I can tell him the only boy I've ever been remotely interested in kissing is sitting right across from me.

Bishop opens his mouth to say something else, but I get there before him. "You said one question, remember?" I remind him. "Truth or dare?"

"I would say dare, but I'm scared you'll make me strip naked and run around squawking like a chicken or something."

I'm in the middle of taking a drink, and water threatens to burst out of my mouth. "Those are the kinds of dares you got at camp?"

Bishop shrugs. "Pretty much. We were thirteen, after all."

"So another truth?"

"It's probably safer."

Hah. Safer. I take a second to think about what I want to know. There are so many things. From the important—what he really thinks about the arranged marriages, how he feels about me, what he dreams of doing with his life—to the mundane—his favorite color, favorite food, how he gets his hair so soft. Stupid, pointless questions. "What was it like growing up in your house?" I ask finally because no matter how hard I try, I can't imagine Bishop roaming those dark hallways. Maybe being raised in that house is why he loves the outdoors so much, forever chasing sunlight through the trees.

"Lonely," he says without pause. My heart clenches. Not because I pity him, but because I understand. I have a sister, but I've been lonely my whole life.

"My father is always busy, always focused outward, on what's happening to Westfall. And my mother is…" He runs a hand through his hair. "Difficult. I think she hoped I could fix something that's missing between her and my dad and when I couldn't…" His voice trails off, tired and sad. "I'm sure she loves me, but I've never felt it. Which is hell on a kid, you know? You're constantly trying to earn love, instead of simply having it. It used to make me angry when I was younger, until I realized that didn't change anything. Eventually, I just stopped trying."

"Yeah, I know," I say. I wish he would teach me the trick of stopping. Instead, I'm caught on the endless loop of needing my father's affection but not wanting to do what's required to earn it.

Bishop stares at me, and something is happening between us, something swirling and forming in the still, humid air. I'm terrified of it, of him, but I can't bring myself to run from it this time, either.

"Truth," I whisper, because I don't trust my voice.

"Were you scared of me that first night?" Bishop asks. His question surprises me, as does the wrinkling of his brow, the seriousness in his eyes.

"Yes." There's no point in lying about it.

A shadow floats across his face. "I wouldn't have…I wouldn't have touched you, Ivy. Forced you."

"I know that," I say. "Now."

"I wasn't ready for that, either," he says. And now it's his turn to look uncomfortable, his cheeks flushed in the semi-dark. I've never seen him unsure before, this boy who is always so self-contained. "Just because I'm a guy doesn't mean…" He looks down at the floor. "Are you still scared of me?"

I swallow. It feels like I have a rock stuck in my throat, jagged and sharp. "No," I say. Which isn't exactly the truth. I'm not scared anymore that he'll touch me. I'm scared because I want him to.

His eyes are dark in the candlelight and they burn into mine. I think he might lean forward and close the distance between us. I don't know whether that's my prayer or my fear. Electricity crackles in the air around us, but he doesn't move.

"I think it's my turn," he says. His voice is deep and rough, like he, too, has something snagged in his windpipe. "Truth."

"Again?" I try to smile, but it's a wobbly effort at best. "We're not much for dares, are we?"

"The truth is more interesting," he says. "Anybody can do a naked chicken dance."

"Why did you pick me instead of my sister?" I hadn't realized how much that question had been nagging at me until I finally asked it.

Bishop gives a wry grin. "I'm surprised it took you this long to ask me."

I cross my arms over my chest like armor. "Well?"

"My mom volunteers at the hospital. A couple of days a week. Helping out wherever she's needed." I must look annoyed because he holds up one palm and says, "Bear with me. It's relevant to the story, I promise."

I make a rolling motion with my hand, *go on*, and he smiles. "I used to go with her sometimes, especially when I was younger. One day when I was about fourteen, I was spending the morning there with her. The doors opened and I couldn't really tell what was happening, but I could hear a commotion. Someone crying, someone yelling, calling for a doctor. I looked over and I saw a girl about my age with long, dark hair yelling for help. And one of the nurses tapped me on the shoulder and said, 'That's the girl you're going to marry someday. Callie Westfall.'"

I feel a pain in my chest at his words. I hate the thought of him marrying my sister. She wouldn't be right for him. She wouldn't understand him. She wouldn't bother to try.

Bishop pulls one leg up and balances his forearm across his bent knee. "I remember staring at her, trying to picture my entire future with her. And then she stepped to the side and there was another girl, younger, with waves of honey-colored hair and huge gray eyes." His mouth curls up at the edges, but his eyes are solemn. "Her face was streaked with tears and blood was running down her torn-up arm." His eyes skip to my scarred forearm.

"Me," I breathe, although of course it was me, who else would it have been?

"You," Bishop says. The word spins out into the air like a promise. Like something I can hold on to if I just have the courage to catch it. "I'm not going to lie and say it was love at first sight," he continues. "But it was fascination. You were hurt. You were frightened. But you were still defiant. Your eyes flashed when you talked about that dog. Your face showed exactly what you were feeling, but what you were feeling was unexpected. Like on the day we got married and you shrank away from me." He gives me a small smile. "With clenched fists." Bishop stares at me, his gaze drifting over my face. "If I had to get married, I wanted to marry someone who I was interested in knowing. You're easy to read, Ivy, but the whole book of you is complicated. That's why I wanted you instead of your sister."

My stomach has turned itself inside out. My heart is breaking, but all its millions of shattered pieces are soaring. I can't breathe, but I can still feel, every nerve ending in my body set on high alert. If he touched me now, I might disintegrate. Or fly to the stars.

"You fascinated me that day," Bishop says quietly. "And you still do."

All my life, that damn dog bite has been the one thing I wished I could do over, had some self-control and not ended up bitten, forever marked with a sign of my impulsiveness. Those silvery scars a constant reminder of what a disappointment I have the potential to be. But Bishop sees them as something else entirely. A badge of honor. Evidence of my strength. A source of fascination. He doesn't condemn my recklessness or my inability to hide my emotions. My worst personality traits transformed into my best.

"Dare," I tell him. I move before the thought even reaches my brain, find myself kneeling on the hard floor next to him without really knowing how I got there. My face is mere inches from his. I put a hand on the wicker couch beside his head for balance.

"What are you doing?" he asks, voice low.

"Be quiet." My throat makes a dry, clicking noise as I swallow. "If I don't concentrate, I'll chicken out."

His eyes sparkle with amusement. "I didn't give you a dare yet."

I take a deep breath. "I gave myself one," I say. And then I'm kissing him. His lips are softer than I imagined, the stubble on his upper lip rougher. For a split second he doesn't respond, and I have time to think I've made a huge mistake, regret and embarrassment welling up in me like blood rushing to the surface of a wound. But just as I'm about to pull back, his hand comes up and threads through my hair, pulling me closer instead.

It's not a gentle kiss, not tentative the way I thought my first kiss might someday be, all chaste mouth and dry lips. It's wild and raw and sloppy. It's like every time I've felt that flare of heat with him over the weeks and ignored it or turned away, it didn't die the way I thought it had. It stayed alive inside me, burning, growing, and now it's exploding, too big for my body to contain. My desperation would embarrass me, if he didn't seem desperate, too.

He pushes me backward, onto the floor, and the wood scrapes my back where my shirt's ridden up. His weight is on me, his long body cradled between my legs, both his hands lost in my hair now. I kiss him until I can't breathe, until I have to pull back or die and it's still a close call which I'd prefer.

He's breathing as hard as I am, his face hovering above mine. I raise one hand and trace the line of his eyebrow with my finger, let my hand go lower and run my fingers over his kiss-swollen mouth.

"I'm sorry," he murmurs against my skin. "About the possible overzealous use of tongue. Apparently, I didn't learn my lesson in summer camp."

I laugh and he does, too, dropping his head so his face rests in the hollow of my neck. His breath feathers across my skin. I stroke the back of his head, running his short hair through my fingers. "It wasn't overzealous," I tell him. "I'm not exactly an expert, but the tongue-to-lip ratio seemed perfect." He laughs again, raising tiny goose bumps on my body.

"I've wanted…I've wanted to do that for a long time," I whisper. "Kiss you." It's easier to get the words out when he's not looking at me.

He raises his head. "Me, too." He kisses me again, softer this time, gentle. One of his hands has snuck behind my neck, his fingers stroking lightly. I arch up into his touch. "Me, too," he repeats against my lips.

These kisses go on and on, drugging my blood instead of igniting it. But the end result is the same. He is as close to me as he can get, his heart beating against my breast, his legs wrapped in mine, and it's still not close enough. For once, my conflicted mind is quiet. There are only the flickering candles, and the scent of fresh cut grass from outside, the ghost of a breeze in the trees, and his mouth on mine.

19

Victoria couldn't have picked a better day to give me the afternoon off. I wasn't able to concentrate all morning between sheer exhaustion and thoughts of last night on the porch with Bishop. I'd finally fallen into bed after midnight, after a few more stolen kisses in the hallway, then laid awake half the night, far too aware of him sleeping on the other side of my bedroom wall.

On the way home, I decide to swing by President Lattimer's library to pick up some new books. I know there is a council meeting at City Hall today, so I should be able to avoid Bishop's father and Erin will make herself scarce if she gets wind I'm in her house. I doubt she's any more eager to run into me than I am to bump into her.

I let myself in the front door with the pass code Bishop gave me weeks earlier. As always, the front hallway is dark and still. I close the door and wait, hear nothing. *Step four, find the codes,* Callie's voice whispers. I've been delaying this step, but there's no good excuse with the house empty around me. There is a keypad on the wall outside President Lattimer's office. My heart is beating so fast I feel lightheaded, have to take a deep breath to steady myself before I walk quietly across the hall. I don't know the code for the office, but maybe it's the same as the one for the house. I'm just raising my hand to try when I hear the scrape of chairs from inside the office, the sound of men's voices. I cock my head, listening. One of the voices sounds like Bishop. I slide backward, turn, and run on my tiptoes across the hall to the library, slip inside, and leave the door cracked.

I can't see anything, but I hear a door opening, a man's booming voice, one I don't recognize, saying, "So, gonna make your dad a grandpa soon?"

Bishop's response sounds light enough, but I can tell he's answering through gritted teeth. "We haven't even been married three months."

The man laughs. "If I remember right, when I was eighteen, three months would have been plenty of time." Another big laugh. "Right, Mr. President?"

"I'm sure they're working on it," President Lattimer says.

There's a hard clapping sound. Someone getting patted on the back? I hope it's not Bishop; he hates that. Would hate it even more from this crony of his father's. They must have moved the council meeting here, rather than holding it at City Hall.

The front door closes. Have they left? I inch forward, and President Lattimer speaks again. "Mike has a point," he says. Their voices are moving away from me. "Your mother would love a grandbaby."

There's a pause. They've stopped walking, I think. "She's only sixteen," Bishop says. He sounds angry. It takes a split second for it to register that he's talking about me.

"That's the whole point, Bishop. The younger the parents, the better the outcome. You know that. Your mother and I were only seventeen when you were born." I can almost hear him smile. "And you're perfect."

Bishop sighs. "I'm not perfect, Dad."

President Lattimer chuckles. "Close enough to count."

I know Bishop suffers under the weight of his father's expectations, the same way I do with my father. His father believes he's perfect. My father believes I'm flawed. But our burdens are similar. Bishop constantly having to live up to some impossible ideal. Me having to constantly prove I can be more than a disappointment. Is he as weary of it as I am?

President Lattimer lowers his voice, and I have to press forward to hear him. "You are trying, aren't you? Everything's okay in that department?" He sounds uncomfortable and it might be enough to make me laugh if I wasn't so angry. I want to storm out into the hall and tell him it's none of his damn business.

"Everything's fine," Bishop says, impatient. "But maybe we're not ready for kids yet." I hear the front door open.

"Ivy gets a say in this, you know. It's about what she wants, too."

"Well, of course it is." President Lattimer is agreeing with his words but not with his tone.

"Besides," Bishop says, "there's plenty of time."

"Less than you think." President Lattimer's voice is sad. "There's always less time than you think, Bishop. So don't waste it."

The door closes and one set of footsteps heads back in my direction. I shrink against the wall, but they stop before reaching the library. Another door closes.

He's gone back into his office. I sneak out of the library, down the hall, and out the front door before anyone else appears.

take the long way home, walking off the excess adrenaline flowing through my veins. I probably could have come up with an excuse if I'd been caught lingering outside President Lattimer's office, but the near miss still scared me. It makes my palms sweat just to think I will have to attempt it again soon.

The house is quiet when I get home, and I think maybe Bishop went somewhere else instead. But faint splashing sounds from the backyard draw me out onto the screened porch. Bishop is kneeling in the grass, washing clothes in the old metal trough. He put too much soap in, as usual, and suds overflow over the sides of the tub and decorate the lawn like miniature snow drifts. I watch him for a few moments, then step outside onto the back steps. It's a beautiful day, not as hot as it has been, but the sun is high in a powder blue sky painted with white streaks of clouds. On days like this it's hard to believe we almost ruined the world not all that long ago.

"You're working hard."

He startles, his hand knocking against the side of the metal tub. He looks up, shaking out his knuckles. I give him a shy smile, one hand shading my eyes from the sun. I don't know why I'm so nervous. But everything seems different since we kissed. I know how he tastes now, how his skin feels under my hands. It shouldn't make that big of a difference, but it does. We're more than just roommates now. More than tentative friends.

"You're home early," he says.

"It was slow at the courthouse. Victoria said I might as well take advantage of the down time."

He smiles at me. "Well, come put your down time to good use."

I slip off my shoes and leave them on the step. "Are they rinsed?"

"Yep. Just need to hang them." He holds up my bra and I snatch it from his hand, my cheeks flushed. "I'll do the sheets," he says, smothering a laugh, and I attempt to give him a stern look that's completely ruined by my grin. "Good idea," I say.

Bishop is on the last sheet when I step up next to him

to help, a clothespin between my lips and one in my hand. "There," I say, once I've clipped them in place. I smooth down the sheet with both hands, making a crisp, flapping sound. We are cocooned between the two clotheslines, a sheet hanging on either side of us. We have made a bedding fort.

He is facing me, close enough that I can see every fleck of darker green in his eyes. "Come here," he says, and the intensity in his voice surprises me. He looks breathless, like I feel, and so impossibly beautiful it makes my chest ache.

I hold out my hand and he takes it, pulls me flush against him. My arms weave their way around his neck. I'm tall enough I don't have to stand on tiptoe when we kiss; a slight tilt of my head and his lips are right there.

My body thrums against his like a plucked string, my mouth not quite relaxing the way it did last night. His hand tightens briefly on my back and then loosens. He's leaving it up to me whether I want to pull away. I know I should. There's a moment where it could go either way, but then I press even closer, my lips part, and his hand on my neck tightens. A tiny sigh escapes my mouth and he catches it with his.

These kisses should feel less intense, in the bright daylight, standing upright instead of lying against each other. But they don't. Shrouded by the sheets from the bed I still sleep in alone, the unforgiving sun on our shoulders, the contact feels more intimate than it did in the private darkness of the screened porch. Maybe because we're slowly beginning to learn each other.

When he pulls back, I keep my eyes closed, the sun

lighting up the inside of my eyelids with a warm golden haze. He cups my face in both hands, runs his thumbs along my cheekbones. "How about that skirt?" he whispers. "And your top? Maybe we should go ahead and throw them in the wash? You know, so we don't waste water." He moves his hands down to lightly grip my hips, one finger finding bare skin under the hem of my shirt.

I open my eyes, and I know without looking that their gray light is shining. I rest my forehead in the hollow of his throat, laughter bubbling out of me. I feel, more than hear, a peaceful hum from deep in Bishop's chest. He tips his head down and rests his lips against my hair. I am content to stay that way and he seems to be, too. And so we do. A boy and a girl holding each other between the sheets.

20

dream about him now. Almost every night. Not good dreams where he's making me laugh or kissing me or touching me with his strong hands. Dreams where I stick a knife in his chest or put a bullet in his brain or smother him in his sleep. Every possible variation of horror I will potentially inflict. I wake with wet cheeks and a pounding heart. In those dark hours of night, when the house is silent around me and he sleeps on the other side of my bedroom wall, I know down deep in my soul that I cannot kill him. That I would rather die myself than be the one to take his life. But I don't know if I can save him, either.

It's taken at least a dozen fittings, all with Erin Lattimer breathing down my neck, but my dress for the president's birthday party is finally done. I'm nervous about the party for a whole host of reasons. The dress being only a small part of my anxiety. I know I'll be on display as the president's new daughter-in-law, everyone watching what I do, the way I interact with Bishop. And my father and Callie will be there, too. Everyone waiting for me to slip up. Although they haven't approached me since the night I found out about my mother's suicide, I know they want the gun safe combination. There are only a few weeks left before the deadline. And a bustling party in the president's house is probably my best chance of finding it.

But beyond all those concerns, there is the simple desire to look pretty in my dress. To watch Bishop's face when I walk into the room. It's a waste of time, but I can't stop picturing the moment. *You're being ridiculous, Ivy*, I tell myself, before finding myself back in the same daydream five minutes later.

The day of the party dawns warm and rainy. I know the bulk of the party is supposed to take place on the back terrace and yard of the president's house, but I don't imagine the turn in the weather ruffles Erin. She's the type of woman who expects things to happen as she wants them to, so I'm not surprised at all when the storm clouds move off and the sun shows up in the late afternoon. Her wish is the weather's command, apparently.

Bishop disappears from the house after lunch and,

almost immediately afterward, a woman I've never met before arrives, saying she is there to help me dress and do my hair. I would argue, but I know better. I have to pick my battles, and this one isn't worth it. Besides, I want to look pretty, but I'd never say it out loud. To anyone.

The woman, whose name is Laura, won't let me look at myself until she's done. But she listens to me when I say I don't want my hair all pulled up. Or, at least, she's listened to what Erin told her beforehand. The dress is a work of art, and I'm not sure I'm going to be able to pull it off. But once I have it on, Laura claps her hands in front of her mouth and smiles. "Perfect," she says.

She turns me with her hands on my shoulders and then steps back, out of my reflection. I was worried I wouldn't recognize myself, but I still look like me. Just a more elegant version. The front of my hair is upswept, but the rest trails halfway down my back, its usual wild waves smooth and shiny. But it's the dress that really captures my attention. It hugs my body more than I thought it would, but it's not skin-tight, the skirt floating out from my hips to skim the floor. My right shoulder is bare, my left partially covered where the lilac material gathers. I've never had a dress that was made for my body and not my sister's. This dress makes me glad to be tall, for once not ashamed of my height and curves or anxious to conceal them. Tonight I see a pretty girl in the mirror, one at home in her skin, and I hope Bishop sees her, too.

I don't even notice Laura's left the room until I hear her voice from the front of the house and Bishop's deep voice in response. I turn from the mirror, unsure. Should I stay where I am? Walk out to meet him? I'm breathing too fast and my palms are damp. I imagine this is how a real bride is supposed to feel on her wedding day, which makes my anxiety even worse.

Bishop saves me from having to decide what to do when he appears in the bedroom doorway. He stops when he sees me, leans one shoulder casually against the doorjamb. His eyes travel down the length of my body before journeying back up. He's wearing a black suit and a coveted white shirt, open at the throat. No tie. I remember the day we met—how I looked at him and catalogued his features so objectively. I understood he was handsome, the same way I knew a pretty sunset or lovely flower when I saw it. But his beauty didn't touch me. Now, when I look at him, I just see Bishop.

And he takes my breath away.

He pushes off from the doorjamb and crosses to where I stand, my hands clasped in front of me. He takes them in his, smoothing out my curled fingers. "So, is this the dress my mother made you crazy over?"

I nod. He nods in return. "Remind me to thank her," he says. He releases one of my hands and cups my cheek, lowers his head and kisses the curve of my neck right below my ear. "You're beautiful," he whispers, "but that's nothing new."

"You don't look so bad yourself," I say and feel his smile against my skin. I hook a finger into his open collar and pull lightly. "No tie?" I tease.

He pulls back to look at me, his arms looping around my waist. "Hate them," he says with a grin.

"Your mother won't be happy."

"She'll get over it." He tightens his hold on me. "Or we could stay home and really piss her off."

I laugh, shaking my head. "Absolutely not."

He sighs and turns for the door, my hand clutched in his. "Can't blame a guy for trying."

Erin instructed us to be early, but we end up being some of the last to arrive, walking up the drive with a few other stragglers. Bishop doesn't seem concerned, but I don't want to give Erin any additional ammunition against me.

Candles in tiny paper bags sparkle along the edges of the driveway and on the front steps of the house. As if in solidarity, fireflies flicker above the grass. When I was younger, there were summers you could scoop handfuls from the air without even trying, enough to fill a jar for a nighttime lantern or to make a glowing ring if you had the will to pluck the shimmering tails from their bodies. I never did, but Callie would do it for me. There is a lesson in there somewhere, if I care to think about it.

From the corner of my eye, I can see the hulking shadow of the tree where my mother died. I don't turn my head to look at it, but Bishop must sense my focus because he gives my hand a reassuring squeeze. We have somehow reached the point where we can read each other without words, and I'm not sure when it happened. One more thing about Bishop Lattimer that has snuck up on me.

Bishop's parents greet us almost the second we step through the entryway. His father gives me a hug and a kiss on the cheek, tells me I look radiant. Erin is her usual standoffish self, but I catch a gleam of approval in her eyes as she takes me in. "Very nice," she tells me. It's the most I'm likely to get from her, and it's enough.

"You're late," she says to Bishop with pursed lips.

"My fault," I say before Bishop can take the blame. "Trouble with the dress."

Erin graces me with a polite smile. "Better late than never, I suppose."

Bishop leads me through the front hallway and out onto the back terrace. It's the same twinkling wonderland as the front, ringed with candles and the lilting sound of laughter. On the far side of the terrace, there is a bar set up, and Bishop nods toward it. "Do you want a drink?"

"Sure," I say. It would be nice to have something to do with my nervous hands. I can feel the stares of the other guests on us, everyone wanting to see the president's son and the founder's daughter. I like it better when we are alone, inside our tiny house, safe from prying eyes.

"I'll be right back," Bishop says. I watch him move away from me, taller than everyone else, his lean body cutting through the crowd. I work at not feeling self-conscious as people mill around me, a few offering kind smiles as they pass. If my father and sister are here, I haven't seen any sign of them yet.

Bishop is waiting in the line for drinks, and he looks back over his shoulder, his eyes finding mine. He gives me a small, intimate smile that heats my skin. I don't look away from him, even when someone sidles up next to me.

"Well, you two seem to have gotten cozier," Callie's voice says.

I tear my eyes away from Bishop's and look down at my sister. She is wearing a yellow dress that makes her complexion sallow, but her face is still beautiful. "He can't keep his eyes off you," she says, running her own gaze down the length of my dress.

"I thought you'd think that was a good thing," I say, annoyed.

"I would. But you can't keep your eyes off him, either."

I turn away from her. I want her focus off Bishop. "Where's Dad?"

Callie points with her half-empty champagne flute to a far corner of the lawn. "Over there."

I can just make out my father's profile among a group of men clustered around a high table decorated with more candles. He is laughing, his head thrown back, like he doesn't have a care in the world.

"He wants the combination to the gun safe," Callie says, her voice lowered.

"He said he'd give me time," I say, not looking at her.

"He already has." She taps my forearm with her glass. "Time's up."

I glare at her and she cocks her head, like she's studying a particularly intriguing, but ultimately smashable, bug. "I told him you wouldn't come through. I must have said it a thousand times. That we'd end up having to do it all ourselves because you wouldn't be able to handle it. You're too soft, Ivy. You always have been."

"Shut up, Callie," I say, fists clenched. "I said I'd get the code and I'll get it. So just *shut up*." I whirl away from her before I do something I'll regret, like scream in her face or slap the smirk off her mouth.

I push my way through the crowd and back into the house. I don't even know where I'm headed, so long as it's away from Callie.

"Hey, where are you going?"

I turn, and Bishop is standing there with drinks in his hands and a puzzled expression on his face. He guides me to an empty spot at the base of the stairwell. "I saw you talking to your sister. What happened?"

I force a smile onto my face, not sure how successful I am in the effort. "Sibling thing," I say as lightly as I can. "Sometimes being an only child is a blessing."

He's watching me, his eyes probing mine. He hands me a champagne flute and grabs my free hand. "Come on." He leads me up the staircase and down a shadowy hall lined with closed doors.

"Where are we going?"

"To my old room." Bishop stops outside the last door, hand on the knob. "You look like you could use a break."

"Your mother is going to have a fit if she figures out we're hiding up here," I tell him.

"Added bonus," he says and opens the door.

His room is large and faces the front of the house. Through the sheer curtains, I can see the flickering candles along the driveway. He doesn't turn on the overhead light, only a small lamp on his desk, leaving most of the room in darkness. Across from the desk is a double bed, made up with a patchwork quilt in shades of blue and gray. The far corner holds an armchair and a small bookcase. The room is spotless and impersonal. It doesn't tell of Bishop's love of the outdoors or his dreams of the ocean. In one glance, I know his mother decorated this space and that she doesn't understand who her son is at all.

"Ah, much better," he says, sinking to sit on the bed. I lean back against the edge of his desk, my fingers fiddling with the stem of my champagne flute.

"I always wanted a sibling," Bishop says. "I imagined having someone around who always understood me. An automatic best friend." He catches my eyes across the room. "But I'm guessing it's not always like that."

"Maybe for some people it is," I say. "But not with Callie and me." He stares at me without speaking, and I know he's waiting for more. "We're just…different. Our personalities. Life would be easier if I were more like her." Tears spring to my eyes and I blink them back frantically.

"Hey," Bishop says gently. "Easier on who? Her?" He stands and walks over to me. "That's her problem. Maybe she's the one who needs to be more like you. Or maybe she just needs to accept who you are." He braces his hands on the desk on either side of my hips and leans into me. His lips are warm and firm and his mouth tastes like champagne.

He starts to pull back and I thread my hand through his hair and hold him still, rest my forehead against his. Our breath mingles on the exhale, our lips a heartbeat apart.

"You're my best friend," I whisper. I don't realize those words are waiting to be said until they arc out of my mouth. They reveal too much, and yet they are the very least of what I want to say to him.

"Ivy," he whispers back. "Open your eyes."

I do and find him staring at me, his gaze serious and dark. I'm terrified of what he might say, words that can never be taken back or forgotten. Words that will kill me to hear. So I press forward and stop his voice with my mouth. He makes a frustrated sound in the back of his throat, but his hands lift from the desk to my waist, pulling me tighter against him.

The knock and the opening of the door occur at the same moment, so there's no time to spring apart, to pretend we've been doing anything other than what we've been doing. For his part, Bishop doesn't even try. He keeps his arms wrapped around me, his lips at my temple, even as his mother fills the open doorway.

She radiates icy disapproval as she stares at us. "People are asking for you," she says. "This is a party to honor your father. Not to hide away up here…doing God knows what. I expect you both downstairs in five minutes." She turns and her high heels click away down the hall. I realize it is the sound I most associate with her.

"Busted," Bishop says under his breath, and a laugh spills out of me as I bury my face in his shoulder.

We heed Erin's not-so-veiled threat and make our way downstairs within the five-minute time limit. I don't doubt she'd come back up and drag us down by our earlobes if we disobeyed. The foyer has cleared out, almost everyone in the backyard where food has been laid out on long tables.

"Hungry?" Bishop asks.

I am, starving actually, but there's something I need to do first. Find the codes. I can still hear Callie's voice in my head, accusing me of not having the will to carry out my mission, so sure I'm not strong enough. "Why don't you get us some food," I tell him. "I'm going to use the bathroom. I'll be right out."

I wait until he's gone before walking quickly toward the front of the house. I bypass the bathroom, though, and without thinking too much about it, press the code into the keypad outside President Lattimer's office. I'm still not sure it's the same one as on the front door, but with the general lack of security, I have a feeling it is.

As I suspected, the lock releases with a quiet click. I open the door and slip inside, closing the door softly behind me. My heart is beating in my throat, threatening to choke me, and I tell myself to calm down. Breathe.

The room is dark, and I know I'm taking a risk by turning on a light, but I have to be able to see what I'm doing. Luckily the heavy drapes are closed and the windows face the side of the house. I'll just have to hope no one outside notices the light.

I try not to think about what I'm doing and what it means. I tell myself I'm helping my family. I'm helping the girls who will come after me. But Bishop's face is all I can see. *What are you doing, Ivy?*

I crouch down behind President Lattimer's desk and

pull out one deep drawer. It's filled with files, all neatly labeled, thank God. I skim through the tabs with my fingers, but nothing about the gun safe, weapons, or defense. I have to hurry. Bishop is going to come looking for me any second. And I have absolutely no good reason to be in this room, let alone hunched behind the desk like a thief. *Maybe you want to get caught. Maybe that would make it all easier.* But I push that thought away and move to the next drawer.

Bingo. The files in this drawer are what I'm looking for. My trembling fingers fly through the tabs until they land on WEAPONS. I pull the file out and open it on the floor. Page after page of inventory sheets, it looks like. Every type of gun and model the government owns. My father would love to have these, but it's too risky to take the file and there's no way I can memorize the information. I keep flipping through the pages, my eyes on the file but my ears on the door. *Hurry up. Hurry up.* If it's not here, then I'm going to have to give up for now and try again later.

I'm about to forget it and shove the file back in the drawer when I reach the page with the code to the gun safe neatly typed out. It's a memo to President Lattimer from Ray. 21-13-6-18-57. Same code for both the outer door and the safe. Sloppy, but better for my purposes. And these words at the bottom of the memo: "The final digit increases by an increment of three every month until the New Year, when the entire series will be replaced." Memo dated January 1 of this year. It's early August now. So 78. 21-13-6-18-78. I close my eyes and the numbers scroll across my eyelids.

I'm sick to my stomach suddenly, hit with the almost

irresistible urge to vomit. I rest my forehead against the desk, cover my mouth with one hand. Is this who I am? A girl who will do anything for her family? A girl who will sacrifice an innocent boy to prove she's not soft? I don't know. I don't know anything anymore.

There's a noise in the hall, the sound of footsteps. I shove the file back into the drawer, hoping it's in approximately the same spot it was before, and slide the drawer shut. I turn off the lamp and cross to the door in darkness, lean my head against the cool wood. I don't hear anything other than the distant sound of voices. There's no way for me to know exactly what waits on the other side, but there's no advantage to staying in here any longer.

I take a deep breath, open the door, and walk out. And run smack into a man's chest.

"Ivy?"

I look up into my father's face, relief coursing through me. He reaches behind me and shuts the door, then puts his hands on my upper arms.

"I got it, Dad," I whisper. "The last digit goes up by three every month."

His eyes glow. He pulls me in for a hug and I hug him back, my chin on his shoulder. Bishop is at the end of the hall, and he smiles when he sees me. I close my eyes and my nose fills with the familiar scent of my father, wood smoke and paper. I remember the winter he taught me to read. And the afternoons after that we spent reading separately but in the same room. The times I felt closest to him always involved a book in my hand. Unbidden, Callie's face flashes through my mind. For all her faults, she's always protected me, even if her methods might not have been the ones I would choose. I open my eyes and watch through a veil of tears as Bishop walks toward me. And Bishop. With his deep laugh and his strong hands. The boy who dreams of the ocean and feeds people beyond the fence. What do I owe each of them? What do I owe myself?

21-13-6-18-78. I turn my head and press my lips close to my father's ear. "21...13...6...18," I whisper. Hesitate. Bishop hovers on the edge of my vision. "87," I say, and pull away from my father.

It's an honest mistake. The kind anyone could make. The type of mistake that buys me time to figure out what to do before they figure out I'm doing anything at all.

21

I am quiet on the walk home. I hold Bishop's hand and make *hmmm* noises as he talks, but I am somewhere else. Still back in my father's embrace, stuck at the moment when I was faced with two choices. And I chose the boy walking next to me instead of my own family.

"Oh, I talked to the head of the Matching Committee," Bishop says. "He told me that Dylan and Meredith both put their names in again for next year."

"Great," I mutter. "Now Dylan will be able to make some other girl's life hell."

Bishop squeezes my hand. "I don't think so. I hinted that they might want to make sure he doesn't find a match."

I breathe a little sigh of relief. "I can't believe Meredith wants to go through that again, either. But I guess it's her choice."

"It is," Bishop says. "Maybe she'll have better luck this time."

"Can't get much worse," I say and Bishop smiles.

I trip over an uneven patch of sidewalk, and he puts out his free hand to balance me. "Whoa." He looks down at my feet. "Why don't you take those off?"

His words bring me back to the day we met, the day we married, and he said the very same thing about my high heels. We've come such a long way since then. Further than I ever dreamed possible. Further than I ever wanted to journey. I hold onto him while I slip off my shoes. This time he takes them from me, hooking the straps over his fingers.

"What?" I ask when he doesn't start walking again.

He lets go of my hand to smooth a lock of hair back over my shoulder. "You look prettier now than you did before the party. I like your bare feet. And your hair falling down."

Even with the chaos inside my head, I can't help but smile at him.

"I'm glad you got to see your father," he says, once we start walking again.

I glance at him, debating what to say. "It was good to see him. I haven't talked to him since that day I found out about my mother."

"Are you still angry with him?"

"Yes." I don't think I'll ever fully forgive my father for not telling me the truth about my mother's death. Because that lie was the catalyst for so many of my decisions, so many twists and turns on the road I've taken. I might have chosen a different path if I'd known the truth from the beginning. My father's cause might not have so easily become my own.

"I understand why you might want to keep your distance from him for a while," Bishop says. "But I don't want to be one of the reasons."

"What are you talking about?"

Bishop's thumb glides over my hand. "I know our fathers haven't always gotten along. I don't want the fact that you're married to me to drive a wedge between you and your family."

"It won't." I already knew, but his words prove it. Bishop is a good person. A better person than all the rest of us. He doesn't understand how rare he is, how everyone else is angling for something right below the surface of every interaction. He's the only person whose motives I trust completely.

I tip my head up to the sky as we walk. The stars wink above us, shimmering slightly in the humid air. They say before the war, you could hardly see them at night because of the light from thousands of cities. Now, they are laid out above us like a vast carpet, bright in a pitch-black sky. For all the death and hardship the war brought, I'm not sorry about being able to see the stars.

I take my shoes back from him on the front porch. "I had a good time tonight," I tell him, but forcing my mouth into a smile takes work. I have betrayed my family and put my own desires above what is best for the group. I have decided that Bishop's life is worth more than a hundred girls' futures. I've turned a corner into a whole new world and there is no easy way back.

My fancy dress ends up in a crumpled heap in the corner of my bedroom, shoes tossed on top of the pile. I crawl into bed in a tank top and underwear and listen to the sound of Bishop brushing his teeth, hanging his clothes on the back of the bathroom door so he doesn't disturb me by putting them in the closet. His routine has become as familiar to me as my own.

"Bishop?" I call as his shadow passes by the bedroom door.

"Yes?"

I shift onto my side. I know what I want, but I don't know exactly how I should ask, what words I should say. It turns out it doesn't really matter, because all my words have disappeared. Instead, I pull the sheet back, uncovering the empty spot in the bed. My heart beats slow but hard, like a bass drum inside my chest. The rhythm so deep it's almost painful. Bishop's eyes move from the bed to my face.

"I don't think I'm ready for…to have sex," I say. I clear my throat to get more weight behind my words. The truth is, I'm not scared of the act itself, not really. Not if it's Bishop and me. And, in a different world, I probably would be ready to have sex with him. But here, in the tangled web I'm trapped in, I'm scared of taking that last step, the one that will bind our bodies together in the same way the rest of us has already merged. But I don't want him on the other side of the wall anymore, either. "I don't want to sleep in this bed alone," I tell him.

"Ivy…" He sounds uncharacteristically nervous, and

that makes me brave. He won't be the one to ask for this. He's been waiting for me.

"I want you next to me," I say.

It takes him four steps to get to the bed, and then he hesitates. He is dressed only in a pair of boxer shorts, and I'm hit with a sudden attack of nerves. Maybe I should have suggested this when he was fully dressed. *Who are you kidding, Ivy?* My hands itch to touch; my fingertips throb with need.

"Are you sure?" he asks me.

"Yes."

He climbs in beside me, the sheet puddled around our ankles. He mirrors my position, on his side, one arm under the pillow where his head rests, knees bent. Our legs are both so long that our knees bump, and after a second's awkward hesitation, I slide a leg over both of his. He puts his free hand on the hollow of my waist before moving it lower to rest on the curve of my hip. His thumb glides along my skin, back and forth over my jutting hipbone.

I inch closer. His eyes glitter in the near darkness, his hair tousled from the pillow. I move closer still, until my body is flush against his. I twine both arms around his neck. Climbing him like my namesake.

We kiss until I'm drunk with it, drunk with the taste of him. His hands are fisted in my tank top, pulling it halfway up my sides, my leg hooked around his waist. And it doesn't matter what either one of us said about not being ready, if we don't stop soon, we aren't going to be able to stop. It will be like trying to put out an inferno with a thimble full of water.

"Ivy," Bishop whispers against my mouth. "There's a fine line between self-control and masochism and right now we are walking it." His voice is husky and breathless but laced with amusement, too.

I tug lightly on his hair. "Lying in bed with me is a form of torture?" I ask, laughing.

"When we're both half naked, it is."

One of my hands has found its way to his bare chest and my fingers play lightly over his skin. It's warm and smooth, and I like the way his muscles shift under my curious hand.

"Stop," he groans, catching my hand as it drifts toward his stomach and raising it to his lips. "Now you are torturing me."

I hadn't thought a touch like that would affect him so much. But then I imagine him touching my bare chest the same way, and heat pools in my stomach, leaving me dizzy and short of breath. "Sorry," I whisper.

"It's okay," he says, tipping his head down to look at me. "There's just a limit to what I can take."

I lean up on my elbows and give him one last kiss. I turn over, pulling his arm across my waist. I fold his hand between both of mine. We're not kissing anymore, but I'm not sure this is any less dangerous, having him pressed against me, his chest to my back.

The full moon is visible through the curtains, its cool glow painting the room in silver. I trace the long lines of Bishop's fingers. "Why didn't you stop trying with me?" I tell myself that if he's asleep, I won't ask again.

He's not asleep. "What do you mean?" His breath tickles the tiny hairs on my neck.

"That night we played truth or dare. You said that after a while you stopped trying to earn your mother's affection." I pause. "Why didn't you give up with me, too?"

"You know why," he says quietly. I close my eyes. I do know, but I'm not sure if I'm ready to hear it. But some part of me must be, because I wouldn't have asked the question otherwise, not of Bishop, the boy who never chooses to say something easy just because the truth is hard. Maybe I want to hear it so that I will know, once and for all, that there is no going back.

"Because I'm in love with you, Ivy," he whispers. "Giving up on you isn't an option." He lifts my hair away from the back of my neck and kisses the delicate skin there.

My breath shudders out of me. The silence spirals into the dark room, and maybe it was foolish to ask the question, but I'm not sorry. I uncurl his hand and kiss his palm, his skin cool and dry. I place his hand over my heart, cover it with my own.

We fall asleep that way. His lips on my neck. My heart in his hand.

22

When the end comes, it comes quickly. I am not prepared, although I should be. Every second of my life has been leading to this moment. Its arrival should not surprise me.

I'm leaving the courthouse for the day, mind on Bishop and home, when the man from the jam stall at the market approaches. He's walking in my direction, pushing a small cart loaded with his wares. I pretend not to see him, like a child who thinks if she doesn't look in the closet a monster won't be hiding there. But refusing to look doesn't save me.

"Jam?" he calls after me as I pass. "Ma'am, could I interest you in some jam?" His voice is loud enough that I can't ignore him, not without drawing attention to myself.

"No, thank you," I say over my shoulder. "Not today."

"But ma'am, I have raspberry. At a good price."

I have no choice but to stop and turn with a false smile

stretched across my face. "One jar," I say.

He sidles up next to me, raspberry jam already in his hand. He passes it to me, along with a small slip of paper, and I hand him a wad of crumpled vouchers. "Thank you," he says. "Enjoy."

I shove the jam into my bag, keeping the note in my fist, and walk away fast. I wait a block, then two, before I stop and open it. *Bridge in the park. Now.* Callie's handwriting.

It's almost a relief, after all these endless weeks, to finally be getting down to it. I suppose I could ignore the summons, but that would only delay the inevitable. So instead of continuing straight toward home, I turn left at the corner and cut across the park, the brittle, late summer grass crunching under my feet.

Callie is already waiting for me on the bridge. She's standing against the railing, leaning out slightly over the hazy water. A few ducks swim lazily below her, but even they are subdued by the heat. She waits to speak until I'm next to her, my bag lowered to the bridge between us.

"It's time," she says.

I don't say anything, keep my eyes on the far edge of the pond. She is holding something out to me, but I refuse to turn my head and look at it.

"You need to put this into his food," she says. "Most of it. Take a little yourself so they won't suspect you of doing it. But only a little. A few drops."

"What is it?" My voice is a dead thing, flat and dry.

"It's a poison that mimics a virus."

This is not what I expected. Something more dramatic

that involved sharp knives or bulging eyes. Some method where I would be forced to use my hands to take his last breath.

"We're going to have some put into food at the market, too." Now I look at her, my eyes wide. "Not enough to kill anyone, but enough to make some people sick. Everyone will think it's another epidemic. They happen often enough."

I stare at her. "And the fact that only Bishop dies? No one's going to be suspicious of that?"

"Suspicion is a long way from proof." Callie shrugs. "And besides, there's no way to know how much people might eat. Bishop may not be the only death." Her nonchalance sends a dagger of ice through my chest.

"Why do we have to kill him?" I ask. "Why is that the only way? If Dad believes a democracy would be better, why can't he convince people to follow him instead?"

"Because people are stupid," Callie hisses. "People do what's easy. They do what they know. Look at all the families who line up on the wedding day with smiles on their faces while their children marry strangers. No one's going to risk their necks for change."

I take the small vial from her hand. The liquid inside is a dark purplish-red color. The color of an old bruise. Ancient blood. Callie rests her hand over mine. Her fingers are cold and wiry. "Think about the end result, Ivy. Once this is over, we'll have the power. And you can do what you want. Work at an important job. Get married again to someone you choose. It'll all be different."

I look into her dark eyes. "What if he's the one I would

choose?" I ask. "If I had the choice?"

Callie rolls her eyes. "Give me a break. If you had it to do over, you'd still want to get married at sixteen? Have all your decisions made for you?"

She's right, of course. No matter what I feel for Bishop, I wish I wasn't married. That the government hadn't forced us into it before we were ready. "No," I say. "I don't want to be married. Not now. Not yet."

But someday, I would still want it to be him.

"See?" Callie's eyes spark to life. "That's what I'm talking about. We'll have choices once Dad's in charge. It'll all be worth it."

"If Dad wants people to have choices, then why is he stepping into President Lattimer's place? How is that a democracy? Shouldn't we let people vote the way they used to?"

Callie's face tightens. "So now that we're down to the end, you suddenly have a million doubts? Dad does want a democracy, but there's no one else better prepared to run Westfall, and you know it. After he has things back to the way they should be, then we'll think about voting. One step at a time, Ivy. And right now we're at your step in the plan."

The vial in my palm burns against my skin. How do you measure the life of one person against the greater good? Can it ever be the right thing to sacrifice an innocent person? And how do you know what the greater good really is? None of us is being tortured. No one is starving or sold into slavery. So is it worth killing someone to make it better? What if that death results in saving the futures of countless girls? Gives thousands of people back their free will? In the end, the answer to all those questions doesn't matter, though. Because I'm not capable of what she's asking me to do.

I can't kill him. I won't.

"So, what's the plan?" I ask her. "What happens with President Lattimer?"

Callie stares at me for a long time before she speaks. "Once Bishop is dead, we'll move in to take control of the guns while President Lattimer is grieving. His death will come after that. Once people see he can't even ensure their safety, can't keep control of his own weapons, they'll be a lot more likely to embrace us."

"So he's going to have to suffer through the death of his son," I say slowly.

"Yes."

I nod. "Is that part of Dad's plan, too? Making sure President Lattimer loses someone he loves, the same way we lost Mom?"

"Yes," Callie repeats. "And it feels like justice to me."

I close my eyes. All along I've been motivated by a desire to see things change. To give people a voice in their government, a say in their own lives. And I still believe my father would be a better leader than President Lattimer. But now I fear he may have been motivated by vengeance, the desire to watch President Lattimer suffer the loss of his son, while my father stands back and relishes the pain. "How are you going to kill President Lattimer?" I ask. "Isn't everything already set in motion?"

"Not exactly," Callie admits after a pause. "It will be

once Bishop is dead."

"Then why was there a timeline? Why…" My voice fades into nothing as I finally understand, "It was a test, wasn't it? You were *testing* me?"

"It wasn't a test, exactly," Callie says, and has the decency to look at least slightly uncomfortable. "But we couldn't have you dragging your feet. We always knew this would be hard for you, Ivy. We couldn't afford to wait forever. But you did great, finding the guns and the codes. Better than we ever hoped. Now there's just one thing left for you to do."

I bark out a laugh. If only she knew the code I gave our father was wrong. "When?" I ask, holding up the bottle.

"The exact timing is up to you, so long as it's in the next week."

That doesn't give me much time. "What about Mrs. Lattimer?" I ask.

"She'll be irrelevant once they're dead," Callie says. "We're not wasting energy on her."

I have no illusions about the relationship between Erin Lattimer and me. It is not made up of warm, fuzzy emotions on either side. But my heart still breaks a little imagining her left behind, husband and son both dead. Her entire world destroyed in the blink of an eye. The very indifference to her suffering an especially vile form of cruelty.

"Our family has waited years to be back in power," Callie continues. "And no one is going to take it away from us."

"Power over what? A bunch of scared people who are trying to pretend the world hasn't changed? Everyone too terrified to even ask what else is out there? This little patch of land with ten thousand people, that's what we're fighting over?" I look out across the park, try to imagine what lies beyond this tiny bit of earth we all claim like it's the only scrap left. Maybe it is. But we don't know that for sure. "Is it worth it?" I ask.

"Of course it's worth it!" Callie exclaims. "This is all there is. And it's supposed to be ours. A Westfall founded this place and a Westfall should be in charge."

That doesn't sound much like democracy to me. I put the vial into my bag. "Good-bye, Callie," I say. I grab her and hug her hard before she can protest or push me away. After everything, she is still my sister. I still love her. And I always will. But I realize now that Callie and my father have been holding me down my entire life, never allowing me the freedom of my own thoughts or actions for fear they would differ from their own desires. They are not so different from President Lattimer.

And it is Bishop who helped me break free. He didn't save me, though. He allowed me the freedom to save myself, which is the very best type of rescue.

I've gone over every possibility a dozen times. Thought about telling Bishop what my father and Callie are planning. But as much as I want to stop them, I cannot go that far. I cannot be the one who dooms them, even if they might deserve it. And doing nothing is also not an option. I could smash the vial and continue on with my life, but they will still find a way to kill Bishop, with or without my help. No matter how I come at the problem, the fact remains that in the end there will have to be a sacrifice. If I won't allow it to be Bishop and I can't stomach it being my family, then there is only one choice left.

It will have to be me.

23

leave the note where I'm sure they'll find it. If not tonight, then early tomorrow when Victoria arrives. She'd never miss it; she's too good at her job. Afterward, I walk home and put the vial in the bottom drawer in the bathroom, behind the washcloths and a jumble of soaps and shampoos. I don't know if they will go to the trouble of checking the vial for fingerprints, but I wipe it off carefully just to be safe, so only my prints will remain.

I smile at dinner and try not to think that it is my last night in this house. I listen to Bishop's laugh and try to forget I will never hear it again, that by tomorrow he will hate me. But he will be alive and that is a fair trade. Or as fair as either of us is likely to get in this lifetime. And at bedtime I don't linger in the bathroom, don't allow panic to set into my bones like the poison hidden in the drawer. I crawl into bed beside him and reach for him in the dark. I don't let myself think that any second there could be a knock on the door, that any moment could be the last.

"Ivy?" he says. I want to memorize the sound of his voice. "Why are you crying?"

"I'm not," I say, swiping at my cheeks with angry fingers. I push against him, rolling him onto his back, and swing myself over so that I straddle him. His eyes look almost translucent in the moonlight. "We could leave," I find myself saying, my breath hitching out of me on a sob. I am wound tight, my body trembling. I feel like the only thing connecting me to the world is the warmth of his hands around my hips, tethering me. "Go beyond the fence. See what's out there. Find the ocean."

He watches me, forehead furrowed. "What's wrong?" he says finally. "Talk to me."

But I can't. I shake my head. "Never mind," I whisper.

His hands tighten on my hips. "Someday," he says. "We'll see the ocean together, I promise."

I nod because I cannot open my mouth, have no idea what might come pouring out. A different kind of ocean maybe, one made of words that would drown us both. So I brace my hands on the pillow beneath his head and lean down to kiss him instead. The softness of his lips, the taste of his tongue, the strength of his hands. I store them up inside of me for a time when they are no longer mine.

I want to tell him I love him. But that would be selfish of me. To leave him with yet another memory he will only question later, a hard-won truth he will only remember as the worst, and final, lie.

I'm asleep when the knock comes, loud and insistent. Bishop is curled around my back, one hand pushed underneath my tank top to rest flat against my stomach.

"Bishop." I nudge his arm. "Someone's at the door." The first hazy streaks of sunlight are poking their way through our gauzy bedroom curtains.

"Hmmm?" he mumbles, his breath warm against my shoulder. The knock comes again, harder this time. They won't wait long. "Who the hell is here this early?" he says as he pushes himself up, throwing the sheet off our tangled legs.

As soon as he's left the room, I sit up, take a deep breath, and palm my hair off my face. I have to be stronger now than ever before, braver than I knew I could be. Voices float in from the living room, Bishop's, another man, and is that... Erin? This is going to be even worse than I anticipated.

I throw on a pair of shorts and pull a T-shirt over my tank top. I just have time to pull my hair up into a messy ponytail when Bishop and a uniformed man appear in the doorway. The man is agitated, face red and veins bulging in his neck. Bishop, with his sleep-rumpled hair and bare chest, just looks confused.

"Ivy," he says. "My parents are here. And the police." He indicates the man next to him with a curt nod. "They say they received an anonymous note saying..." His voice trails off and he looks at the cop. "This is ridiculous. I can't believe we're even having this conversation."

"The note said you planned on poisoning him," the cop says.

"They want to do a search," Bishop tells me.

"Go ahead," I say. I wish the rest of me was as numb as my voice.

The cop backs out of the room, and a few seconds later, I hear the sounds of cabinets opening in the kitchen, his voice barking orders. Bishop is staring at me and if I don't look away, I'm going to cry. I sit down on the edge of our bed, keep my gaze on my clasped hands.

"I don't understand what they're even doing here," Bishop says. He sits down beside me, so close our bare legs touch. He scrubs at his face with both hands. "Weren't we asleep five minutes ago?" He lets out a raspy laugh. "Maybe I'm dreaming."

"It's not a dream," I say. My voice sounds very far away to my own ears, like I'm speaking through a curtain of clouds.

"Well, they need to hurry up and get out of here," Bishop says. The anger in his voice is hiding something else—fear, maybe, or doubt. My heart drops into my stomach. I wish there was a way to save him that didn't involve hurting him. But it's a choice between pain now or death later, and he'll get over the pain of losing me. I'll make it as easy for him as I can.

Bishops takes my hand in his, following the lines of my palm with his index finger, while we listen to the police ransack our kitchen and living room, pretend we don't notice them moving down the hall to the bathroom right outside the door. Tension races through me like lightning, threatening to shoot sparks from my fingers and toes. No matter what Bishop said to the cop, he's feeling it, too. His body vibrates with nerves next to mine.

There's an exclamation from the bathroom, the sound of rapid footsteps, more talking. I don't focus on the words; instead I try to clear my mind and take even breaths.

"We found something," the cop says, and Bishop and I both swing our heads in his direction. He's holding up a plastic bag with the vial inside.

"What is it?" Bishop asks.

"That's what we'll have to find out," the cop says, staring at me. "But if I had to guess, I'd say it's poison."

It seems like slow motion as Bishop turns back to me, his green eyes locked on mine.

"We need to—" the cop begins, but Bishop doesn't even look at him. Bishop holds up a hand to cut him off.

"Ivy," he says. He's not just looking at me, he's looking into me, probing me with his gaze. He doesn't believe. He's waiting for the explanation, waiting for the words that will make sense of that vial. He doesn't even look that concerned. He doesn't believe in the vial because he believes in me.

A single tear spills over, runs down my cheek. "I'm sorry," I whisper. Every inch of me hurts; even my skin aches. I want to throw my arms around him and never let go. But I stand on steadier legs than I deserve and face the policeman who is coming toward me. I don't resist as he grabs my arms, keeping my gaze fixed on the far wall. I don't look when Bishop tries to intervene, pushing against the cop, calling my name as I'm dragged into the living room, past the president, a stricken look on his face, and Erin, who would tear me apart if she could.

I don't look back as I'm escorted out of the house, Bishop's voice a constant, furious counterpoint behind me. On the outside I am calm, a careful blank, but inside my blood and bones and flesh scream out for him. But I put one foot in front of the other, remind myself that every step makes him safer even as it takes me farther away from him.

24

They put me in a cell in the basement of the courthouse. It is clean, at least, and separated from the other prisoners. The cop who found the vial practically shoves me in, but David, who met him at the courthouse door, is kinder.

"I'm sure we'll get this all sorted out soon," he tells me with a worried smile. "Sit tight."

The door clanks closed behind them, but I don't sit. I sink onto the cot bolted to the far wall and curl up into a ball, as tight and small as I can make myself. It's hot in the airless cell, but I shiver uncontrollably, clench my teeth to stop their chattering.

I have to be prepared for whatever happens next. I can't falter now. I tell myself that whoever comes into my cell, I will be ready. It could be my father, the president, Bishop himself. Whoever it is, I will be strong.

I'm not sure how much time passes. Long enough that bright sunlight is slanting in through the tiny window at the top of the cell. It's almost unbearably stuffy now and tiny dust motes dance in the bright shaft of light. If I stare at them long enough, I can pretend I'm floating among them, transported somewhere far away from here.

"Ivy?"

I jerk up to sitting, blood beating against the backs of my eyes. It's Victoria in the doorway. Not who I expected. She closes the cell door behind her and leans back against it. Her eyes are sad.

"Your father and sister are here," she says. "They're upstairs being questioned. Then they'll meet with the Lattimers. They say they had no idea what you were planning." It's not a question, but she asks it like one. Waiting for me to sell them out.

"They didn't know," I say. My tongue is dry and feels several sizes too big for my mouth.

"I assume you don't want to talk to the police without an attorney. So this afternoon, we'll get a lawyer assigned to you. Then you can—"

"No," I say, too loud. I temper my voice. "No lawyer." The legal system is not the same as it was before the war. We are not entitled to an attorney or to refuse to speak to the police. But my friends in the courthouse are giving me special treatment I neither need nor want. Victoria probably thinks she is helping me. "I want to plead guilty. No trial."

"Ivy," Victoria says, taking a step toward me. "I don't

know what's going on. But I do know what will happen if you plead guilty. And so do you."

I nod. Breathe past the terror sitting in my chest like a boulder. "I'm guilty. No trial."

Victoria stares at me for a moment, then reaches behind her and unlocks my cell. "Come with me," she says.

I hesitate. "Where are we going?"

"Come on," she says. "Hurry."

I don't want to leave the relative safety of my cell, but Victoria has never hurt me. I stand and follow her out of the cell. "We'll see what we can do about getting you some shoes," Victoria says, glancing at my bare feet. "And some other clothes."

We walk out of the cellblock and through another door Victoria has to unlock with a ring of keys attached to her belt. David is waiting on the other side, and his eyebrows shoot up when we come through.

"I'm putting her in one of the interrogation rooms," Victoria says.

"Okay." David seems confused, but he doesn't argue.

Victoria leads me to a door on the left of the hallway, indistinguishable from all the rest. The room beyond the door is small, holding only a card table and two chairs. "Sit," Victoria says. "I'll be back." Before she leaves, she flicks a button on the wall intercom. She locks the door behind her.

There is a two-way mirror on the far side of the room, but I don't think anyone's watching me. I sit on the metal folding chair and cross my arms, using my hands to try and bring some warmth to my skin. The intercom on the wall buzzes to life, static shooting through the room, startling me and making me jump in my seat.

"She says she's guilty." Victoria's voice from the intercom. What is going on?

"Bishop! Are you listening? Did you hear what Victoria said?" Erin's voice this time. The intercom distorts the sound, making everything fuzzy and slightly indistinct, but I still recognize the voices. I pick up my chair and move it closer to the wall.

"It doesn't matter what she said." Bishop. He sounds exhausted. "She didn't do it. She wasn't going to kill me."

"Then why was there poison in your house?" Erin demands.

"I don't know," Bishop says with a sigh. "I don't have an explanation for it, but I know she's not guilty."

I want to reach through the intercom and touch him. It's a kind of torture knowing he's right upstairs and I can't get to him.

"She says she is, though," President Lattimer says. They must all be here. Are my father and Callie up there, too?

As if the thought summoned her, I hear Callie speak. "I didn't want to say anything before. But now I think I have to."

"What is it?" President Lattimer asks.

"Ivy's always been…different," Callie says. My hands curl into fists in my lap.

"Different?" Erin's voice is sharp. "What do you mean?"

"Unstable," my father says, and with that word I hear the last brick fall. My fate well and truly sealed. It's what I wanted. It's what had to happen. But my family's betrayal still cuts like a sharp blade. "We did what we could for her," my father continues. "But she's always been up and down, impossible to predict. We hoped that she would outgrow it. That it wasn't a permanent part of her personality."

There is silence for a moment, and then Erin bursts out, "Just like her mother. Crazy like her mother!" I am glad we are not in the same room, because right now my fists have a mind of their own.

"Erin, stop it!" President Lattimer barks.

"Ivy is not crazy. And neither was her mother," my father says. "But…it's not completely out of character for her to do something like this."

"She felt very strongly about the arranged marriages," Callie says. "That they were wrong. She might have thought this was an appropriate response. There's really no way of knowing exactly what was going on inside her head."

There's a moment where no one speaks. "Bullshit," Bishop says flatly into the silence. "That's utter bullshit."

"Bishop!"

Even with my entire life spiraling out of my hands, I have to smile at Bishop's words, at his complete faith in me, at his mother's appalled response. He can still, after everything, make me smile when I least expect it.

"I don't know exactly what's going on, but what you're saying about Ivy isn't true," Bishop says. "Either you don't know her at all or you're lying. I lived in that house with her every day. I slept next to her. And there is nothing wrong with her. She—" His voice breaks and I turn away from the intercom. I know how carefully Bishop guards his emotions, protecting them from those who don't deserve to see beneath his surface. I hate that I am the one who has forced him to reveal himself this way.

"We lived with her, too, Bishop," my father says. "For a lot longer than you. No one knows her better than we do."

"Then how could you let her marry our son?" Erin demands. "Knowing that she's unstable?"

"That wasn't our decision, if you'll recall," my father says. "He was supposed to marry Callie. But he chose otherwise. It wasn't up to us." So smug, so confident, even with his plan falling to pieces around him. There's no way he can kill Bishop now, or at least not in the near future. After what I've been accused of almost doing, my father can't risk the finger of suspicion pointing back at our family so soon.

"Regardless, you had an obligation—"

"Be quiet." Bishop's voice whips out of the intercom and everyone falls silent. "Just be quiet." There is a pause, and I hear a chair scrape back. When he speaks again, his voice is louder. Closer to Victoria? "I want to see Ivy."

"No," I say before I can stop myself. I spring out of my seat, clawing at the intercom, but they can't hear me. "No!"

"I want to see her," Bishop repeats. "Now."

"Give me a minute," Victoria says. "And you can't go inside the cell."

"Thank you," Bishop says. More rustling and the murmur of voices. The intercom goes dead.

25

'm curled into a ball, facing the wall, when he arrives. Victoria never came back to get me, but David escorted me to my cell. I tried to tell him I didn't want visitors, but he said that wasn't up to him. The late afternoon light coming from the tiny window gives the cell an autumn glow, even though we're still in the last hazy days of summer. I close my eyes against the burnt orange light when I hear his voice.

"Hey," Bishop says softly. "We need to get you out of here. There's definitely not room on that cot for both of us."

It takes me a long time to turn over, push myself to sitting. His is the last face I want to see. The one face that will undo me, that has been undoing me from the very first moment we met.

I finally look up, and his familiar, beautiful face looks back at me. "Bishop…" My voice is hoarse, like I haven't spoken in weeks. "You shouldn't have come."

He wraps his hands around the iron bars separating us. "Of course I was going to come. Where else would I be?"

I choke out a laugh. "Anywhere?"

"Come here," he says. "Closer to me."

I shake my head, keep my hands white-knuckled around the metal edge of the cot, like he might somehow find a way to drag me toward him if I'm not careful. I am scared his touch will make me weak when I need so desperately to remain strong.

"What's going on, Ivy?" he asks. "I know you weren't going to poison me. So why are you taking the blame?" He pauses. "Was it your dad? Did he put you up to it?"

"Why would he do that?" I ask, my eyes on the floor. "He may not like your father's policies, but they've managed to get along for decades."

Bishop lets that sink in, studying me. "I saw him upstairs a few minutes ago. With your sister. He said you're unstable. Callie said they weren't all that shocked you'd do something like this."

So, as I suspected, he didn't know the intercom was on. A little gift from Victoria. She probably hoped that hearing what my family said would make me spill my guts. And now Bishop is here, trying to provoke a reaction from me that I can't let him have. My throat works, but I don't respond.

"Why would they say that? We both know it's not true. I've lived with you, talked to you every day. You're the least unstable person I know."

"They lived with me longer," I point out, the same thing

my father said.

"I don't care!" he practically yells and I can hear how hard he's working to keep himself under control. "I would know." He lowers his voice. "I know you."

He is right. He knows me better than anyone ever has. Than anyone ever will again. I would have stopped it if I could have. But I've learned the hard way, we can't choose who we love. Love chooses us. Love doesn't care about what's convenient or easy or planned. Love has its own agenda and all we can do is get out of its way.

"Where'd you get the poison?" he demands. "If this was your plan, who gave it to you?"

I shake my head. "The person who gave it to me didn't know what I wanted it for. It doesn't matter where it came from."

"Oh," Bishop says, "well, that's convenient. Was the person who gave you the poison the same person who just happened to leave an anonymous note on Victoria's desk? Amazing how that worked."

"Stop trying to figure it out, Bishop," I say. "Just let it go."

"Are you serious?" he demands. "There's no way I'm letting it go. This isn't some stupid argument about whose turn it is to clean the bathroom. This is your life, Ivy!" His voice is getting louder with each word. "You know what's going to happen, don't you? If you plead guilty?"

I keep my head down, my mouth closed.

"Goddamn it!" Bishop explodes. "Look at me! My father will put you out. Beyond the fence. Do you understand that?"

"I know," I say, voice quiet.

"You know? *You know?*"

I paste on a pained smile, try to look at his face without my heart splintering in my chest. "Maybe I'll be okay. Maybe I'll make it to the ocean."

He gapes at me. "*Maybe* you'll be okay?" he repeats finally. "Maybe you'll…" His voice trails off, and he rests his forehead against the bars. "Will you please talk to me," he says in a defeated voice. "Tell me the truth so we can figure out what to do. What the hell is going on?"

I stare at his bent head, remembering the feel of his hair sliding between my fingers. "I didn't want to get married. I didn't want to marry you. And your father wouldn't listen. He doesn't care about all the girls forced to have babies before they're ready or marry boys they don't know. We don't have any freedom, not even to decide who we love." I take a deep breath. "I wanted him to know what it felt like to lose something. The way we've lost all of our choices."

He doesn't move for a long time, and I think maybe I've done it, convinced him of my guilt by repeating the same reasons Callie gave him upstairs. And they're true, up to the point they become a total lie. He lifts his head, and his eyes lock onto mine. "I don't believe you," he says.

Why does he have to make this so difficult? Why can't he accept the worst about me, the way so many other people do? Why doesn't he just give up on me and walk away like my family has already?

"Are you honestly telling me it was all a lie? You faked

everything between us?" He shakes his head. "You're not that good an actress. You're no good at hiding your feelings, even when you try. It's one of the things I like best about you."

I turn my face away, and the tears I've been holding back begin to fall. Slowly at first, then floods of tears, gushing out of me. I don't even attempt to wipe them away, letting them drip off my cheeks and chin where they spatter on the concrete floor like a tiny rain shower.

"Look at me," he says, his voice low and desperate. "Look at me and tell me none of it was true."

"Don't." My voice catches. I can't look at him.

"*Say it*," he demands. When I look at him through a blur of tears, I can tell he thinks he's won. He knows I cannot look him in the eye and say I felt nothing for him. And if I can't do that, he'll know the poison is a lie.

He doesn't take his eyes off me as I stand. I walk toward him, stopping right before I reach the bars. "It was all true," I say through my tears. "Every second. The times I resented you. The times I was angry at you. The times I was afraid of you." I take a long, unsteady breath, my eyes on his. "The times I loved you. It was all true."

I see the relief run through him, the sheen of pain and confusion in his eyes fading into hope. He opens his mouth to speak, but I reach out and wrap my hands around his on the bars. The touch of his skin is like electricity, pinning me in place.

"But the poison is true, too, Bishop. And nothing that I just said changes that." I squeeze his hands. "I was going to kill you."

I will my words to be truth, even though I know they are the vilest deception, I set my jaw, keep my gaze steady. I don't want him to find a lie no matter how hard he looks. His eyes search my face with an intensity now so familiar to me, I feel it in my bones.

"Remember when you told me I fascinated you? How the first time you saw me I was scared but still defiant? How I was easy to read on the outside but complicated underneath?" He doesn't respond, his eyes boring into mine, still digging for the lie. And if I don't convince him soon, he's going to find it. Desperation makes me cruel. "I'm still that same girl," I tell him. "The one who could love you. And kill you anyway."

There's a moment of charged silence, acceptance slowly flowing into his eyes like brackish water, turning them dark and cloudy. I loosen my grip on his hands. He yanks them out from under mine, holds them up like I'm pointing a gun at him as he steps back from the bars. My skin still tingles where it touched his.

"Do you believe me now?" I ask, cold as ice. Finally, after all this time and when I need it most, I've found Callie's voice inside of me.

He does.

Life is one sick joke after another, I'm discovering. Because it hardly seems fair that it should hurt so much to finally get exactly what I've been wishing for.

26

I spend the next three days alone, other than Victoria, who stops by periodically to give me updates on what's happening in a careful, professional tone and leaves so fast she practically trips over her own feet. And David, of course, who brings my meals and actually smiles at me. Sad, sorry smiles that are somehow worse than if he glared at me or spit in my food. They remind me of the looks you'd give a lamb right before slaughter. Which is fitting, I suppose.

My father does not come. Callie does not come. They've cut their losses and moved on. And although I'm not surprised they've chosen to save themselves—it's what I wanted, after all—the ease with which they've abandoned me leaves me brokenhearted. From the beginning, I was only a pawn in their quest for power. The thought of sacrificing themselves for me has probably not even occurred to either one of them.

I am not so selfless, or so brave, that I haven't considered telling the truth about my family during all the endless hours in my cell. I know how easy it would be to point the finger of blame in their direction and a part of me yearns to do it. But I want to be better than the lessons they taught me. I want my love to be greater than my hate, my mercy to be stronger than my vengeance.

Bishop does not visit me again. I don't want him to; I could hardly bear it the first time. The look on his face as he jerked his hands out from under mine, backed away from me like I was contaminated. I wouldn't be able to stand that again. I would break under that look and confess everything. So I tell myself it's better that he has finally lost his faith in me.

I never deserved it anyway.

On the morning of the fourth day, Victoria arrives and informs me I'm going in front of the judge this afternoon. She pauses outside the cell. "It'll be fast, Ivy," she says.

"Okay." It usually is when someone enters a guilty plea.

She looks up at the ceiling, anywhere but at me. "No, I mean…after your plea is accepted, you're going to be sentenced. Today."

"Oh." The timing doesn't really matter. What's done is done, but I thought I'd have more time. "And when will they put me out?" I ask.

Again, her eyes land on everything but me. "I don't think they'll wait for the next scheduled day. Mrs. Lattimer is pushing to have you put out immediately. She says you're too big a threat to keep here. And they want to use you as an example. Keep this type of thing from happening again."

I nod, although my neck is stiff with fear. "Thank you for telling me."

Victoria's gaze finally finds mine. "If there's anything you want to say, now would be the time to say it. It's not too late to have a trial."

"No, no trial," I say, for what feels like the thousandth time. "You turned the intercom on that day, didn't you?"

"Yes. I was hoping it might shake the truth loose. That it might remind you who is worth protecting. And who isn't."

I don't respond, and she sighs, the sound more frustrated than disappointed. Like she knew already she wouldn't get anywhere with me.

"Will I get a chance—" I pause and clear my throat. "Will I get a chance to say good-bye to my family?" Even after everything, I still love them. They are still my blood, and although we've disappointed each other, I would like to see them one last time, hold them in my arms and kiss their cheeks good-bye.

Victoria's eyes flare before she looks away from me. "They haven't asked to meet with you, Ivy. Not even after sentencing."

"Oh...okay." My voice is very small.

"But Bishop has asked if he—"

"No!" I exclaim. "Not Bishop." I have no idea why he would want to be in the same room with me ever again. He once said giving up on me wasn't an option, but I hope to God he's changed his mind about that. I thought I had forced him to. *Maybe he still loves you, a traitorous little voice in my head whispers. Maybe he's not ready to give up.* A flicker of hope sparks inside me, but I stomp on it, smother it. Hope like that will destroy us both, and I have to kill it where it lives. "I don't want to see him," I tell Victoria. "But can you give him a message for me?"

"What?"

"Can you tell him that I'm sorry." I pause, debating how much I can say without giving everything away. But I have to take the chance. "And tell him to be careful."

Victoria steps closer to the bars. "Careful of what?" she asks.

I don't think my father will try to kill Bishop again, not when he came so close to being caught. He'll figure out some other path to get what he wants. And the truth is, there is no way to keep someone safe forever. The world is full of a million dangers, both realized and never considered. But this is the best I can do. "Tell him to be careful about trusting people," I say. I manage a wobbly smile. "Although that probably goes without saying at this point."

After a long moment of silence, she gives me a quick nod. "All right." She steps back from the bars. "Good luck, Ivy."

I don't think luck is going to help me, but I give her a small smile. She has always been good to me, even now.

Once she's gone, I curl up on the cot. My default position in the cell. I have every crack on the cinderblocks memorized, can tell how long it is until my meal trays arrive by the slant of light through the window above my head. But as hard as I try, I can never hear anything from outside. Just the clank of doors and sometimes the sound of footsteps. No matter what, it will be nice to smell fresh air again and hear the wind in the trees.

I trace my finger across the rough cinderblock, remembering the warmth of Bishop's skin under this same finger. I hope that someday he is able to forgive himself for loving me. I hope that he finds another girl, one better than me, to guard his heart. One who deserves the faith he puts in her. I hope he touches the ocean and tastes its salty sting. Tears pool in my ear and the hollow of my neck, and I'm glad there is no one here to witness them.

Bishop asked me once who I wanted to be, and I think I know the answer now. I want to be someone strong and brave enough to make hard choices. But I want to be fair and loving enough to make the right ones. After everything, I can't be sorry for loving Bishop. And I'm not sorry for saving him, either, even if I sacrificed myself in the process. It was my choice and I'm proud of it. If that makes me soft, then it's a softness I can finally live with.

They leave me handcuffed to a bench in a back hallway while I'm waiting to be escorted to the courtroom for my plea hearing. I'm staring straight ahead, trying very hard to think about nothing, when my father rounds the corner and sits down beside me.

"Dad?" I say, not entirely sure he's not simply a figment of my imagination.

"We don't have long," he says, "The guard said only five minutes." He lays a hand on my cheek.

"I'm so glad you came," I tell him, trying to smile.

"Oh Ivy," he sighs, his voice breaking, "what have you done?"

My throat tightens at his words. "What I had to do, Dad." We're speaking in a kind of code, neither of us sure who might be listening. But it feels like we've always communicated this way, never able to come at anything honestly, always circling around the truth.

He shakes his head, drops his hand. "They're putting you out."

"I'm sorry, Dad," I whisper. "I love you."

A tear trails down his cheek. I've never seen my father cry before. "I love you, too," he says.

"But not enough to save me," I say, my voice harder than I expected it to be.

My father stands and stares down at me. "You made your choice, Ivy."

"Yes," I say, meeting his eyes. "And you made yours."

The courtroom is packed with people when they bring me before the judge. Everyone craning for a look at the traitor. A few people hiss at me as I walk by, but I keep my eyes straight ahead and my chin high. Generally, nowadays, crime is not a spectator sport, but I must be an exception.

I'm marched to the defense table and, after I take my seat, the two guards flanking me step back. Victoria's colleague Jack Stewart is already seated at the table. He came down to my cell once, to tell me he is representing me. Victoria obviously ignored my request to proceed without an attorney. It doesn't make much difference, though. His job should be short and sweet. He gives me a grim smile before turning back to the front of the courtroom. From behind us, I can hear the buzz of voices, but I don't focus on the words. I doubt I want to hear them.

The courtroom, with its dark cherry wood and high ceilings, lends a formality to the proceedings before they've even started. Any illusions I've had that my fate will not be determined today fade in the presence of the courtroom's authority. My future is in the hands of the judge who will sit behind the high bench in front of me. There is a kind of relief in knowing there is nothing left for me to do.

The voices behind me rise, and I tell myself not to turn. But my curiosity is stronger than my apprehension, and I swing my head to the left. President and Mrs. Lattimer have entered the courtroom, followed by my father and Callie. Bishop brings up the rear. He looks in my direction, his eyes remote. But he doesn't take his gaze off mine as he joins the rest of them in the front row behind the prosecutor's table. No one sits directly behind me. The empty bench a testament to how far I have fallen.

I can still feel Bishop watching me, even after I turn

back to face the front of the courtroom. I keep my eyes on the door through which the judge will enter and pronounce my sentence.

"All rise, the Honorable Lawrence Lozano in session."

Jack puts a hand under my elbow, but I stand on my own. I'm not afraid of what's going to happen in this courtroom. I'm only afraid of what will come after.

Judge Lozano looks to be in his late forties, with short, salt and pepper hair and wire-rimmed glasses. I never formally met him during my months at the courthouse, but from a distance, he always appeared friendly enough. Today there is no evidence of that friendliness.

"Mr. Stewart," he says, looking at Jack over the top of his glasses. "I understand your client wishes to enter a guilty plea?"

"That's correct, Your Honor."

Judge Lozano glances at me and beckons me with a sharp curl of his fingers. My stomach does a hard forward roll, but I manage to contain my nerves. I walk up to the bench, and Judge Lozano points me to the witness box next to him. There is no chair inside the box so I stand, facing the gallery full of spectators. My eyes skim over the faces and finally land on Bishop. He is still staring at me, his face grave. I have absolutely no idea what he's thinking. It takes me back to those first days of our marriage, when every word he said or gesture he made was a complete mystery to me.

"You have been charged with attempted murder in the first degree. What's your plea?" Judge Lozano asks me, voice loud, and I jerk myself back to reality.

"Guilty," I say without hesitation.

Everyone knew my plea, but hearing it out loud, from my own mouth, sends a ripple of unease around the room. I am thankful that I will be spared having to outline my crime in detail, the way it used to be done before the war. No one is as concerned with a defendant's rights anymore. If you say you're guilty, they take you at your word. They must figure you'd be a fool to admit guilt and risk being put out unless you actually committed the crime.

"Given the unusual nature of this case, the president has requested that I pronounce your sentence and have it carried out immediately." Now the ripple has turned to outright shock. Apparently, the speed of my punishment is news to the gathered crowd. Most of them look thrilled to be witnessing such excitement. Bishop, too, seems surprised. His head whips toward his parents, and then he leans forward, hands gripping the wooden balustrade separating the gallery from the courtroom.

I try to tell him with my eyes that it's all right. The last thing I want is for him to worry about me. I want him to forget me and move on. Be safe and happy. He doesn't need to worry. I am prepared for what's coming. Or as prepared as I can possibly be.

"Ivy Westfall Lattimer, you are hereby sentenced to be put out beyond the fence. Sentence effective immediately following these proceedings."

The courtroom erupts, even though my actual sentence can come as a shock to no one. Over the din, I hear Bishop call my name, and although I know I should not look at him, I cannot bear to leave without seeing him one last time. But when I let my gaze travel to his, I wish I had turned away. He is standing at the balustrade, his face pale and drawn, and Callie's hand is on his upper arm, her face tipped up to his. She is whispering urgently to him. Her touch is too familiar, her face too kind. She is playing a part to get what she wants.

Something snaps inside of me, something that's been pulled taut for days, weeks, maybe forever. I see Callie clearly now—her heart is cold; her quest for power, her need for revenge, is even stronger than my father's. She is not going to let this stop her. To her, Bishop is not a person worthy of love or empathy. To her, he is like the dog that bit me, the one she choked on the end of his chain. Bishop is a nuisance. He is in her way. And whatever it takes, she is going to find a way to hurt him.

I charge out of the witness box and get halfway to her before the guards realize I've moved. One grabs me by the arm and wrenches me backward, but I don't stop, straining and kicking against him. I'm a wild thing, feral and out of control. If I can get free, I have no doubt I can kill her with my bare hands.

I scream, a long, mournful howl that silences the rest of the room. Another guard joins the first, and they drag me toward the side door of the courtroom even as my feet drum against the floor. I scream and scream until my lungs are empty and bright dots dance before my eyes. I scream as I hear Bishop yell my name. I scream until I'm shoved through the door into a hallway and something hard and heavy hits me on the side of the head and my world fades into black.

It is dark. Inky dark. My head throbs in time with my thudding heart. Something sharp is pressed into my cheek. Even my eyelids ache, but I manage to open them. More darkness, although it's not so black. Shot through with pale streaks of light. I roll my eyes upward. The moon. I'm outside. How did I get outside?

I tilt my head and groan as pain slides through my skull like a hot knife. I turn my head carefully to the side, lift my cheek off the rock cutting into my skin. There is something glinting in the darkness beside me, a silvery sheen. I can't figure out what it is. It hurts too much to think. I snake a hand out and reach with trembling fingers. Cool metal, thin and smooth. It rattles against my hand. I know what it is, but my mind fights the knowledge. My fingers curl around the metal the way Bishop's did the day we stood on the opposite side.

I am beyond the fence. And I am alone.

27

It's the thought of the dead girl that finally gets me moving. I know that no one is coming. My father and Callie are not going to appear on the other side of the fence with a new plan, this one destined to save me. Bishop is not going to crash through the trees, his hands full of water, his face full of forgiveness. But still I remain against the fence, the metal pushing between my shoulder blades, my head thick and throbbing.

As the sun rises high in a cloudless blue sky, the only sound the relentless thrum of hungry grasshoppers in the high grass, my mind turns to the girl Mark Laird killed. Her body lies somewhere along the perimeter of this fence. And I know if I don't move soon, I will end up just like her. Abandoned, forgotten. Left to rot. Because the longer I sit here, eyes glassy and gaze unfocused, the easier it becomes to stay.

I have no idea which way to go. Or even how to take the first step. When I was in the cell below the courthouse, I told myself that I could handle this eventuality. But now that it's here, I think I overestimated my own strength. A few listless tears mingle with sweat on my face, and I lower my head to my upturned knees, even though it makes the pain in my head worse, like two knives behind my eyes, probing for a way out.

There are only two choices. Stay here and die. Or get up and see what happens next.

I don't want to end up like the dead girl. I don't want to give up like my own mother. I may be her daughter, but I am not her. I lift my head and hook my hand into the chain-link above my head, use it to pull myself upright. My leg muscles scream in protest after more than twelve hours on the ground, and black dots dance across my vision.

I remember Bishop saying that the river is to the east. I made sure to pay attention to which way the sun rose this morning. Water. That's my first priority. Find water, and worry about everything else after that. The only way forward is one painful step at a time.

The going is slow, my arms and legs not quite moving in sync. I probe gingerly at the back of my head, and while my hair is tacky, there is no fresh blood flowing. I wonder how many times they hit me before they threw me out here, whether they had any qualms at all about dumping a teenage girl out into the dark, alone and unconscious. Probably not. After all, I tried to kill the president's son.

Instantly, Bishop's face flashes in my memory. I grit my teeth, push him from my mind. He is not mine to remember anymore. He might as well be a million miles away from me, rather than somewhere not so far beyond the fence that separates us. I have to find a way to forget him, even though just the thought of it makes it hard for me to breathe. He's elemental to me now, as much a part of me as my skin or my aching heart. But surviving alone and beyond the fence is going to take everything I have. I can't afford to waste a single second thinking about anything, or anyone, else.

The ground is rough and uneven, sloping slightly down-ward and just begging me to step wrong and twist an ankle. I give a little silent thank-you to Victoria for making sure I got a proper set of clothes before I was put out: jeans, closed-toe shoes, a tank top and sweater, even though it's way too hot for one. At least my clothes give me a fighting chance. I doubt I'd last very long barefoot and in the pa-jama shorts I was wearing when they first threw me in jail.

The going would be easier if I moved away from the fence, but I'm reluctant to release my hold on it. My left hand skates across the surface as I walk, metal bumping underneath my fingers. As a child, the thought of the fence frightened me. But now it feels like a security blanket I can't let go of. Stepping away from it means stepping into the abyss. I may wander so far afield that I can never find my way back.

I don't have any real idea of how far away the river is from where I was put out, but I can't imagine it's too far. Thinking of the river reminds me of Bishop again, and I stumble over a divot in the ground. I give myself a mental shake. Not even five minutes after I promised to forget, and I'm already breaking my vow.

I try to empty my head of thought, concentrate solely on putting one foot in front of the other. Something warm and wet slithers down my neck, but I tell myself it's sweat and not blood and refuse to allow myself to check. There's nothing I can do about it if I am bleeding again, so it's better not to know. Once I'm at the river, I can douse my head with water, wash away the blood that itches where it's dried to crusty patches on my skin and tangled in my already matted hair.

From the north—the Westfall side of the fence—I hear the faint sound of voices, and I stop cold, my heart hammering its way up into my throat. I press against the fence, my fingers curling around the warm metal. It's two children, probably forty feet in the distance, playing some kind of game among the trees. I doubt their parents know they have wandered so close to the fence.

"Hello," I call, but my voice is rusty and weak and they don't look up. I try again, clear my throat and yell a little louder. This time they both see me, scrambling up to their feet in unison. The older one, a girl, pushes the smaller boy behind her.

"Can you help me?" I ask. "Please."

The boy's hand comes around and fists in the girl's sundress, one eye peeking out from behind her hip.

"Go away," the girl yells. "Get out of here!" The words themselves are strong, but her voice wobbles, her eyes bright with fear. Her pale blond hair skates across her face in the breeze.

I know they can't do anything for me. That my very presence is terrifying to them. But I can't bring myself to walk away. A sudden fierce desperation grips me, the knowledge that when these two children flee, I will be completely alone in the world.

"Please," I say, barely a whisper. "Please."

The girl bends down and grabs something from the ground. She pulls her arm back and throws it at me. The rock bounces off the fence just above my hand, the metallic clang loud in the surrounding silence. She grabs the boy by the arm and retreats into the trees. In only seconds they have disappeared from view, the woods once again empty save for me.

I lean my head against my hands. My skin is filthy, dirt caked in uneven patches. My forearm is painted with streaks of dried blood. I'm sure I looked like a monster to those children. Something evil beyond the fence, the child-stealing witch their mother always warned them about.

Tears slip down my cheeks, their salt stinging my lips. I give in, allow myself to weep for everything I've lost, for the fear of what's to come. I grieve the daughter I was, the wife I never wanted to be, the killer I refused to become, the traitor I pretended to be.

I am none of those things now. I raise my head and wipe my eyes. Daughter. Wife. Killer. Traitor. They are all old versions of me. Now I will become a survivor.

I take a deep breath and let go of the fence.

ACKNOWLEDGMENTS

A massive thank you to: my editors, Alycia Tornetta and Stacy Cantor Abrams, for their keen insights and for helping me make this book better; everyone at Entangled Publishing for giving me this opportunity; Rebecca Mancini, for working her foreign rights magic; my husband, Brian, for loving and supporting me even when I'm at my craziest and for always being my constant; my children, Graham and Quinn, for hardly ever complaining when making dinner takes a backseat to writing and for making me laugh every day; my mom, for reading to me when I was young (just one more!); my family, near and far, for their encouragement and enthusiasm; Holly, for being the sister I never had and the best friend I couldn't live without; Meshelle, Michelle, and Trish for our monthly margarita lunches which both keep me sane and force me to get out of my writing clothes (i.e., sweatpants) once in a while; and last but not least, my cat Larry, who keeps my legs warm while I'm writing.

1.0

Beginnings are tricky things. I've been staring at this blank page for forty-seven minutes. It is infinite with possibilities. Once I begin, they diminish.

Scientifically, I know beginnings don't exist. The world is made of energy, which is neither created nor destroyed. Everything she is was here before me. Everything she was will always remain. Her existence touches both my past and my future at one point—infinity.

Lifelines aren't lines at all. They're more like circles.

It's safe to start anywhere and the story will curve its way back to the starting point. Eventually.

In other words, it doesn't matter where I begin. It doesn't change the end.

1.1

Geeks are popular these days. At least, popular culture says geeks are popular. If nerds are hip, then it shouldn't be hard for me to meet a girl.

Results from my personal experimentation in this realm would suggest pop culture is stupid. Or it could be that my methodology is flawed. When an experiment's results are unexpected, the scientist must go back and look at the methods to determine the point at which an error occurred. I'm pretty sure I'm the error in each failed attempt at getting a girl's attention. Scientifically, I should have removed myself from the equation, but instead, I kept changing the girl.

Each experiment has led to similar conclusions.

1. **Subject:** Sara Lewis, fifth grade,

   Method: Hold her hand under the table during social studies,

   Result: Punched in the thigh.

2. **Subject:** Cara Whetherby, fifth grade, second semester,

Method: Yawn and extend arm over her shoulder during Honor Roll Movie Night,

Result: Elbowed in the gut

3. **Subject:** Maria Castillo, sixth grade,

   Method: Kiss her after exiting the bus,

   Result: Kneed in the balls.

After Maria, I decided my scientific genius was needed for other, better, experiments. Experiments that would write me a first-class ticket to MIT.

I'm tall and ropey with sandy blond hair so fine it's like dandelion fluff—the kind of dork that no amount of pop culture can help. Which is how I already know how this experiment will end, even as my hand reaches out to touch the girl standing in front of me at Krispy Kreme donuts.

There was a long line when I walked in this morning, so I'd been passing the time by counting the ceiling tiles (320) and figuring the ratio of large cups to small cups stacked next to the coffee (3:2). I'd been counting the donuts in the racks (>480) when I noticed the small tattoo on the neck of the girl in front of me.

It's a symbol—infinity. There's a cursive word included in the bottom of one of the loops, but I can't read it because one of the girl's short curls is in the way.

Before I realize what I'm doing, I sweep away the hair at the nape of her neck. She shudders and spins around so fast that my hand is still midair. Flames of embarrassment lick at my earlobes, and I wonder if I should be shielding my man parts from inevitable physical brutality.

"What's your problem?" Her hand cups her neck, covering the tattoo. Her pale skin flushes and her pupils are black holes in the middle of wild blue seas, but since I'm not coughing up my nuts, I'm already doing better with this girl than any before.

She's waiting for me to explain.

It takes too long to find words. She's too beautiful with that raven-hued hair and those eyes. "I wanted to see your tattoo."

"So, ask next time."

I nod. She turns back around.

The curl has shifted.

The word is "hope."

"Rapido, Chuck. J's pissing his pants because we're going to be 'tardy,'" Greta says, using her shoulders to wedge the door open so she can make air quotes around James's favorite word. "God, it smells good in here."

Greta McCaulley has been my best friend since our freshman year at Brighton. On the first day of Algebra II, Mr. Toppler held a math contest, like a spelling bee only better. I came in second, one question behind Greta. Since then, her red hair, opinions, and chewed-up cuticles have been a daily part of my life. She has a way of ignoring the stuff about me that makes others want to punch me. And she's equal parts tenacity and loyalty—like a Labrador/honey badger mutt.

She'd also beat the crap out of me if she knew I'd just thought of her as a hybridized breed of animal.

Outside, her boyfriend James unfolds himself from the cramped backseat of my car, and rips open the heavy doors. "People of Krispy Kreme, I will not be made tar—" He takes a quick breath and loses his concentration. Krispy Kreme's sugary good smell remains invincible.

Greta stands beside me in line, while James drifts toward a little window to watch the donuts being born in the kitchen. Greta and

James have been together since the second quarter of ninth grade. If I wanted to continue to hang out with Greta, her Great Dane of a boyfriend would have to become part of my small circle of friends.

Actually, it's not a circle. It's a triangle. I'd need more friends to have a circle.

The girl with the tattoo steps up and orders a glazed and a coffee. She's about our age, but I don't know her, which means she must go to my sister's high school, Sandstone. It's for the regular kids. I go to Brighton School of Math and Science. It's for the nerds.

Greta leans into my shoulder, and I know I'm not supposed to notice because a) we've been friends for a long time, b) James is four feet away, and c) I just fondled a stranger's neck, but Greta's left breast brushes against my arm.

"So what's with the girl?" she asks. "I saw her turn and—"

My ears feel warm. "Shhh."

Mercifully, Greta whispers, "I thought she was going to punch you."

"Me, too."

"What'd you do?"

"She has a tattoo," I say, shrugging.

"And?"

"And, I may have touched it."

Greta's mouth hangs open, a perfect donut.

"Fine. I touched it."

"Where?" Greta quickly turns and scans the girl. "Oh, thank God," she breathes, touching the correlating spot on her own bare neck. "I thought maybe it was a tramp stamp."

I must look blank because Greta points to her lower back, just below the waistline of her khaki uniform skirt.

"God, no," I say, too loudly. The girl with the hope tattoo glances over her shoulder. Greta and I both look at our shoes.

James steps in front of us, and for once I'm thankful that the width of 1 James = 2 Charlies + 1 Greta. His large frame blocks us from the girl's glare. James taps the face of his watch.

"I know," I say. "Look, both of you go back to the car. I'll be right there. We have plenty of time to make it before the first bell."

They turn to leave just as the girl is stepping away from the counter, coffee in one hand and donut in the other. I should let her walk away and be thankful she didn't punch me, but without thinking, I touch her arm as she goes by. I can feel the muscle of her bicep tighten under my fingertips.

I'm locked in place, like when an electric shock seizes all the muscles in your body so that the only thing that can save you— letting go of the electrical source—is the only thing you can't do.

"Yes?" she asks, her jaw looking as tight as her bicep feels.

"I wanted to apologize."

"Oh," she says. Her muscles relax. "Thanks."

She smells amazing. At least, I think it's her and not the warm donut in her hand. Either way, I have to force myself to focus on what I was about to say.

"So, I'm sorry." *Now, walk away. Go, Hanson.* "But I'm afraid you're mistaken about infinity. Infinity is quantifiable. *Hope* is immeasurable."

Her expression shifts, like Tony Stark slipping into his Iron Man mask. She shakes her arm free from my slack grip. "So if it can't be measured, I shouldn't count on it? That's bleak, man. Very bleak."

She turns and pushes through the door.

```
Subject: Girl with the hope tattoo, first day
of senior year,

Method: Grope her neck. Follow with a lecture
on topics in advanced mathematics,

Result: No physical harm, but left doubting
whether I'll ever figure this relationship
stuff out.
```

Check out more of Entangled Teen's hottest reads...

FRAGILE LINE

by Brooklyn Skye

Sixteen-year-old Ellie Cox is losing time. It started out small... forgetting a drive home or a conversation with a friend. But her blackouts are getting worse, more difficult to disguise as forgetfulness. When Ellie goes missing for three days, waking up in the apartment of a mysterious guy—a guy who is definitely not her boyfriend—her life starts to spiral out of control. Now, perched on the edge of insanity, with horrific memories of her childhood leaking in, Ellie struggles to put together the pieces of what she's lost.

PERFECTED

by Kate Jarvik Birch

Ever since the government passed legislation allowing people to be genetically engineered and raised as pets, the rich and powerful can own beautiful girls like sixteen-year-old Ella as companions. But when Ella moves in with her new masters and discovers the glamorous life she's been promised isn't at all what it seems, she's forced to choose between a pampered existence full of gorgeous gowns and veiled threats, or seizing her chance at freedom with the boy she's come to love, risking both of their lives in a daring escape no one will ever forget.

WHATEVER LIFE THROWS AT YOU

by Julie Cross

When seventeen-year-old track star Annie Lucas's dad starts mentoring nineteen-year-old baseball rookie phenom, Jason Brody, Annie's convinced she knows his type—arrogant, bossy, and most likely not into high school girls. But as Brody and her father grow closer, Annie starts to see through his façade to the lonely boy in over his head. When opening day comes around and her dad—and Brody's—job is on the line, she's reminded why he's off-limits. But Brody needs her, and staying away isn't an option.